The Angel of History

The Angel of History

Bruno Arpaia

Translated by Minna Proctor

CANONGATE
Edinburgh · New York · Melbourne

This edition first published in 2007 by Canongate Books

Originally published in Italian as *L'Angelo della Storia* in 2001
by Ugo Guanda Editore SpA

1

This English translation was supported by
The Italian Cultural Institute, Edinburgh

EDIMBURGO

British Library Cataloguing-in-Publication Data
A catalogue record for this book is available on
request from the British Library

ISBN 978 1 84195 983 2

Typeset in Perpetua by
Palimpsest Book Production Ltd, Grangemouth, Stirlingshire
Printed and bound in Great Britain by
Clays Ltd, St Ives plc

www.canongate.net

To Iaia and Alfredo, the angels of my history

It is, however, characteristic that not only a man's knowledge or wisdom, but above all his real life — and this is the stuff that stories are made of — first assumes transmissible form at the moment of his death. Just as a sequence of images is set in motion inside a man as his life comes to an end — unfolding the views of himself under which he has encountered himself without being aware of it — suddenly in his expressions and looks the unforgettable emerges and imparts to everything that concerned him that authority which even the poorest wretch in dying possesses for the living around him. This authority is at the very source of the story.

— Walter Benjamin (from 'The Storyteller', in *Illuminations*, English translation copyright Harcourt Brace Javanovich, Inc.)

'Why the fuck are you asking questions up and down every street in town? What the fuck is all this gossip-collecting for?'
    'So I will know what I'm doing when I lie.'

— Mario Vargas Llosa (from chapter 8 of *The Real Life of Alejandro Mayta*, translation copyright by Farrar, Straus and Giroux, Inc.)

PART ONE

Chapter One

Before leaving the house, he pressed his forehead up against the window and looked out. Night pushed through Berlin on the backs of clouds and icy winds tossed the stripped, leafless branches of trees lining the boulevard. The Wilmersdorfer Luch clock across the way read six o'clock already. Benjamin set his glasses on his forehead and rubbed his eyes. He had to go. He was in a cold sweat, nailed into the shadow, numbed by pain and sadness, but he had to go. He adjusted his tie, looked lingeringly over the rows of books on the shelves, at the paintings on the walls and his threadbare old sofa. Then he grabbed his bags and went out into the stairwell. A bitter wind worked its way under his coat and cleared his thoughts. For a moment, he saw the coin of his life spinning in the air and hitting the ground with a false note – it fell the wrong side up. He had to go. In the courtyard the dim lights from the windows formed a trap and the ground was sprinkled with the recent rain. He turned the key in the lock, twice, then three and four times, struck by his last doubt, a final awareness of his habits and memories. After that it was done.

Through the window of the tram he watched scattered pedestrians on the boulevard, eyes turned downward, the pavements slick with filthy sewer water, a reckless woman begging on the church steps. The square in front of the station was deserted except for a lone patrol, standing stiff and bored under the opaque illumination of the street lights. Benjamin couldn't turn back now. With effort he lugged his suitcases to a checkpoint where two soldiers stood watch.

'Papers,' ordered the older of the two. He was SA, blond and thin, his uniform seemed to hang off his shoulders.

Benjamin pulled them out of his coat pocket and handed them over the barrier. He wasn't trembling but he still didn't dare look him in the face. The blond soldier took his time. He showed the passport to his partner, turned it over, unconvinced, and then stared hard at the traveller – that pointy chin, those mean, chilly eyes boring into him.

'Go on,' he concluded.

It was some time before Benjamin caught his breath. He didn't feel right again until he got to the middle of the enormous atrium. Panting, he set his bags down on the ground. The silence around him was broken only by the puffing trains idling on the tracks and the wind sneaking in through the tunnels, the creaking of a sandwich cart. He moved forward, keeping some distance between himself and the soldiers with their rifles slung around their necks, staying away from the unpopulated waiting rooms. The train was practically empty and no one waved from the platform.

Benjamin was still thinking of nothing when the train pulled out. Several hours later he looked out the window at the Cologne station. It was midnight. Standing right outside on the

4

platform was Carl Linfert, a historian he'd met in the *Frankfurter Zeitung* offices.

'Herr Benjamin, where are you headed?'

'To Paris, and you?'

'Oh, I'm staying right here,' Linfert answered with a shake of his head. 'I just came to see a friend off.'

The conductor at the end of the platform swung his lantern and the train slowly started moving.

'Have a safe trip and good luck!' cried Linfert.

Linfert was the last familiar face Benjamin saw on German soil. After that, just lights streaming past in the night through the dirty glass, and the clinging stubborn preoccupations that kept him from sleeping until he got to the border. It wasn't until later, after the day had started breaking over the country-side and the listless French sunlight began to creep into the compartment, that Benjamin realised how much he had to lose. Perhaps he had already lost it forever.

Chapter Two

What's that, my son? Still going on about your German, your philosopher? His name was Benjamin, wasn't it now? He must have really been someone – a very important person if you came all the way to Mexico from Italy, all those thousands of miles, just to talk to a poor old man like me. Yes, I'm very old. Do you know that this October 26, I'll turn seventy-eight? Have I already told you that? You'll have to forgive me. Andrés, my grandson, the boy who let you in, he's always making fun of me because I can't keep things straight. I never remember what happened yesterday or the day before. He says that I have diseased arteries and that I'm incurable. What can I do about it? I'm certainly not going to let it bother me. Let him talk. If I were really sick, people wouldn't joke about it. Instead you'd all treat me with those pious little smiles that people reserve for jackasses. It's better to play along. You want to know what I really suffer from? The affliction of time. Just like my grandfather, may he rest in peace. After a certain point, he'd answer questions that you'd asked him three days earlier. He'd mix up the before and after. But I remember things from fifty years ago as if they were happening now. That's why I remember your philosopher perfectly. As I said, it must have been autumn 1940. I found myself at the top of the Pyrenees in the middle of the night, standing on the French–Spanish border on the Lister Trail. What was I doing up there? Well, that's another story. You should know that I was born in Spain, in Asturias. I wasn't born here in Mexico. But I've been living here for the last fifty years. I came here back in 1941 to save my skin and I stayed, because I couldn't ever go back. At sixteen, in October 1934, I was in the middle of the Asturias revolution. I hardly need to explain that we were fighting for a lost cause. Two thousand dead, fifteen thousand prisoners tortured. There were the legionnaires, the Moors of the African army raping women and burning down houses. My mother died then, struck down by a bomb. It fell on us by accident. Maybe they just dropped it so that they wouldn't have to carry it back to their base, which would make them look bad. It was rotten luck. I didn't have a great time of it either. I spent a month in jail, being beaten and tortured like so many others, and then I made it out. I don't even know how. I managed to escape to France in the hold of a ship carrying cider to La Rochelle. I stayed there for a year, living in squalid flea-traps, or in fields where we'd built barracks for ourselves, running from the cold. We went from Orléans to Dieppe and then to Saint Nazaire. In 1936, when we won the elections, I went home. We didn't even have time to celebrate, not to mention catch our breath, and there I was with a rifle in my hands. I must have been almost eighteen when those bastards rose up again in July of '36. War. That was the only life I knew. It was my trade. I didn't like it but what could I do about it? There wasn't any choice, we had to defend ourselves, fight back.

I knew those men well. Giving up would have been the same as committing suicide. So I slung my rifle over my shoulder and set off again.

I fought in Gijón, my city, and I then joined the offensive against Oviedo in February '37. In July Colonel Aranda claimed he was with us, but he led the rebellion against us – the traitor. He laid siege to the city and wasn't budging. More than thirty thousand of us mounted a counter–attack but those sons of bitches had cannons and fought us off. We lost. I don't know how many men died. It was a disaster. In the meantime, General Mola launched an attack against the Basques and we had to go help them. In May I was made a sergeant and they sent me to Bilbao to protect the city in the *cinturón de hierro* against the raids by German Condor Legion and the Navarre and Italian armies with their carts and cannons. I thought I would never see anything more horrifying in my life. But there's no end, my son, to the very worst.

I was a socialist, even if my company was made up of anarchists. I'd fought with them – the CNT, the anarchists' trade union – years before and I have to say that I was happy with them. They were good people; those guys had balls. And we were united by the fact that for both of us, getting along with the communists, well, let's say it was never wine and roses. My lieutenant was also my friend, Mariano Peña. I've already told you about him. We grew up together, were toddlers together, went to school together, went snail hunting in the marsh along the banks of the Piles river. We started chasing the girls who went parading along the calle Corrida or out on the boardwalk. Then, little by little, we started going to party meetings; there were strikes, weapons, the elections, and then

there we were, part of the revolution. I mean the 1934 revolution. I like to think we were well behaved, even if our
combined age didn't top forty. If you had seen him, standing
on the Gijón barricades directing the men and the battle! How
he did it. He seemed born to it; born to give orders. That's
why they made him a lieutenant in two years, even though he
was so young. And even though he was shit as a person. He
was a nun-chaser, a snake and a hothead. You could tell right
away when he got agitated because he'd start twisting his curls
with his fingers and look you right in the eyes. He had an icy
stare. Lucky for me we were friends.

All that aside, if it weren't for him I don't think I would
have survived Bilbao. They came from the sky, fifty fighter
planes, seventy three-motors, massacring us with machine guns
and bombs. On the ground they deployed three brigades armed
with heavy artillery. You didn't shoot back, you hoped they
didn't hit you . . . hoped you'd be luckier than the guy next
to you. The Basques prayed, but we didn't even do that, because
we were all atheists and had to make do with hand-gestures
to ward off the bad luck. It was one o'clock on the eleventh
of June – I remember it as if it were yesterday. The nationalists broke through our front, but it took them another week
to occupy the entire city, and another two months before we
got to Santander. Our men crumpled before those brutal
cowards – some more, some less – we just let them come at
us without realising that what we needed to do was buy some
time. But Mariano knew that and he deployed our company
the right way; they only got a few of us, who they could, and
we'd stand, doing what we could to hold up another line of
combat. It went on like that until September. Months of eating

badly, sleeping with our eyes open, staring at the sky, ears perked up and our hearts in our throats. We were almost happy when the order came down to retreat back to Asturias – even if we knew that it had gone badly. Back to face our destiny, the cursed destiny of Asturias. Surrounded just like we were three years earlier, barely protected by the remnants of an army that had already lost Bilbao and Santander. We hardly had any provisions and only about twenty planes. Then it was October again. What a coincidence. The German planes came through Infiesto and Arriondas and left maybe four houses standing. Troops in Solchaga, our lines crushed in Ibarrola, and in the meantime the Italians were attacking Avilés. I asked Mariano, 'Why do we keep going? It's over. Shouldn't we just try to save our asses before those bastards sink the only ships we have left?'

We were standing on the front looking out towards Villaviciosa. There were twenty men and two machine guns guarding the bridge. It was drizzling that night but we hardly noticed. Mariano and I were going from one command station to another trying to get ammo. We only had a couple of boxes; just enough for half an hour of steady fire and that wasn't enough. But no matter who we asked, no one wanted to give us supplies. That's why I'd started talking like that . . . and because my stomach was howling for food . . . and because I could see that it was getting harder and harder for us to keep soldiers on the line. So many ran, they went home or went looking for a ship, even a fishing boat, to escape on.

'I'm serious, Mariano,' I said. 'What are we fighting for now?'

I knew he'd start twisting his hair, but I'd never imagined he'd get so pissed.

'Bastard,' he said, 'cowardly bastard.' And then he pointed his rifle at my chest and clenched his teeth. Then he calmed down. He wasn't blind and he knew I wasn't wrong. He just didn't want to admit it.

Chapter Three

As Benjamin tried to get some sleep in the train for Paris, he watched the grey water of the Mosa slide past. The engine whispered through Reims; he could see the spires of the cathedral beyond the long stretch of buildings. Everything he left behind churned in his mind; his memories all seemed to be trying to squeeze through a tiny opening, as if the blackboard of his past was already full. It was March 18, 1933 – six weeks before Marshal von Hindenburg named Hitler chancellor of the Reich. Though for months already the people Benjamin knew no longer slept in their own beds and spent their days out at the cinema or in department stores. He hardly ever put his nose out the front door. He felt safe in his shell, while the other Berlin intellectuals gathered at the Romanisches Café. 'Sitting there,' Hans Sahl would write many years later, 'like animals petrified in the moment, untethered, waiting to be blown away. It was as if they'd lost their identities and were waiting for new ones to come and save them. They scoured over train schedules, hunched over maps, and wrote letters to relatives long since emigrated to America who had made their fortunes it seemed.' It was a long funeral for Weimar Germany, a timid ritual conducted to the rhythm of the word *escape*.

But Benjamin wasn't on the run – at least not yet. He wasn't well-known enough and his writing was too abstruse and esoteric to attract the attention of the Nazi censors or position him as an enemy of the state. And yet his life in Germany ended on January 30, 1933, with an 'almost mathematical simultaneity'. Within just a few days' time all his manuscripts were returned to him, his contacts disappeared, negotiations lapsed, all the letters he wrote asking for explanations were met with silence. Time was short. Benjamin never appeared to lose his calm during those weeks, even if what had befallen his friends should have filled him with terror. On January 20, the SA raided the houses of Horkheimer and Pollack. The night of February 27, Bloch, Brecht, Bentano, Dracauer and Speyer disappeared – all of them went abroad to escape. Ernst Schoen and Fritz Fränkel were captured and tortured.

Those last days he spent in Berlin were a constant attempt to distance himself from this inevitable end that had only just begun. He would be leaving his language and leaving himself. He crept on tiptoe while history was moving in on him like a locomotive. History begged him to follow his friend Gretel's advice and run. There was nowhere else to go but Paris. Over the last twenty years, Benjamin had spent many months there. He spoke the language fluently; he had translated Proust and Baudelaire into German; he knew French literature better than most; and he'd been working on a book, *Passagen-Werk*, about Paris. Where else would he go? Although this time around he wouldn't be making another trip to a city that he thought of, perhaps even more than Berlin, as his own. He would never be able to live there again as he had in 1913 – his first visit – when he'd experienced it 'intensely, the way only children know how to live'.

And yet, he had to go. Benjamin didn't believe that the Nazi spectre would eventually pass; he knew it would last. Nevertheless, all those weeks he spent shut up in his studio, he'd been waiting for something, ruminating on his doubts and apprehensions, until, at last, all of the indecision of the past years and months seemed to evaporate in a moment. He put his affairs in order, sublet the apartment for a year, and left quickly for France. He brought a couple of suitcases with him, filled with more books, manuscripts and notes than clothing. But he was forced to leave his library behind in Germany – the library that he needed for his work.

Benjamin left alone, because there was no one left who could bring him to the station. He arrived alone, because there was no one at the station to meet him. He stepped down from the train pale and exhausted. Sighing deeply, he looked out over the gentle rain, just barely liquid, falling over the Paris sky, and picked up his bags.

Chapter Four

You think it was easy to tell Mariano to his face that fighting was useless, that we had to get out before it was too late? Courage was what we needed back then. But lucky for us, he gave in just a couple of days later. German planes had downed a submarine and a destroyer in the port of Musel. They'd burned our stock houses. Gijón at night was like a scene from hell and it kept burning through the day. Our company abandoned the bridge we were defending and scattered: our front line had been eliminated. There we were, the two of us, at three in the afternoon, walking down the road that ran from Pedroso to Contriz. It wasn't as if Mariano would ever admit that I'd been right. When he saw a car approaching, he abruptly said, 'We'll requisition that car, get to Gijón and head out from there.'

We didn't really want to take the car, but we had to get out. The Musel wharf was in shambles, an obstacle course of shrapnel. You couldn't tell who was in command in that stampede. People weren't carrying permits; no one wore their stripes on their shoulders. Everyone – gunners, drivers, police and *asaltos* – was fighting to be the first on board a ship. But the few ships that were still seaworthy were already crowded with women and children. And the people on board were doing everything they could to keep anyone else off – otherwise they'd sink under all that excess weight.

I didn't even have time to say goodbye to my brothers Marcial and Libertad. We drove right to the wharf, climbed out of the car and headed for an old fishing boat that must have been held together with spit. Three armed soldiers blocked our path.

'You have to stop here, *comrades*.'

The boy pointing his rifle at my chest and staring me down was younger than me. I grabbed the barrel with my left hand and planted my 9-millimetre Star sub-machine gun into his gut and screamed, 'I'll blow you to bits!'

But as soon as we got on board, we joined the others keeping people off. The fact is there were hundreds of us crammed onto that boat, and not even a miracle would have made room for more. I closed my eyes. I couldn't take it. I'd been on the battle-ground just a few hours before. I couldn't count how many days it had been since I'd slept . . . or eaten. I heard some people in the distance agreeing to get off the boat as if in a dream, and then someone else said something about there being no more coal left. Then I realised that the boat was actually pulling away from the dock. Mariano was snoring next to me. Lucky him. He didn't seem to mind the sweat, the stench, all those bodies packed in like cigarettes in an unopened pack, the weeping women who'd left their children behind. The sea was calm enough, fortunately, but then just a few miles out we ran smack into the *Cervera*. It was dark already and the boat circled ours, shining lights at us, and then suddenly their cannons fired, falling in the water not a hundred metres away. That was when Mariano woke up. 'What the hell?' he said. All around us people were vomiting, trying to eat their identification papers, trying to get the captain to gun the engine, while other people were screaming for him to stop.

The *Cervera* came closer and a voice called out 'Who are you?' The guy at the command kept cool. 'Women and children,' he answered. Someone shone a flashlight into the stern and we flattened ourselves against the deck as best we could. The light circled and then went away.

I could hear the order. 'Head towards El Ferrol – we'll follow you in.'

We all started breathing again. The motor rumbled back to life, the night was dark, the wind rushed against the portholes. The *Cervera* kept close behind us. After two hours, they communicated that we should change our course and that another ship would take us into port. They turned and disappeared – out on the hunt for more important prey. Once they left we didn't know what to do. We argued about it. Some people wanted to follow the orders and others wanted to head north to France. We didn't have any food and the *Cervera* had sequestered our water supply to keep us from escaping.

'How long does it take to get to France?' I asked.

'Three days.'

'Is there fishing equipment aboard?'

'Do you see any? This old tub has been retired for more years than I can remember. There's no equipment at all left on her.'

Mariano, who hadn't said a word up to this point, suddenly tried to stand up, his rifle in his hand, but his head crashed into the ceiling. No one laughed. He dug his fingers into his hair and stared at the commander.

'That's enough talk,' he said. 'We'll head to Bordeaux. Anyone who has a problem with that should tell me now.'

They fell as silent as carpets, every last one of them, except for the babies who never stopped whimpering. And so we headed north, tired, stupid, racked with hunger. There wasn't even the shadow of the other ship. It was just sea, then sea, then more sea. Night-time came, dawn, and then daylight brought the wind, lifting the foamy waves high.

'When will we get there?'

The captain didn't answer. He looked up at the horizon. He was almost ready to collapse from thirst and hunger just like everyone else. Even the babies had stopped screaming. The coal started running low on the fourth day and the sea grew angry, the waves mounted. One man went crazy. He grabbed a pistol and started shooting. He wounded two people before someone shot him. And do you know what we did after that? I still get shivers thinking about it. We threw him onto the fire as a substitute for coal. Rest in peace. Thanks to him, though, we saw the coast of Lorient the next day. I think we all had this idea that we'd get a hero's welcome in France. They had a Popular Front government, right? But I already knew what we were in for — history. They treated us like enemies. As if all we were worth was the crust of bread they gave us before they loaded us onto trucks and sent us right back to Spain. Get out from under our feet. So that's how Mariano and I found ourselves in Barcelona. It was December . . . no; it was the end of November 1937 when we stepped out onto the Ramblas.

'All right,' said Mariano, wiping his hands. 'So we start over.'

Chapter Five

Destroying everything took only a couple of years. Just a few years in a country on the skids, feet mired in crisis, head stalked by the Nazis. And yet the few years around 1930 were, as Benjamin himself said, the high-point of his life. He was part of Brecht's circle, working at the national radio station and publishing in two highly regarded literary journals. He wanted to become a top German critic and had come quite close. He completed his long essay about Karl Kraus at the end of 1930, the beginning of 1931, attempting to reconcile his Janus-like mixing of theology and materialism. He never made much money, though after his divorce from Dora Kellner he managed to find himself a place to live. It was a large two-room studio in Wilmersdorf, on Prinzregentenstrasse, attached to his cousin Egon Wissing's house. The two-storey structure stood at the end of a lane, in the middle of a garden and underneath a willow. The entrance was in the back, up a steep, narrow stairway. In the study he'd arranged his library of two thousand books, a little drawing from his son Stefan's birthday, and several devotional paintings: a three-headed Christ (reproduced from an ivory Byzantine bas-relief), a *trompe-l'oeil* of the Bavarian forest, Saint Sebastian, and 'the only prophet of the Kabala, Paul Klee's *Angelus Novus*'.

The move had been costly and each month he struggled to get his rent money together. But he was happy in that house, adapting to the bachelor life and his new working nest. From his window he could see the old Wilmersdorfer Luch clock, which over time became a luxury he regretted having to give up. In the winter he could even see the children on the ice-skating rinks. Instead of sitting at a table, he'd write and work reclining on a sofa inherited from the former tenant. On that sofa, surrounded by his books and pictures — a vision of calm — he'd been able to start his *Passagen-Werk*, a sweeping portrait of nineteenth-century Paris that he'd spent years gathering material on. There were obstacles to spare, but for the first time Benjamin seemed resolute, free from that 'exhausting slowness' that seemed to cling to him. In truth he spent those months reconciling his debts — to himself and to life.

Disappearing, committing suicide, being over and done with everything — this was the thought spinning in his head like a sluggish, trapped horsefly. It pursued him through his travels in 1932 along the Riviera and down to Ibiza and then back to Germany. Sometimes, when he was reading at home on his couch, Benjamin could barely manage to finish a page without drifting into such a total state of disembodiment he'd forget to turn the page. He'd reflect on his project and plan it out. Should he do it at home or in a hotel? Was it really inevitable? The more he thought about doing it the more peaceful he felt. This 'project' dogged him for a year, working its way into his head and making him fluctuate between depression and ataraxy. He never revealed any of this in his letters to friends, despite the fact that it was distracting from his edits on what would eventually and miraculously become the short prose pieces in *Berlin Childhood*. Until he almost did it. It happened in Nice, at the Hôtel du Petit Parc near the end of July in 1932, two weeks after his fortieth birthday. It must have been an awful day – the doomed moment of gathering up all the threads of his life, putting the weights on a scale, everything that was and all that should have been. If he'd looked in the mirror that day, he would have seen a man who women found bodiless, a friend at most, a tired, poor, melancholy man, a stranger in his own world – a world that was slowly evaporating. This is why a few days earlier, when he was still on Ibiza, he'd written to his oldest friend Scholem, who had emigrated to Palestine. Of course he'd revealed it in his own way, with that passion for obscurity and mystery that had set him apart even when he was a young man, sending cryptic, desperate messages hoping that sooner or later his friend would understand. 'To think,' he wrote, 'that I'll be spending my birthday in Nice, in the company of a very silly man who I've met frequently on my trips, and we will drink to my health, unless I decide to be alone.' Who in the world was this man, wondered Scholem, trying to understand. Today, we might suppose that he was writing of the hunchbacked dwarf of childhood nursery rhymes who haunted his worst nightmares – his destiny already formed. Exhaustion seized Benjamin at the Hôtel du Petit Parc. It was as if the entire predicament of his existence were falling on him at once, as if the stars guiding his life had lined up in a perfect trajectory of misfortune.

He spent the day he arrived in Nice sitting on a bench on the Promenade des Anglais watching the sea. There was a heavy, hot sirocco blowing; it took his breath away. The wind mounted and the sea churned, the waves tossed up on the beach, sending up a foamy, brackish odour. And then Benjamin tore his gaze away from the horizon, took his fountain pen from its case and wrote Scholem a letter full of signs, breadcrumbs and clues about the tangled thoughts cluttering his mind. The letter was difficult to decipher. He wrote of looking reality in the face with a solemnity that felt like desperation. He'd had enough of the compromises he'd made in order to continue his life. He closed his bag and walked slowly through the alleys of the old city, working his way through the flower market, inhaling the good smells coming from the restaurants, watching people rush around finishing the day's errands. Just before sunset he counted the money he had left and ordered a croissant in a café on Place Rossetti. Then, his decision made, he returned to the hotel. He was very close to taking the final step. He spent the night stretched out on the bed, smoking his pipe and contemplating the faint ray of broken light that streamed hesitantly through the blinds from a street lamp. Until that yellow light turned golden in the early dawn. Then Benjamin closed the shutters and sat down at the table by the bed and composed his will. All of his manuscripts would go to Scholem. He carefully extracted a few pieces of paper and wrote three short messages to Ernst Schoen, Franz Hessel and Jula Cohn – one of the three most important women in his life along with Dora and Asja Lacis. He wrote to Jula: 'You know that I've loved you for a long time. And standing here on the brink of death, life offers me no rewards greater than those I suffered for you. This farewell must be enough. Yours, Walter.'

When he had finished writing, Benjamin removed his glasses

and rubbed his eyes. They were tired and as fiercely blue as ever. He stood, lit his pipe and then lay down on the bed, his shoes still on, staring motionless at a corner of the ceiling. Outside the July sun beat mercilessly on the old city and over the sea; it snuck into the alleys and worked through his shutters – the sound of the street rising with it. His pipe went out and Benjamin thought to himself that he wouldn't even be allowed to die in silence.

Chapter Six

Of course I haven't forgotten. We're getting to your philosopher. What was I talking about? Ah yes, how we ended up in Barcelona. Well, I would have liked a few days of rest, to steal some time back from that damn war, just walk around the city. But not Mariano. He got angry and stamped his feet and said that it was treachery to sit around with your hands in your pockets at a time like this, to act like a tourist while our brothers were fighting. So the very next morning we reported to the recruiting headquarters. They were very good to us. We were welcomed like rich men at a bank. 'Please come in. A pleasure to meet you. Make yourselves comfortable.' A captain asked us where we were from and then complimented us on our work. In the end, he gave us coupons to eat in any of the mess halls, a travel pass through the Republican zone, ration books, money and cigarettes. Most importantly, we walked out with a thirty-day leave. They said we'd talk about us going back to the front after Christmas. I was almost jumping for joy, but Mariano was practically black in the face he was so mad.

'Don't be upset,' I said. 'Command knows what's best for us.'

It didn't happen overnight, but we started taking pleasure in that life. We'd eat in whichever mess hall we pleased, or at the Basque tavern near the post office. We walked down the Ramblas and around the Barrio Chino, buying pack after pack of toasted almonds. Sometimes we'd go all the way down to the sea to wait for the fishermen to come in and we'd gorge ourselves on fresh sardines. We frittered away our time at the cinema and in crowded bars, until one morning there were sirens and we ran for a shelter. That's where I met her. What do you mean, who? Mercedes! Are you sure I haven't told you about her already? She was from Port Bou, near the border, but she was living in Barcelona. She was a nurse in the Calle Talleres hospital. Brunette – looked a little Gypsy with her high cheekbones and those green eyes. And if you could have seen her ass. She reminded me of my first girl, Pilar, who I'd taken when I was sixteen, by the barricades. They even had similar temperaments. But Mercedes was more hot-headed. To think she was an anarchist who was forced into marriage as a girl with an old fascist lawyer! She did away with him herself during the first days of the insurrection. But I didn't find out about that until much later. I didn't know anything when I saw her for the first time, sitting on a bench, in the dull lantern light, her legs crossed like a queen in the middle of all those hundreds of people cowering in the shelter. She was with a friend, Ana María – a pretty piece of work herself. Outside we could hear the bombs whistling and the explosions getting closer. We were all quiet and tense, but those two girls acted like nothing special was going on, whispering together. It's a mystery to me how women always find something to talk about.

I might have stood there forever watching her like an idiot.

Lucky for me, I had Mariano. You could tell that he liked Ana María. He nudged me with his elbow and then put his hand on my back.

'Let's go,' he said.

He had to push me physically because he knew what a disaster I was with girls. My stomach got all twisted and words would get stuck in my throat. He never thought twice about plunging right in. I kept quiet, but by the time the bombing was over and we left the shelter we were already laughing and joking together as we walked them back to the hospital. In reality there wasn't much to laugh about. You couldn't even count the dead and wounded. The smoke and dust was everywhere, the ambulance sirens were screeching all around. Entire buildings crumbled like cookies. Craters gaped in the street. Water shot from broken pipes and swirled around the bodies of the godforsaken people who hadn't made it to the shelter. We helped; we did what we could and then went to the Carl Marx mess for lunch. That night we saw Ana María and Mercedes again on the Ramblas and an hour later we were all in bed. That's how it was back then. People living under death's shadow do things intensely. Is my grandson Andrés still around? Good, so I can tell you. That girl would have made a corpse stiff. She wanted it; she was hungry and open to anything. I didn't have much experience but I was the happiest man in the world. You know what? Get closer, so I don't have to shout. I thought I should just stick it up her ass and throw away the key and burn the receipt. That was such a great life. Nights in bed with Mercedes. And then during the day while she was working and our men were falling by the thousands in Teruel, we were off raising hell with our buddies. Even Mariano was happy. But it all ended on the fourth of January when they called us all to the barracks. There were two hundred of us altogether – mostly Spaniards, but not only. There were Czechs, Brits, Poles, French, Italians and Finns.

'Get undressed,' ordered the officer.

After our shower they gave each of us two uniforms, two berets, a coat, a poncho, linens, even cigarettes and a pouch of American tobacco. Two thirty, in the middle of a downpour, a military train was heading out from the Francia station, destination unknown. Mariano and I were on that train. Ana María and Mercedes were down on the platform waving their handkerchiefs. There were no tears shed. I felt more angry, nostalgic and sick. It was like my stomach was eating itself. Mariano, on the other hand, was acting like he'd just come out of a long sleep. It didn't take much. Maybe he could already smell combat and that excited him.

'And we're back in business,' he said rubbing his hands together.

I looked at him and then turned away to look out the window at the factory smokestacks getting smaller in the distance, the fields outside Barcelona reduced to swamps under the completely grey sky and the rain beating against the glass. I imagined myself back in the trenches – the cold, the cannon fire.

'You're out of your mind,' I told him and then went to sit down.

Chapter Seven

Benjamin performed an about-face and completely abandoned his plan to take his own life in that little room at the Hôtel du Petit Parc in Nice. His reasons remain a mystery. Over the months that followed, he hunkered down and worked, taking full advantage of his incredible capacity for concentration and fishing through his 'reservoir of profound serenity' – nothing seemed to upset him. It was as if passing through death and looking it in the eyes, he'd passed some kind of initiation ritual. After that, life couldn't present him with anything worse. In the meantime, living was worthwhile.

And yet, a year later, after his escape from Berlin to Paris, he'd spent only a few days in the shadow of the Eiffel Tower before descending back into turmoil. In bed, at a hotel on rue de la Tour in the sixteenth arrondissement, Benjamin watched his pipe smoke curl up toward the sink and the cracked mirror on the wall in front of him; it filled the grimy room, spread greyly over the grey walls. He'd come back to Paris from Ibiza at the end of September 1933 tormented by a fever that came over him in waves. Malaria, claimed the doctor. A hearty quinine

28

cure lowered his body temperature but his strength didn't come back. He squandered the little energy he had writing letter after letter. 'This illness,' he wrote to his friend in Palestine, 'has left me just enough strength to recognise the wretchedness of my situation – but not enough strength to extricate myself from it. I'm not even healthy enough to climb the stairs of the cheap hotel where I've been forced to take lodging.'

Lying on that bed, covers pulled up to his nose, he listened carefully to the growl of the city beyond the closed blinds – snarling and ready to pounce. This wasn't the same city that he'd once known. But then he wasn't the curious carefree tourist of a few years before either. For a person like him, alone and without money or a home, without a country or a language, for a Jew running from the Nazis, Paris showed another face, a harsher, harder face. Benjamin didn't even need to go to Ibiza and then come back to France in order to comprehend the situation. He'd already predicted it to Scholem two months earlier: 'The Parisians are saying "*Les émigrés sont pires que les boches*," and that should give you an accurate idea of the kind of society that awaits one there.'

He wasn't wrong. With the exception of a brief period under the Popular Front government, the émigré life in France just kept getting harder. There were expulsions and arrests; it was impossible to process any kind of paperwork. As if that weren't enough, the group of exiles and intellectuals who had gathered in Paris so committed to proving that there was another 'better' Germany drew far too much attention from the Brownshirts. They were put under surveillance – terrorised, robbed, assassinated. The exile centres filled with spies compiling lists, watching activities, furnishing information and trying to discourage the leadership. It was dangerous to be too politically exposed and talking to anyone you didn't already know very well was a risk seldom worth running.

Benjamin was hardly prepared for that battle. Which is why (following the shadowy contortions of his complex temperament) he simply absented himself and avoided growing attached to anyone. He preferred to stay away from the in-fighting of the communist movement or the oblivious pettiness of the various émigré groups. He was reserved, yes, but he ended up alone, choosing isolation. And for years he wrote the saddest letters to his friends, who were by now scattered to all four corners of the world, regretting that loneliness. He wrote letters pretending that letter writing wasn't anachronistic. Letters allowed him, as Adorno explained, 'To reject the separation and remain no less far away, no less separated.' He wrote confessions without revealing to himself that he felt profoundly more alone than ever before and that he still preferred not to join the other émigrés at the café. In the end, for someone like him, it was almost better to be lost in the anonymity of a giant foreign city.

It was difficult. Benjamin was really distressed by the conversations he had with his few, highly selected friends from Berlin. The number of people he associated with in Paris could be counted on one hand: Hans Sahl, the photographer Gisèle Freund, Hannah Arendt (philosopher and distant relative), Stephan Lackner and Fritz Lieb (Karl Barth's student) whom he addressed almost immediately in intimate terms while it had taken him almost ten years to speak like that with Scholem, a bosom friend and companion since youth. Later on, Walter would become involved with Adrienne Monnier, Sylvia Beach, and Arthur Koestler – that was after he returned from Spain and left the Communist Party — and Pierre Klosowski and Georges Bataille. But it's not possible to replace friends you've had for twenty years, the people you discovered the world with. Those friends were all out of reach. Scholem was in Palestine. His ex-wife Dora was in Italy, Jula Cohn, whom he'd loved in the years leading up to the divorce, was in Germany with her husband Felix Noeggerath. And Alfred Cohn was in Spain. This is another one of the blows that exile delivers — it takes everyone along the path of their own individual diaspora. It shatters the collective spirit. Not much remains afterward. You're left alone to settle your accounts, ruminating over the same crop of thoughts every day, cultivating them in solitude. Perhaps the only thing left afterward is your work.

'Until it was written,' said Sahl in his memoir, 'it was still being lived. Until it was written, Hitler hadn't won yet.' But what if you were like Benjamin, racked with such a pitiful vision of yourself that it's almost suffocating? 'Living among the émigrés is unbearable,' he confessed to Scholem on the last day of 1933. 'A solitary life is not more tolerable. Living in a French world is impossible. All that is left then is work. Although nothing is more threatening to work than the plain recognition that work is the entirety of your inner life.'

But that was what allowed him to keep going, to persist. In March 1934, Benjamin resumed work on his Parisian *Passagen-Werk* — threshold spaces, places where ancient myths and the merchandise of the modern world came together. And he felt like he could only work in Paris. That book full of quotations and images, built like an enormous kaleidoscope, took root in books that had already been written. This is how Paris was for Benjamin, 'the great reading room of a library divided by the

Seine.' It was a library that Walter plundered without scruples, copying sentences, illustrations, notes and references with boundless energy into his notebooks. The material he accumulated became more and more cumbersome while the project began to seem perhaps interminable. Benjamin worked on *Passagen-Werk* almost ceaselessly during those years of exile, stopping only to work on some essay commissioned by the Horkheimer Institute – for Adorno, who was supplying the small grant he was living on. But it was his essay 'The Work of Art in the Mechanical Age' that seemed most promising. For years his allusive, esoteric projects had kept him out of fashionable conversation, but this essay led him to believe he might be influential in the debate over the future of Marxist aesthetics. Benjamin would be at the middle of a global discussion and wouldn't feel so alone anymore. How wrong he was. That essay may be his most famous work today, but it had a catastrophic reception at the time – even from his staunch supporters: Scholem was non-committal, Adorno critical, Brecht was even offended and the audience – mostly Communist Party members – at the two evening panels organised by the association of exiled German writers where Benjamin and Hans Sahl discussed the essay listened as if in a silent bubble, almost a boycott. This was late June 1936.

'That's it. It's all over,' he said to Hans Sahl as they walked home together at the end of the evening. The moon was hidden behind a pitch-black cloud. Blustery wind rattled the lamps over the deserted streets. It was a peculiar wind for a humid June night – a grim wind, fat with rancour and rain. Leaving the station on the metro, the lights of the station were quickly swallowed by the dark tunnel.

'What's over?' asked Sahl.

'It's over for them. You saw their faces? The *comrades*? And their leader, Müzenberg . . . they're jackasses and I don't mean just aesthetically speaking.'

In Weimar Germany Sahl had been an important theatre and film critic, among the first to believe in film as an art form. Benjamin's essay brought new perspective to bear on his hunch and yet no one seemed to appreciate it.

'You'll see, Walter,' he said as they stood on the steps of the station leading up to the road. 'They'll give it its due in the end. You're too far ahead of your time.'

It was late by the time they reached the rue de Vaugirard, Benjamin's pace was slow and uncertain and his head was bowed. He'd stop periodically but continue talking, shaking his head and never looking up at Sahl, who was having some difficulty following but couldn't figure out how to interrupt.

'I made a mistake, I made a mistake . . .' he kept repeating in the grimy darkness of the night. He was worn out and panting. This was a man used to being in control of his feelings. He never liked to reveal too much and worried about saying the wrong thing. But that evening he seemed short of illusions. And was slowly pulling the white flag of surrender from his pocket.

Suddenly he burst out, 'Enough of this,' and embarrassed drops of rain began to fall. Sahl opened his umbrella and stood closer, trying to keep Benjamin from getting wet.

'Maybe we should leave,' he whispered. 'I've already seen a couple of uniforms around. Are your papers in order?'

'What does it matter?'

It was god only knows what time of night and they'd been standing there for a long time under the soundless rain shower.

And then two policemen out on their rounds appeared from around the corner.

'Bonsoir,' said one, lifting his fingers to his cap. 'You've been standing here for quite a while now. Who are you and what are you doing?'

Sahl didn't have time to answer because Benjamin jumped in, 'We are two German Jews standing under an umbrella talking,' he said very seriously. Then he twirled his fingers in the air and made off alone through the rain that had begun to seem unending.

After that ill-fated evening in 1936, Benjamin made no further efforts to broaden his circle. Even though he missed intellectual companionship and his loneliness bothered him, he resigned himself to it. He began to concentrate on himself and his few friends whom he didn't spare the smallest detail – not even his constant state of anxiety over his finances – in his letters and in rare encounters. Money became his central concern, his obsession.

After his German remittances were suspended, his only source of income was the money coming in from Adorno and Horkheimer's Institute for Social Research. But that money never seemed enough. There isn't a single letter from that extensive period that doesn't hint at his hardships and deprivations, the difficulty of daily survival, the humiliation he suffered without any promise of remedy. In October 1935, for example, Benjamin wrote to Max Horkheimer, 'Any help you give me will produce immediate relief. I have reduced my living expenses enormously compared to what they were in April when I returned to Paris, consequently I am now living as a boarder with some émigrés. Beyond that, I have succeeded in obtaining permission to take my midday meal at a restaurant that has a special arrangement for French intellectuals. In the first place, however, this permission is temporary and, in the second place, I can make use of it only on those days I am not in the library, for the restaurant is very far from there. I will only mention in passing that I ought to renew my *carte d'identité* but do not have the one hundred francs this requires. Since it involves a fee of fifty francs, I have also not yet been able to join the *Presse Étrangère*, which I was urged to do for administrative reasons.' To Scholem he wrote, 'I don't know how long my powers of resistance will last in view of all the circumstances, since I am provided with only the bare necessities for *at most* two weeks a month. The most trifling purchase depends on a miracle taking place.'

Was he exaggerating? Possibly. Even Scholem, his very best friend, would admit years later that he'd had doubts and harboured suspicions. The truth might have been that when it came to money and other practical things – what it takes to put food on the table – Benjamin was like a man lost in the desert, a time-traveller who stumbled into the present.

'You should have been born in the eighteenth or nineteenth century, like one of your *flâneurs*,' Hannah Arendt told him once. It must have been at the Café de la Paix after she'd returned from one of her trips to Palestine. During that period Hannah was director of the Paris office of the Alijah Youth, which organised the emigration of children to Palestine. 'Really you're an *homme de lettres* and you don't belong to any time,' she sighed as she finished off her tea and tossed her mane of black hair over her shoulder. 'You should have lived in a time when you could have been paid to write what you write without ever thinking about obligations. Wouldn't you like a stipend that had no obligations attached?'

She seemed to grow meaner as she spoke, meaner and more tired. It was as if she was going to tell him everything she thought this time, without weighing her words.

'No, not at all . . .' Walter spluttered.

'Of course you remember that we no longer live in the age of Pascal and Montaigne. Things didn't go in your favour at the university, and then they went badly with Scholem and the Zionists, and badly with your Marxist friend. Will you ever open your eyes?'

She was off and running now. It was a bad sign when she knit her brows like that.

'It's useless to keep trying,' she added sternly. 'You will never find anyone who is willing to give you money so that you can live happily ever after as an *homme de lettres,* a revolutionary aristocrat. I am sorry to be the one to tell you, Walter, but there's not much room left in the world for men like you.'

He could only remember a very few occasions in which anyone had dared to speak so harshly with him. Benjamin looked at her, trying to fight against the onslaught of emotions that seemed to be pressing on him from all sides. The people sitting around them in the café seemed a muffled crowd in the distance, only concerned with what was going on at their table. He thought he should say something, but every sentence that came to mind deteriorated before he could open his mouth.

'One becomes ever more what one is,' he finally mumbled.

Hannah didn't answer. It would have been useless to continue the discussion. It would have been equally impossible to chat about something else. As they left, Benjamin took off his glasses, wiped them carefully, waved at her with some embarrassment and headed for the metro. The thoughts running through his head seemed false, they didn't belong to him – these compact black masses like storm clouds, chaotic and powerful images – the threadbare suit, the wretched room where he lived, the meals made of a croissant and coffee, the nightmares and loneliness, everything that he'd forsaken, the thousand humiliations he'd suffered for the publication of an article, or an essay, even the translation of a novel. Anything to thwart his horoscope. How long could he go on like this?

And of course, over seven years of his exile in Paris, Benjamin had been forced to change house eighteen times, live in a sublet with strangers and fellow immigrants, in the fleapits of *banlieue*, in noisy little draughty rooms and all of this meant that until 1938 he couldn't even keep his books with him or receive visitors. He could only work at the National Library or in a café on the Left Bank, where if you ordered a coffee the waiters would let you sit for hours. Except for the brief period when he visited Brecht in Denmark or took advantage of Dora's hospitality in San Remo, Walter was always in the library or at one of those cafés, biding time as his life slowly crumbled around him.

Chapter Eight

The cold, my boy. It was four below zero centigrade when we got to the front. They brought us to Saragozza in Pina to relieve the soldiers stationed on the Ebro river. There was mud, coagulated mud and mud men — frozen and bundled up in that tangle of trenches. That was the front that winter. On the bright side, things were calm there — a burst of gunfire every so often, an isolated mortar shell — just so we felt useful. Further south, Teruel was a slaughter. Our side had launched the attack but now Franco's forces were fighting back and Italian artillery alongside the Legione Condor were crushing the advance. By the end of February, they'd taken back Teruel and collected interest along the way. They got all the way to Alfambra. We lost ten thousand men; another fifteen thousand were taken prisoner. Mariano was seething. The news kept coming in and making him hungrier than ever for combat. At night he made us patrol the river in that cold that would turn your breath to ice, just to show that we were at war too.

'The men are tired,' I said one morning. 'They know these midnight walks are as good as useless.'

He seemed to think about that. Then he snorted and heaved a glob of spit the size of an egg on the ground.

'Remember that I'm your Lieutenant,' he said and went off to sleep.

Something ugly had come between us but we didn't have any time to clear the air. Franco moved down the front and even those of us at Aragon came under fire. They forced us down with artillery and then charged. We were face to face with the Moroccan soldiers under General Yagüe. He was a tough character, a Falange fascist who had always been commander of the *Regulares d'Africa*. We couldn't have been in a worse situation. Mariano and I had faced the Moroccans in '34 at Gijón, and then again in Bilbao and Santander the summer before. They were worse than animals; they were inhumanly cruel, raped women and cut your throat laughing like possessed men. They even got a kick out of the lowest kind of actions, like occupying a hospital and exterminating the doctors and the wounded with their bayonets, goring them in their stretchers. Now they were advancing along the right bank and coming toward us, razing everything in their path. There weren't many of us and we weren't well armed. Meanwhile our front was collapsing, Belchite, Alcañiz, Rudilla. Colonel Aranda took Montalbán.

We decided that I should go to Barcelona to get more ammunition and bring it back fast. I drove the truck full-speed and pulled into headquarters in the early afternoon. The city seemed numb from a recent bombing. Over the last few months the Italians had gone mad, they were taking off from Maiorca and dropping as many bombs as they could. Barcelona had turned greyer and sadder, people dragged themselves grimly through the dusty streets. A colonel at the command station told me that it would take them all night to load the truck. Six o'clock and there I was waiting in front of the Calle Telleres hospital. Who else would I be waiting for? Mercedes. She was what she was. My woman. With her flashing green eyes, and curves in all the right places. It was like she was made just for me. I had two months to catch up on and just seeing her again triggered something in my trousers. She was happy to see me. Sure. But not happy enough.

'Did you meet someone else?' I asked outright as we walked up the Paseig de Gracia.

She stopped and looked me in the eyes. Then she raised her hand, folded down her thumb and waved her remaining fingers in the air.

'I have four others,' she answered, smiling sadly. 'But that's none of your business. I'm a free woman, got that?'

Free love and all that crap. Do you remember it?

'Please,' I managed to say to her. 'Why would I care?'

Of course I cared and boy did I. My stomach was in knots, my intestines were growling and twisting. But little by little she kept getting sweeter and soon it was just like before. Within two hours we were back at her house in bed. She was on all fours, face in the pillow, and I took her from behind. I already told you that we liked it like that. That was when we heard the sirens and a faraway grumble, that buzz that kept getting louder and heavier and the next thing you knew all you could hear were engines rumbling. Heinkel planes. We could hear the first bombs fall, far away, beyond the train station.

'Don't stop,' she said. 'Keep going.'

Well, that's easier said than done. The troops were already starting to pull out, abandon the front. Plop it went – getting out of the trench. You want to be able to shake it off, but nothing doing. The planes were coming and going low overhead. Mercedes turned around and looked at me, head to toe.

'You're really just a boy,' she said. 'Okay. Let's get dressed now and we'll go down into the shelter.

We didn't know what was in store for us. We ended up staying there for two days, packed in like sardines. Nothing to eat or drink. All that whimpering and snivelling in between the blasts. A dust came down over us every time the walls shook from the explosion. The bombings came in waves, about every three hours, sometimes more frequently, hitting every neighbourhood and every civic and military target. We'd never seen anything like it before – it was the first time there'd ever been a bombing like that, and there I was in the middle. Once we could come out we realised right away that the death toll would be in the thousands. Streams of blood were running down the pavement; there were arms, heads and legs just scattered in the middle of rubble. The smell of burnt earth, stone and flesh got into your nose. I should've built up a tougher skin by then. But I couldn't manage to keep calm. Mercedes looked slowly around and started sobbing. Then I hugged her and we kissed.

'I have to go now,' she said. 'I've got to get to the hospital.'

'When will we see each other again?' I asked.

She shrugged and indicated the disaster all around us.

'When you get back from the front,' she answered and took off.

The front. Damn. They were still waiting for ammo back at the camp. I got there right in time – in time to partake in the dismantling. Mariano shouted when he saw me.

'Back already? You could have stayed on for a while longer.

Our own little lord out on a jaunt and we're back here dying. Three-day lock-up.'

Mariano loved to cut people down. He liked it twice as much when he was doing it to me. But I answered back this time.

'Didn't you hear that they bombed Barcelona? The whole world is angry at Franco and Mussolini and you're taking it out on your friend.'

'Friend my ass,' he yelled. 'Remember that I'm your superior.'

He never got over that. I was about to jump on him when Mariano looked at me and smiled, 'Did you see Ana María?'

'Yes, sure,' I lied. 'She's thinking about you and sends her best.'

The peace didn't last. On March 22, Solchaga and Moscardó's troops attacked between Huesca and Saragozza. It was our turn the next day – us against Yagüe. When I saw the Moroccans coming across the river in their fezzes and white trousers, I realised that it was all over. Even Mariano realised it; and he gave the orders to abandon our position. We ran for kilometres, days on end, we crossed Aragon under air fire, through lines of civilians abandoning their villages and cities, dragging carts filled with mattresses, chickens, goats. And then Lérida fell on April 3. Two weeks later the fourth Navarra Division led by Camilo Alonso Vega reached the sea near Vinaroz. Our territory was cleaved in two.

Chapter Nine

Five years after his arrival in Paris, Benjamin finally scraped together enough money to rent a room for himself. Number 10 rue Dombasle in the fifteenth arrondissement was an early twentieth-century building, a good distance from the centre. A lot of German immigrants lived there under the surveillance of Madame Dubois, an elderly but good-natured landlady. The Hungarian journalist Arthur Koestler, who, after having been condemned to death by Franco for his coverage of the German and Italian participation in the civil war, scandalously left the Communist Party, lived there. Above him lived his lady friend, the very young English sculptor Daphne Hardy. Elsewhere in the building: Fritz Fränkel, a famous doctor who in the past had supervised Benjamin's hashish and opium experiments; a German psychoanalyst; and Lisa Fittko's brother, Hans. Benjamin had met Lisa Fittko and her husband — also named Hans — one afternoon in 1933 at the Café Dôme. The Fittkos with their anti-Hitler activism were a little like a parsley sprig among the leftist exiled intellectuals. But Benjamin never had much interest in them. Though he did spend an evening at the couple's little apartment in Montmartre looking out over an intersection of rue Norvis, rue de Saules and rue St-Rustique that had been often painted by Utrillo. Since Hans lived right above Benjamin, he came to appreciate him in time – tall and handsome and a theoretical physicist. Without his favourite chess opponent, Brecht, Benjamin spent many winter evenings playing with Hans instead, bombarding him with questions about his research but never revealing the first thing about his own.

Five years to secure an apartment and gather his papers and books. Yet Benjamin never managed to resolve the problem of furnishing those few square metres. Despite his best efforts, the room stayed bare and uncomfortable. The only thing Benjamin really had was a splintered mahogany desk on which he kept a leather briefcase that had belonged to his father. On one wall hung the only painting he'd managed to keep, Klee's *Angelus Novus* – his secret emblem.

It was fine. Sometimes, sitting at his desk looking through his books, his light adjusted low almost on the desk, Benjamin would think back with disgust on the places he'd lived during his years of exile. The last one had been a small ground-floor room, dank and dark, looking over one of the main thorough-fares out of Paris. The roar of trucks getting onto the highway had actually kept him from working on his Baudelaire essay. Here on rue Dombasle, the lift just on the other side of the wall made a racket that drove him to distraction. On very hot days, when he opened the window, the street noise managed to drown out the squeaking pulleys and hollow hum of the motor, permitting him several hours of concentration.

Gershom Scholem visited him in that room late in February. He'd been invited to New York to give a series of lectures on

Jewish mysticism and organised a five-day stopover in Paris so that he could see his old friend. The encounter had been cancelled so many times, left up in the air and postponed, that Walter had written that he was starting to think of it as 'the meeting of leaves torn from their distant trees in a storm'.

They hadn't seen each other for eleven years. Benjamin even let himself be hugged before settling onto the bed and smoking one Salomé after another. Pipe tobacco had become so expensive that he only allowed himself a very occasional pipe, and in the meantime settled for the dreadful, cheap Turkish cigarettes instead. Sitting uncomfortably on the least shredded of the chairs, Scholem sized up his friend. Walter looked older than his forty-six years; he'd grown rounder, his moustache was thicker and neglect speckled his sober bearing. Under his now grey hair, his face had turned ashen, his brow was heavier, and a hint of a double chin appeared when he nodded. His knuckles were pale and swollen. Scholem assumed it was due to poor circulation or his heart.

'You look well,' he said at last.

'Liar,' responded Benjamin disconsolately. 'That's what you say when it's not true anymore. You know what Lisa Fittko calls me? She's Hans's sister – the man we just met on the stairs. She called me old Benjamin. A lot of people do. They just don't know that I know.'

When they went out later for a stroll, Benjamin clung to Scholem's arm. Scholem was significantly taller and younger too.

'Are you trying to kill me, Gerhard?' he said, using Scholem's childhood name. 'Go slower. Remember that I'm old Benjamin.'

It wasn't an easy encounter after so many years. Intense years that hadn't chipped away at their friendship so much as assailed the ideas they once had in common. If they disagreed now, sparks flew. They fought on rue Dombasle, in the cafés along Boul'Mich', and they fought on the street. They argued about Walter's friendship with Brecht, about his essay on the work of art in the mechanical age, about Céline and anti-Semitism, about the trials in Moscow that the world was watching with bated breath. Benjamin was reticent. His responses were torturous, he treated Scholem as if he were a party member, a 'class enemy', despite the fact that Scholem had never officially joined up and often disparaged the communist leaders. He may or may not have known then the fate of Asja Lacis, the revolutionary Latvian that Benjamin had met on Capri in 1924, the woman that he perhaps loved best of all, and who in the end fell victim to the great Soviet purification.

Benjamin continually side-stepped things, avoiding, even dodging the subject of his arrangement with Horkheimer and Adorno's Institute, which Scholem was not enamoured of. His friend attempted to engage him, but Benjamin brusquely and stubbornly shut him out.

'I'm very happy with them,' he'd say with conviction. Then, not half an hour later, he would admit that he could neither stand nor respect Horkheimer. 'I don't know. He's not trustworthy, even on the theoretical level. Not a small thing . . .'

On their last evening together, the two sat on a bench in the Luxembourg Gardens, resting. It was already getting dark, and it was cold. The sky was gritty and an angry wind announced that winter was on its way. Straining for breath, Benjamin stared at the branches of a nearby lime tree that looked unhealthy.

'Under the roof of the institution,' he announced as if talking to himself, not looking at his friend, 'the tattered thread of my life is lost.'

'Kafka?' asked Scholem, sinking his chin into his collar.

'Exactly,' smiled Walter. 'Two years,' he added with a sudden seriousness. 'I would really need two years of not having to depend on the Institute. To be able to concentrate on *Passagen-Werk*. It's not even a viable option here in Europe, but if you were able to rustle up some kind of appointment for me, something, then I could liberate myself from Horkheimer. I swear I would. Could you ask your editor friend, Schocken, if he would let me write a book about Kafka? Then I could at last come to Palestine.'

The light in the sky slackened and seemed on the verge of disappearing. Lower on the horizon, just over the tree line, darkness was gathering. Scholem looked angrily at his friend, as if the shadow of a cloud had crossed over him. His expression read vexation and pain as if some old decay had suddenly emerged.

'You remember Magnes?' he suddenly asked.

'Magnes who? Your chancellor in Jerusalem? Him?'

'Yes, him,' replied Scholem.

They weren't looking at each other as they spoke but staring at the gravel by their feet and at the hedges along the street. But Scholem could imagine his friend's face gone red with anger and embarrassment.

'You remember,' he added to fill the silence, 'don't you, that ten years ago I asked him to lend you money so that you could study Hebrew and come to Palestine? You changed your mind, but you never returned the money. Now you want me to ask again on your behalf?'

The last sentence seemed to come from Scholem's feet, as if he were trying to subsume his anger.

'I can explain that. I can explain everything,' muttered Benjamin, watching a dog go into a flowerbed at the end of the path.

'Of course you can explain. But how do you explain it to me, Walter?'

Benjamin looked up and tried to smile now.

'Do it for a friend,' he said. 'It's the last favour I'll ask.'

Scholem didn't blink for a long, a very long minute.

'Okay, I will try,' he answered.

Walter looked at him hopefully. He was struggling to keep down another thought that he knew should surface – he had to hide it. Just a little while before this he'd scolded Adorno when he left for New York. 'You have to stay,' he told him. 'You have to stay here. If we all leave, Europe will cease to exist.'

But now he'd reneged even on himself. He sat with his gaze cast down, and pushed the pebbles around with his toe. The park was slowly emptying. Beyond the gate, the street lights of rue de Fleurus had already come on.

'It's late. I have to go,' said Scholem with a sigh.

That was the last time they saw each other.

Chapter Ten

You know, we didn't have a chance of winning and we should have admitted it back then. Think about it. While Franco was attacking Aragona, Hitler swallowed Austria whole – in a single night. While everyone – France, England – they all just shut up, sat back and watched. This whole line we got handed of non-intervention. If it weren't also a tragedy it would be a farce. It wouldn't have even taken much; a child could have seen it. Hell if Mussolini and Hitler weren't going to intervene. After Austria, people started admitting it, but didn't concede it. As if no one could see what the Germans were up to. Everyone was too busy fawning over them. Adolf pointed and everyone else saluted. Even Stalin. And believe you me, the idea that he was our ally should have been looking dubious by then. France opened its border for a while, just enough time for us to get some arms in, but then they closed right up again. Europe was abandoning us. And then what did they go on to do?

Don't look at me like that. I know this is the sort of stuff you say afterwards. The situation was not perfectly clear back then and in any case it wasn't like we could just open the battle up to those sons of bitches. We didn't have any choice back then. We had to fight anyway, and all we could do was pray for god knows what – a miracle. Or that no one had the last word yet.

After the retreat, Mariano and I walked around Barcelona as dejected as could be. During the day we hung around headquarters waiting for the platoons to be reorganised and for someone to tell us what to do. At night, lucky us, we'd be with Ana María and Mercedes. But something had changed, though I didn't know what. You could see it in the way we smiled, the way we talked. It was just like before but wrapped in a sadness that wouldn't go away if you scraped it. Mercedes and I kept up like before but something was prickly between the other two. Then they had a fight one evening when we were heading to the movies near Paralelo. Mercedes and I were walking ahead. Ana María must have said that she didn't love him anymore or something like that because suddenly we heard Mariano screaming from behind us, 'There's someone else, isn't there? Admit it.'

'Yes,' said Ana María. 'So what if there is?'

I turned and saw Mariano, fist digging into his curls, staring at her.

'I'm the one who should be asking so what. I'm out there freezing my ass on the front and you're running around, and meantime, you ugly bitch, you're sending me messages. "I think of him all the time, send him my love." What a tramp.'

'Messages? What messages? What are you talking about – when ever?' she started to say.

Oh god, I thought, now I'm going to get dragged into it. I squeezed Mercedes' hand hard and we walked ahead. The only reason I got out of that was because Mariano had already gone too far, twisting his hair and glaring like that. He wasn't accustomed to broken promises, and that's why he fell to pieces so quickly. He was begging, sweating, ranting.

'What about all those things you said about free love?' we heard him say.

'Precisely. It's free,' she said, 'and I don't want to be with you. Do you get it or not?'

We never got to the movies and over the next days my buddy's mood was so ferocious that he'd have poisoned you if he bit you. I ended up sneaking around with Mercedes so that he wouldn't suffer seeing us together. Brimming with anger and hungry for revenge, he ended up doing everything he could to get transferred into an offensive strike unit. He told them that he wanted to lead a counter-offensive commando squad to run raids and sabotage the enemy's line before our guys even got there. It was a way of committing suicide, that's what it was. But amazingly they took him seriously because of his merits on the field. In late April, they green-lighted his project. He threw himself into the preparations and I didn't see him for days. I took advantage of the time to visit Mercedes. By now we'd become used to the air raids; my soldier kept up his work and she got so excited when the planes passed low overhead. It was going well with us and would have kept going that way if Mariano hadn't caught us one afternoon eating ice cream in a café on the Ramblas.

'I've been looking for you for three hours,' he said.

It was a clear May evening, a light breeze swept the air, so softly it seemed to be strolling. Mercedes shifted in her seat and grabbed my hand under the table. She knew what was going on. Mariano didn't even sit down. Standing over me like a grenadier, he stared right at me, avoided Mercedes' eyes.

'I'm all set,' he said. 'I'm leaving the day after tomorrow with my division. I picked out my men, guys with balls. You're on board, right?'

What could I say? I looked at her for help but her expression gave away nothing. I knew what she was thinking though – it's fine to have fun and take advantage of every instant. But when it comes time to fight, only a coward hangs back. And I would have said the same thing. To keep living this quasi-life would be a sentence to cowardice and mediocrity.

'Okay,' I whispered. 'I'll see you tomorrow at headquarters.'

The light from the street lamps on the Ramblas was shining against an almost black sky. A few stars twinkled on. That sky was so beautiful it made you curse the day the damned war started. There were people crowding around us, soldiers, mothers with their children about to go in for dinner, idlers. A van passed, anarchist flags waving, full of recruits heading for the station.

'Let's go home,' Mercedes murmured. I put my tongue in her ear and a hand on her ass. 'If they bomb us tonight, it won't matter,' I said quietly.

Chapter Eleven

We spent two weeks training in a quarry near the Pyrenees and then set off. We travelled by Russian Sturke jeeps, three of them, for a day, then through the night with our headlights off, and half of the next morning. There were sixteen men in our unit. I drove the first car with Mariano, our captain. With us rode: a Swiss cook, our look-out Jimmie, a blond Irishman, and Alfonso, Italian, second sergeant. He was a bit of a fool but was a genius with explosives. The rest of the unit was in the other cars: two Andalusians, a Galician, three Americans — one black — two German Communists and who else have I forgotten? Right, the Englishman and Jan, he was Dutch and a mortar expert. Then there was Lech, a short Pollack — a bundle of nerves he was and an ace at gunning down planes. Mariano had chosen his men well; they were all adventurers, sure, but they were good companions too. Most importantly, they were good with weapons, could move from grenades to machine guns without blinking and then change again to rifles, knives, pistols.

Right before noon, we came to a village that had been bombed to the ground. There was no one there except for some rabbits, goats and chickens picking through the rubble. We caught a jackass and two mules and loaded them up with arms and provisions and started climbing the mountain. After three hours we hit the top and found an abandoned monastery, the pantry still stocked to the brim with oil, rice, beans, chickpeas, wine. So we decided to pitch camp there. Since we didn't have trenches, we took our positions in the craters that the bombs had left. We overlooked the Ebro from here and could watch the enemy stacked out on the opposite side of the river. Yagüe's Moroccan *Regulares* were here, the Guardia Civil, Carlist *Requetés*, the Italian volunteers and the Spanish Foreign Legion. It was quiet on the front. They only shot if we went to get water at the spring, otherwise it was as calm as could be. If only we didn't have to patrol for miles in order to cover the ground between us and the next unit – there were so few of us out there.

We lay low for a week, watching the troops' movements, and marking the positions of their cannons. Then we started crossing the river at night. It was easy. The water was low and there was hardly any current. We'd take their guards by surprise and beat them, then break through their lines with grenades. We came back with a prisoner almost every night. One time we went pretty far and found the Moroccan camp. One was playing the flute next to the fire; others were sleeping half-naked on the ground.

'Now,' said Mariano.

We attacked. We launched twenty grenades and sprayed them with two machine guns followed by rifle gunfire. It was a massacre. They were furious. As we were retreating across the river mortar shells starting falling in the water around us and then the machine-gun fire started showering on us from every direction. Frankie, an American, took one in the shoulder, but it wasn't serious. I almost broke my foot getting up the bank. We barely made it across the river and into the ditches dug by mortar fire along the bank. We were out of bullets.

'Only shoot if they try to get to this side,' ordered Mariano.

Soon, Jimmie the Irishman came to tell us that there was an entire column getting ready to cross. Moroccans, two or three hundred, maybe more, a whole battalion. It was like they'd gone mad, shrieking and throwing their rifles into the air. The kind of stuff that makes you shiver under a full moon.

'Wild men,' said Alfonso, spitting on the ground. 'Should I get some dynamite ready?'

Mariano was stretched out behind a dry wall, twisting his hair. He looked at me and then at the Moroccans, then back at Alfonso, and then at the Moroccans.

'No,' he said. 'Let's get back up to our ditches and wait for them. Once they've crossed the river and are out in the open we'll attack.'

They thought we'd retreated so they were almost casual as they waded through the knee-high water. They moved forward in groups. It looked like they were dancing in a carnival parade. Our first mortar shot dug a hole into the rear of their group, they kicked into action with the machine guns and we responded with rifle fire. They fell like mutton. But there were so many of them and they didn't stop. The mortar fire whistled around our ears. They hit one of the Andalusians and another American. They were thirty metres to my right. I didn't have time to even scream.

'Shit,' I said.

'Shut up and shoot,' said Mariano.

We fought for two and a half hours. The Moroccans stood their ground in front of us, but the firing was coming from both sides.

'They're coming in from the sides,' I yelled. 'What the hell do we do now?'

'If you spent less time yelling,' Mariano said calmly, 'you would have already noticed that.'

Then he motioned behind us with his head. I turned. Shit, it was true. Two Russian tanks, our men, were coming down the path and behind them there was an entire company. Not bad. We emerged from the ditches shooting straight ahead, while the two tanks headed right into the water and then split in different directions. Fifteen minutes later you could have crossed the river walking on dead bodies and you wouldn't have got your feet wet. They lost six hundred men and we took two hundred prisoners. We'd only lost two men and had one wounded. But we still had to hide that night in the cellar of our monastery because they came in with planes and cannon fire. It went on continually throughout the day and night. But who cared? Everything outside was shaking. But we were safe and calm, our bellies full. The brothers had a lip-smacking dark wine in their cellar. When the truck came to pull us out four days later, we were happy and a little drunk. We had learned that we'd thwarted an offensive with our action, so we'd been celebrating. When we got to the new camp near Tarragona, the brigade commander called Mariano into his tent for a meeting. He had a scowl on his face when he came back two hours later.

'What happened?' I asked.

'Up yours,' he said.

He lay down on his cot, his face was so long it brushed his feet. He closed his eyes and went quiet like a mummy.

'So,' I insisted. 'Are we going to make a night of it or are you going to tell me what's going on?'

He showed me a crumpled piece of paper.

'Service orders from Command,' he said. 'Lieutenant. They're making you one too. They say that you fought well back at Ebro. Crazy shit. I can't believe it.'

Shit was right. I'd been promoted. I was an officer now too. But boy was my buddy upset; he was practically shaking with anger.

'You shouldn't take it so hard,' I stuttered. 'You'll always be the chief, the commander.'

Now what? His face had collapsed into a grimace.

'Of course I'm the chief,' smiled Mariano handing me another piece of less-crumpled paper. 'See,' he said. 'You're a lieutenant now too, but as for me, precious boy, I've been made a captain.'

Then he started laughing to make your blood curdle, that son of a bitch. He was still laughing when he told me that there was more. The whole platoon had been given a fifteen-day leave. By now the others had already heard and they were jumping for joy.

'I bet that someone around here,' he said looking at me meaningfully, 'is going to go running off to Barcelona.'

Actually we all went – obviously. First thing when we got to Carl Marx headquarters we hit the kitchen and shored up to return to our life as gentlemen. They'd handed out a good supply of cigarettes and paid us on top of that. We all went walking together through Barcelona, showing off in our uniforms, looking for trouble in the bars and out on the street. I saw Mercedes on the second day, when we all went to visit our buddy in the hospital. This time she gave me a big smile, with her mouth and her eyes and heart.

'How long are you staying?' she asked, kissing my neck and stroking my scalp with her fingers. She was proud of me and my new rank. I felt that little by little she was starting to love me for real – not the way people love during war-time, defensively gambling, trying to cheat death. That kind of love clung to you like a flea on a dog.

I slept with her every night that she wasn't on duty at the hospital. The Italians did some bombing but we never went down to the shelter. I admit that I'd started getting a taste for those shivers too. I was so happy that I almost forgot about the war. Alfonso was the one who had to come and remind me. He knocked on the door early one morning. It was still dark out. Mercedes and I were cuddling drowsily, my fingers stroking the hair between her legs.

'You in there, Professor?' called Alfonso from the other side of the door.

I struggled to stand and barely managed to put on my trousers. The minute I opened the door he burst inside excitedly.

'Hurry up, won't you? Don't you remember we're moving out today?'

Shit, he was right. I was about to tell him to hang on when Mercedes walked through the room naked.

'Good morning,' she said, heading over to the bathroom, a big smile on her face.

Alfonso was enchanted. He stood stiller than a statue, and I had to nudge him to make him shut his mouth and remind him that I was standing right there.

'You look like you think you saw the Madonna.'

'*Quasi*,' he answered in Italian.

He was still thinking about it when we were on the truck heading back to Ebro.

'Your Mercedes is really the best piece of ass I've ever seen.'

'Except for your sister,' I growled.

PART TWO

Chapter Twelve

A few months later, penning the story of Scholem's visit to Paris in a letter, Benjamin's tone was off-hand. 'Our philosophical debate whose time was long due,' he wrote, 'proceeded in good form. If I am not mistaken,' he added, 'I gave him an image of me as something like a man who has made his home in a crocodile's jaws, which he keeps pried open with iron braces.' The image wasn't far from the truth. For years now, Benjamin had been gathering adversity around him like a 'pack of wolves'. The hunchbacked dwarf had never stopped chasing him and Benjamin knew that. However much trouble he took trying to foresee danger he always seemed to end up, with the uncanny precision of a sleepwalker, in the middle of trouble. Even his nostalgia, that coward, betrayed him making the happiest moments disappear from his memory. He started thinking that his life had been reduced to shards that endlessly piled up around him. The more he tried to look backward the more burdened he felt by harbingers of the future. The Angel of History spoke to him, sent signs that Benjamin interpreted quite clearly. He hardly marvelled at all when, on March 12, 1938, not a month after Scholem's visit, Hitler invaded Austria. It was dumb fact that the world's history and his own personal history should cross like paths in a forest. His son Stefan was at that very time studying in Vienna.

Stefan wore his twenty years poorly. He was an isolated and rebellious man, traits that were exacerbated by the absence of a good father. Stefan risked being trapped in the Reich's newest territory. As a Jew and a communist living in a Nazi-occupied city, the best he could hope for was a concentration camp. The only thing that Benjamin could do from Paris was to pester Dora in San Remo for news. He spent his last money of the month on agitated telephone calls. And then the telegram he'd been waiting for arrived. Stefan had managed to escape to Italy by the skin of his teeth and he and his mother were going to move to London soon. With the Fascist racial laws, Dora had to sell her pension and wanted to open a boarding house in London.

Only then, forcing himself to feel reassured, Benjamin resumed work on the Baudelaire essay. At least he tried to. But there were obstacles: the lift at rue Dombasle, chronic migraines, a stubborn laziness that clung to him like a leech, and a gripping in his chest that sometimes left him breathless. He needed a bit of fresh air.

He became convinced of this need to breathe freely while coming home from the library one day. The bright light of the May afternoon fell on him as he came out of the métro. Benjamin inhaled the sparkly air, trying to catch his breath. Those few stairs had been enough to make him wheeze. He crossed rue de Vaugirard with small steps, as if the light were blinding him, and ducked into Madame Suchet's store. Koestler had first brought him to that dark little store with its dusty shelves and pungent smells. 'The owner is intolerable,' he warned. 'She behaves as if she could stand around and talk until the end of time. But she gets certain cheeses.'

Upon entering, Benjamin ventured a nod.

'Bonsoir, Madame Suchet. May I have a baguette and a piece of Camembert?'

'A light dinner tonight, Monsieur *Benjhamèn*?'

She was teasing him. And how she went on with that *Benjhamèn* . . . If only one Frenchman could prove himself capable of pronouncing his last name. Just for him – as he cared so much about names. Many years earlier hadn't he written that 'the name is the most intimate essence of language itself,' the only trace of the divine in human language. But he was too tired to correct her.

'So this Hitler of yours . . . will 200 grams be enough? So do you think there will be a war? I lived through one already, lost two brothers to it, one in Ypres and the other at Verdun.'

'Forgive me, madame, but Hitler hardly belongs to me and as to whether or not there will be a war, I don't know. Who's to say? I only need 150 grams, thank you.'

'There won't be a war, you'll see. The *boches*,' she said, again mutilating the word, 'I mean, the Germans know perfectly well that we hold the Maginot Line and it would be useless to even try . . .'

Out on the street the light dusted the slate roofs with a weathered gold and the skirts of girls riding by on bicycles swelled in the air like sails. What a sight, though it didn't last long. Upon returning home he discovered that the lift was broken again. This was too much, even for one such as him. He had to get away, at least for a while. When was the last time he'd been to Skovsbostrand? Two years, he told himself as he faced the staircase. Two years to the day. The moment had perhaps finally come to accept Brecht's invitation to Denmark. He'd collected almost all the material he needed for the Baudelaire essay. He just needed another two weeks to gather his notes and then he'd go off to that fishing village where he would be able to write in peace, and all that aside, the cost of living was much less up there.

He stopped, panting, on the first-floor landing. He was convinced that he should leave perhaps immediately. But after another flight of stairs, standing by Hans's door, he'd changed his mind again.

He ruminated and ruminated for a month, torn by the desire to see Brecht and the fear of having to depend on him financially – between his desire for tranquillity and the strain of changing his habits. Until suddenly, as usual, he resolved it was time to pack up his few items. It was June, a tepid morning that already smelled of summer, when he boarded the train heading north.

In Skovsbostrand he rented a garret right next to Brecht and his family. He didn't need much to make him happy: a long heavy wood table to write on, a window from which he could watch the sea and the Sund, and the dotting of sailboats and little ships. There was a dense forest of fir trees on the opposite shore. At least, there was silence around him. The weather was ugly and didn't really call one out for strolls. The sky was the colour of a donkey's belly and the sun barely ever made an appearance. So much the better. This way he could work for eight or nine hours a day non-stop, able to concentrate. In the evenings, for distraction, he'd play with Brecht's two children, listen to the radio, dine and then face Brecht in an endless game of chess that he almost always lost.

'I'm just not able to concentrate,' he'd say, brushing off the defeat. *Baudelaire* was his justification – the essay was a despot, demanding total loyalty, requiring a degree of commitment that kept him even from reading his friend's latest novel, *The Affairs of Herr Julius Cesar*, which was nearing completion. Brecht was understanding, he knew Benjamin needed that isolation. In the evening they spoke of Russia and the bad news coming in from Moscow. Certainly Brecht was balancing on mirrors – the exigencies of Stalin's politics could be explained, the trials. The siege of the homeland. But gradually, as time passed and the long northern nights fell on the other side of the window, they both let their guard down and admitted that everything they had committed to politically over the last twenty years had ended in catastrophe.

Now and then Brecht would ask about his work. 'How is it going?' he'd venture. And Benjamin would nod. If it was going well, he might elaborate about how the essay seemed to be growing under him, taking him to unexpected places, little by little turning into a ponderous book that stretched its tentacles in so many directions, lighting up new and scintillating thoughts.

Walter believed in his *Baudelaire*. But there was another shadow, a mischievous and evil shadow extending over his work and robbing his sleep. Standing in the garden in front of Brecht's house one day, posing for a photograph, he was incapable of hiding his dark mood. His eyes can't lie and his eyes, captured by the snap, were tense, vexed, staring and uneasy under that grizzled tangle of hair.

It was impossible not to be thinking about Hitler's move into Sudetenland, about Chamberlain flying over to Berchtesgaden all ready to make concessions to the Führer, or of General Franco in Spain conquering one republican territory after another. Fortunately the newspapers arrived late in Skovsbostrand, so one felt less apprehensive opening them. When the Munich agreement was announced over the radio on the evening of September 29, the news was like a betrayal that came with the force of a dagger in an already open wound.

'We're fucked,' said Brecht running his hands through his short shaggy hair. Benjamin sat in front of him worrying his chin with a finger and rocking back and forth in his seat.

'Fucked. Fucked . . .' He couldn't seem to think of anything else to say.

At least his book was done. 'I felt I was racing against the war,' Benjamin wrote to Adorno in early October, 'and, despite choking anxiety, I nonetheless experienced a great sense of triumph when I finally wrapped up the *flâneur*, after almost fifteen years in gestation and just before the end of the world (the fragility of a manuscript!).'

With no little regret, Benjamin's visit came to an end. The book was dispatched to New York. Benjamin used his last few days in Denmark preparing the hundreds of books in his library that had been in Brecht's care to be shipped to Paris. Something in the air, however, gave him the impression that his efforts were in vain. 'I am increasingly coming to feel, however,' he wrote to Adorno, 'that this destination will have to become another stepping stone for me and the books. I do not know how long it will still physically be possible to breathe this European air;

it is already spiritually impossible to do so after the events of the past weeks.'

If he only had known that great historical events weren't the only things set to ambush him. Back in Paris, he found his sister, the other Dora in his life, now living close by him, had fallen gravely ill, and there was bad news from San Remo, as well. Stefan's emigration to London was snarled in bureaucracy – it seemed that it had become harder to leave Italy. And then there was *Baudelaire*.

It was Adorno who wrote to him after a rather suspicious delay, a long, cautious, carefully worded letter expressing the opinion that Benjamin would have to reconsider the structure of the essay. It didn't work – didn't work at all. He'd imposed an 'ascetic discipline' on himself by 'omitting everywhere conclusive theoretical answers', he'd hurt himself trying to give a nod to Marxism, denying space to the most courageous and fruitful thoughts with a kind of preventive self-censure inspired by mat-erialistic categories. 'If one wanted to put rather drastically, one could say that your study is located at the crossroads of magic and positivism.'

It was a devastating blow and he was hurled into a deep depression. Born under the melancholic sign of Saturn, Benjamin would often even renounce eating, staying for hours and hours in bed, ruminating on his misfortunes and cursing the hunchbacked dwarf from the nursery rhymes who never left him alone. He forced himself to respond to Adorno and hash through his agreements and disagreements concerning *Baudelaire*. He decided to seriously pursue becoming a naturalised French citizen. He went about it, as he said, 'with discernment, but without illusions'. He would write, 'If before the only uncertainty was hesitation, now even the utility of this process has become problematic. The collapse of human rights in Europe makes legalisation of any description effectively illusory.' Benjamin was among the few German émigrés who recognised this. And as always, his ability to understand the state of the world didn't help resolve practical matters. Despite the help of Paul Valéry and Jules Romains, Benjamin never did obtain French citizenship. And yet in that enormously difficult predicament in which staying in Paris at all was a deadly gamble, did he ever really consider leaving the country? His ex-wife Dora, who came to visit at the end of December, couldn't even convince him. Stefan's problems meanwhile had been remedied and now mother and son were moving to England.

Dora had been an extraordinarily beautiful woman and hadn't lost any of her charm as she grew older. She still had the energy and determination to face life that she always had. While the man she had been married to seemed to find pleasure in every delay, and felt perfectly comfortable with every indecision, it was profoundly irritating to her by now. Though she couldn't help but worry about him.

'You can't stay here,' she announced harshly one evening. They were in a café on Montmartre, two cups of steaming tea on the table between them. An icy wind blew scattered pages of an old newspaper down the street, the Christmas decorations strung between two buildings shook. 'Why don't you come to London with us? We'll put you up for a while. You would certainly find something to do . . .'

Her offer might have been laced with pity and Benjamin very well may have felt that lace wrap him up. He grew aggravated.

'Let's not speak of it,' he sharply answered. 'Let's not talk about it again. The only place I can work is in Paris.'

He stood, put on his coat, the same coat he'd worn through the last seven winters, and then he leaned down and stroked her face, pushed his fingers into her hair. She leaned against his hand, squeezing it between her cheek and her shoulder. Walter stood for a while looking at her.

'Bon voyage,' he finally said. 'Tell Stefan to forgive me if he can.'

Back on the street, he dug his hands into his pockets and walked with his eyes on the ground. As he headed up the steep pavement, he could feel the cold air on his teeth and his heart struggling to beat.

Chapter Thirteen

That evening Mariano told us to pitch the tents under the almond trees in a field near Falset. There were sixteen of us again, because they'd assigned us three new men: Jacque was French and had a pointy nose and pomade in his hair, Luigi was an Italian communist who instantly hated Alfonso for belonging to a different party. And then there was Sepúlveda – I never did learn his first name. He was CNT – anarchist union – from Maros, a little village in the province of Jaén. What a character: dark, hairy, outspoken, he ate priests for lunch. Just think, every morning he'd wake up and run down into the town to piss. Where? Against the church – the prelate would chase and curse him for centuries and he'd yell right back, 'Homo! Go kiss a rich person's ass! Parasite!' We'd try to make a point of going to see the show before starting our exercises on the hill. We hunted rabbits in the afternoon. There were thousands of them and we ate a lot, and traded others with farmers for fruit, onions and tomatoes. I couldn't say how long we were there. War's like that. You live in the day and you don't have much use for calendars. Until the moment when

72

you're forced to wrestle time again. That happened the day we saw the disinfection truck parked in the village square. They distributed the new uniforms. The day of the attack was getting closer.

The next day, July 24, I remember it well, we were heading up the road running alongside the Ebro. It was almost dark when we settled into a cane field south of Mora near Miravet. The order to cross the river came down at midnight. This time we were serious; we were attacking en masse. There were a hundred thousand men covering a ten-kilometre-long front. Our mission was to push through their lines, get on the road to Saragozza and cut the Moroccans off as they were retreating. Alfonso could barely stay in his skin. He was the one who had to carry the ropes over the river so that we could cross and mark the route for the boats coming in with the rest of our troops. It was a dark, moonless night.

'I can't see shit,' he said and jumped in. Fifteen minutes later we got the signal. He'd tied the thick rope around a fig tree on the other shore and was waiting for us. The water was high, but not too cold. While the 11th division was transferring boats, we got out of our wetsuits and put on Franco's uniforms. The others were getting into position as we left and headed west toward Corbera.

'Forward march,' ordered Mariano. 'And I'll shoot the first person who talks.'

An hour later we were in our positions, grenades and machine guns ready in ditches by the side of the road. We were near a river. Orders were to shoot on sight anyone who tried to pass. It would be impossible to make any mistakes, our men would head north from the Ebro; the only people passing over our bridge would be enemies retreating. And they came. In groups and then in waves. We took them by surprise and sent them back in the same direction they came from. Pale, ragged, scattered: Guardia Civil, the *Tercio de Extranjeros*, *Requetés*, Italians and the *Regulares*. The only ones we had mercy on were the conscripted men, the Spanish, everyone else . . . Alfonso worked them over with the grenades and Lech the Pole mowed them down with the machine gun.

'A hundred and eighteen, a hundred and twenty-five, a hundred and forty-six,' he counted.

You couldn't tell how he managed to count in the middle of all that smoke and the darkest dark.

'What in the hell are you counting, you ass?' yelled Sepúlveda.

'That's enough,' said Mariano. 'We have to get to the gates of Corbera now.'

We marched through the night Indian file, until dawn, and then we started seeing the houses of the village in the distance. There was a wet, humid haze hanging over the road. A motorcycle sentry arrived and told us that the orders were to take Corbera.

'How? There are only sixteen of us,' Luigi protested.

'You're a lowly turd, that's what you are,' said Alfonso.

We had to force the two Italians apart – and we barely managed. Luckily Mariano intervened, his fingers in his hair, his eye steely.

'Finish it up, you two. We can do it. We just need to buy enough time so that the other units can get here to back us up.'

We went in two rows, marching down the pavements of the main street. Then they started shooting from a bakery window.

Just two steps in front of me the English guy got hit from behind and he fell to the ground. I saw him leaning up against the wall, his chest bloody, his breath hoarse. He tried to cover the wound with his hand, maybe he was trying to block the blood getting into his throat. He didn't make it. He died with his eyes open and we launched grenades into the bakery. When it was silent, we went in. It had been a woman shooting at us. Now she was lying dead on the ground, tattooed with shrapnel, the machine gun still in her hands. We found three pilots in the basement, Germans. We shot them there and then and resumed our advance, bullets whistling by our ears. I don't know how we got to the other end of the town, to the cemetery. We'd lost the Andalusian, the black guy and the Galician. Luigi was wounded on his arm, not badly. It must have been ten in the morning when the planes arrived. They were sweeping the ground with machine-gun fire, like demons, they even hit their own soldiers as they ran. There were six planes, then ten, then six again. Luigi was happy. This was his specialty. He planted his weapon and began shooting. He waited until they drew near and then showered them with fire. He got two; they spiralled and exploded in mid-air.

'There goes one, and two . . .' he counted.

'He knows how to count,' Sepúlveda whispered to me as we squashed up against a wall.

At one o'clock under a deadly heat, our men took Corbera, but the battle wasn't over for us. They gave us replacement soldiers and ammo and sent us south toward Gandesa.

'We're leaving immediately,' Mariano announced.

'Wait,' argued Sepúlveda.

'What's the matter? Are you busy?'

'I'll be back in two minutes,' he said, disappearing around the corner.

I knew what he was up to and so I followed him. There he was, motionless in front of the church steps, his trousers around his ankles. He was relieving himself and muttering curses like an old anarchist. But this time no priest emerged to yell at him and he seemed almost disappointed as he walked back toward me, buttoning up his trousers.

'Sorry, Lieutenant,' he said. 'But I made a promise, a vow.'

We got to Gandesa too late. Our men had already occupied it just before dawn. Good. But our advance had been too quick. There were still troops behind us and those of us at the front – our unit, for example – had to wait for new orders. Exhausted, we rested up for three days in a grove. There were some bombers and a few tussles with scattered groups of Moroccans or Italians, and then one day a communications officer told us to head over to Sierra de Pandols, which Franco's men had just taken back the day before.

We left right after dawn, at six thirty, and we walked for hours. To fight a war in those days you had to have strong legs. It was hot. Mariano had us drink a lot of water before we left, and then save water during the march. We moved slowly; we didn't rush, the sun along the way practically made the rocks squeak.

'What's the point if we get there too late?' I asked.

'It's better to arrive refreshed,' answered Mariano. 'A tired man is a dead man walking.'

'I'll write that down,' I said, falling back. Lucky for me, he grinned.

We passed a battalion climbing up to the front and then we

slid into a deep, walled ravine that opened onto ten caverns. It was like a ring of hell, I swear it was, with all those ambulances coming and going. The grottos were full of wounded men, and others were stuffed with corpses. They'd built a mess hall in one grotto down near the bottom. We filled up on hot soup and bread and then set off again. At the far end of the ravine, passing another clearing that was about two hundred metres long, carpeted with dead and wounded soldiers, we saw Sierra de Pandols. It was a tall, heavy-walled fortress, stippled with the scars of bombs and grenades. Up top there was a blockade where the enemy was positioned. At the base of the wall there were a couple of units, ready to attack. And another unit was hidden under the jutting cliffs about halfway up. Everywhere there was the stench of dead bodies left to rot.

It was sheer luck that the mortars didn't get us as we crossed the plain and started climbing up the left side of the Sierra. Our orders were to get as close as we could to the top, observe the enemy and pass on instructions for the attack. But we stopped about halfway.

'We can't get any closer right now,' said Mariano. 'We'll wait for nightfall and then go.'

It was brutal how slowly time passed under that unforgiving sun. There was nothing to drink. And the machine guns would start up in periodic angry bursts. Then our tanks arrived and there were more grenades. One by one our companies joined the formation. But it didn't make any difference. It was a massacre. We were coming in from the front, out in the open, and they were positioned above us in the hundreds. We'd get close and they'd start shooting. They even shot at the guys trying to get the wounded off the field. Mariano sent Jimmie the Irishman up ahead. There had to be some other route to the top. In fact Jimmie came back in about an hour and told us to come and see.

It was incredible. From where we stood, even higher up, hiding in the shrubs, we could see out over the whole company. It was like an ant farm teaming with Moroccans and the Spanish Foreign Legion. Mariano looked at me and smiled.

'We've got them now,' he whispered.

I was the one who had to go back down and convince a major and a captain that we'd have to change our strategy that night. And I was right behind Mariano when at around two in the morning we launched our attack with grenades. Directly behind us, hidden, there were two units waiting for our signal. We took a nest of gunners by surprise, and Lech set up his own weapon to cover our descent into the barricade. They ran, shot, and fled in every direction. The Dutchman threw up a green flare and our men got within a few steps of the top. Poor Jan though. He still had the rest of the flare in his hand when the first bullet hit him, but he kept on shooting as if he weren't feeling any pain, as if he'd never felt that bullet take a piece out of his lungs. He must have screamed when the second bullet got him, but his body didn't settle down for an instant. He took the third one in the face and fell. He had red mush for a face by the time I got to him. I guess ever since then I've been afraid in some way, because it's hard to erase the image of his face. But how can I explain something like that to you?

When we slowly filed down at dawn, there were only nine of us left: Mariano and me, Luigi, Alfonso, Jacque, Sepúlveda, Lech, Jimmie and the Swiss cook.

'All things considered, it's still going well for us,' muttered Luigi.

'Why don't you ask the opinion of the other guys – the ones we left up there?' answered Alfonso.

They were speaking Italian but Mariano and I could understand them. At least we got that sparks were about to start flying again. They calmed down instantly when a mortar shell landed just a few metres from us, reminding them we hadn't reached safety yet.

'Christ,' they said almost in unison and lowered their heads.

We were heading back to the ravine but we were advancing slowly. The Fascists had figured out it was a camp and were pounding it from the air. The caverns were full of soldiers and we must have been drawing too much fire outside. Mariano ordered us into an overflowing grotto. We stood at the entrance, almost outside, when a downpour of grenades and mortar fell on us. And where do you think the shrapnel got me? Here, on my right butt cheek. I felt a little pang and then nothing. I thought that I hadn't even been hit, but I fell down in pain as soon as I tried to get up. Alfonso, Lech and Jimmie were right near me and they looked bad too. Mariano saw I was wounded and squinted. I thought he was going to come at me twisting his hair, but instead he tore the sleeve off his shirt and started bandaging me. Later on, when they were loading us into the ambulance he put his mouth up to my ear, grinned and said, 'So you found a way, right, you figured out how to weasel out of this. I always knew deep down that you were a bed wetter.'

He was teasing. But it's true that my battle of Ebro ended there. I spent almost two months in the hospital after that, sharing a room with Jimmie and Alfonso. The shrapnel had gone all the way to the bone and had hit some nerves.

'Amputate. Cut it off,' said one French doctor, a blowhard with a goatee. 'If we don't, we may risk total nerve damage.'

Lucky for me there was another doctor there, an Englishman who was convinced he could save my leg. He operated on me cold, no anaesthesia – medical supplies were low. Hurt like the devil but may the god of medicine always protect that English doctor because you see my leg? I still have it and it works pretty well, almost.'

I couldn't get out of bed for a long time, but I ate like a fancy gentleman – a priest served me and waited on me. And Mercedes, even if that wasn't her section, would come visit every two hours. She tended to my bottom, cuddled me. She loved me. If it weren't for all the bad news coming in from the front I would have signed up to stay. But instead I just shook with anger there in my bed, getting news that those sons of bitches had razed Gandesa and Caposines; and that we were pulling out. Then one morning in late September I was released. I was brewing indecent fantasies in my head – not that I really wanted them to bomb us, I just wanted to find some special way of celebrating the occasion. But then I got the newspaper and went white before I even had time to read it. France and England had dropped their trousers for Hitler again in Munich and Hitler was swallowing Europe, bite by bite. They had abandoned us. We were alone again.

Mercedes was waiting for me at the house, she'd even made my favourite dessert, but her smile faded when she saw me.

'What is it? What happened,' she asked.

I didn't say anything. I just spread the newspaper out on the table. She just glanced at the headline and pushed her hair back.

'We're fucked,' she said.

'Fucked — yes, we're fucked.' All I could do was repeat it.

Chapter Fourteen

Benjamin doesn't look at the camera; his eyes are lowered, concentrating on his writing. Gisèle Freund frames him in the slyly taken shot at the National Library in Paris and yet he seems to be fading into the background, shrunken and bent over his papers. Old Benjamin, in his grey suit and waistcoat, just starting to look frayed. Distracted, almost circumspect in his peaceful setting. He grips a fountain pen in his right hand and holds the pages of a book open with his left. His unusually high forehead is crowned by wavy, unruly hair, which age had – as Gardel sings in an old tango – sprayed with 'the snow of time'. His sharp nose protrudes under his glasses; his meaty, slightly flaccid cheeks belong to a man who has passed middle age but just barely, dragging a stubborn load of tiredness with him. There is an open inkwell and large sheets of stained blotter paper in front of his hands, which are expressive and stubby, like a child's hands.

Freund's is an intense portrait, with a perfect harmony of geometry and the position of the elements: catalogue files, shelves full of books – and yet the image conveys unease, the same kind of unease that many of his friends and contemporaries must have felt when faced with Benjamin's extraordinary intelligence. 'He was one of the most bizarre, and most genial people I ever met,' wrote Arthur Koestler. But he never totally revealed his intelligence. Benjamin hid behind minute details, criticism, commenting on the work of others. It was ten years from Walter's first meeting with Gershom Scholem, who became his closest friend, to the day in 1921 when he finally conceded to addressing him with an intimate form of 'you'. Benjamin cultivated mystery and erected protective barriers around the most futile and innocuous things: his ritual of gestures, his courtly manners, the hints of despotism in his character, the fatalistic and resolute way he drew toward the end with little steps; the way he looked at you, at once determined and lost, the stare of a man who takes reality too literally. Details, scraps. But no one knew better than Benjamin how to reconstruct his own story and make sense of it, building something out of these 'by-products', this 'hill of broken crockery' that made up his existence.

In truth, Benjamin limped through life, trying to mask his ineptitude at living. When he wrote to Scholem about Kafka in June 1938, he could have been speaking of himself: 'To do justice to the figure of Kafka in its purity and peculiar beauty,' he wrote, 'one must never lose sight of one thing: it is the figure of failure. The circumstances of this failure are manifold. One is tempted to say: Once he was certain of eventual failure, everything worked out for him en route as in a dream.' And again, 'He was of course speaking about himself,' Hannah Arendt would write, 'when, in complete agreement, he quoted what Jacque Rivière had said about Proust that he "died of the same inexperience that permitted him to write his works. He died of ignorance . . . because he didn't know how to make a fire or open a window."'

Perhaps during the years of his exile, from 1933 to 1940, moving between Ibiza, San Remo and Skovsbostrand, the only place where Walter Benjamin found himself truly at ease, at home, was at 'his place' at the table in the National Library of Paris where Gisèle Freund took his picture. Housed in that building were the only territories Benjamin could move through with the surefootedness of the consummate explorer. He moved among those tables without the slightest indecision, almost suspended by the 'light breeze of curiosity'. He discovered halls and corridors, forgotten foundations, he ventured into the *Cabine des Estampes* to the images that confirmed his imagination. He even managed to get himself admitted to the *Enfer*, the section where the obscene books were kept.

However much circumstances conspired against him and however determinedly events seemed to force him away from Paris and the library, Benjamin never let go – not, that is, until the German army was standing at the doors to the city. Not until the last moment, months after the war had broken out and once his life was clearly in danger. Until then he took stubborn refuge in that silence, when the sky painted with summer colours glowed in through the window of the reading room. It was only there that he managed to escape from the 'psychosis of noises' that had tormented him for years, in every house and every room where he ever lived. Many of his letters are full of despairing descriptions of trucks passing on the road, elevators breaking his concentration, curses against the unlucky destiny come alive in a piano never heard before, the inconsolable lamentations of someone suffering something like a dreadful toothache who simply can't imagine anything worse. 'I am now seriously considering whether it wouldn't be better to work only at night, which would bring in turn numerous other inconveniences. But there must be other people who manage to find some kind of peace – aren't there?'

He almost never found it. As he drew near to the final chapter of his life it became more and more elusive. But Benjamin never wanted to acknowledge that, not until it was too late. Immersed in his books about Paris from another age, he stuck to his place at the library, watching fearfully and almost stealthily as the world rushed around him. Wavering images and uncertain figures like the Kaiserpanorama that he'd seen as a child, half-shadows that seemed to offer a 'heartbreaking quality of farewell'. Unfortunately, those shadows were real, and they'd set a date with him on the final frontier.

Chapter Fifteen

Yes. Fine, Benjamin. But think about the story I'm telling you.
There aren't many of us left who can still tell this story. And
any story, even one about my meeting your philosopher, has a
'before' and 'after' even if it seems that we're all in such a rush
these days and there's a damned craze for forgetting. So listen,
just be a little patient and we'll get to Benjamin. First off, there
were the last months in Barcelona when we already knew that
it was all lost and the ration card went down to a few grams
of lentils a day, when not even the bombings, which got worse
and more frightening, seemed to bring back the urge to screw.
There was sadness and resignation everywhere. Then I lost my
heart to my trousers. I met Pilar again – my first girl, the one
I did it with in Gijón in '34. It was mid October and I was in
a café on the Ramblas. I hadn't had news of her for years but
when I saw her again it was as if all that time built up in my
head was reduced to nothing, a cigarette butt, a glob of spit.
She was still beautiful, but her face had grown hard and there
was a bitterness about her mouth that didn't go away even when
she smiled. She was a captain now, a Valladolid communist. She

said she'd been angry as hell when they didn't let her go to the front line too. Because women couldn't fight! Was it a left-wing government or not?

'Of course. You're right,' I said, stuttering because that girl still got right to my heart. My heart. I finished up my *cortado* and made up an excuse to leave.

I was sorry but not too sorry. I was leaving the next day. Since my leg still acted up they'd given me a desk assignment in Sabadell. I was working on the payroll in the offices. The good thing about the job was that I travelled all day and often got back to Barcelona and Mercedes. That's how I happened to be in the city when they were sending the International Brigades home. After the Munich agreement there was no reason for them to be here, they were useless. Arrivederci, thank you, and here's a kick in the ass to everyone who fought harder for Spain than we did, thousands of them never leaving our trenches. Now the veterans were filing along the Diagonal. We hugged them and threw flowers, we saluted them with closed fists. Mercedes and me and Ana María had planned to meet Jimmie and Alfonso in the Plaza de las Glorias Catalans. When we got there Jimmie was crying a river and Alfonso was sitting all hunched up on a wall, he looked like he was in mourning, worse than an undertaker.

Ana María went over to comfort Alfonso and that's how I found out that they'd been together for some time. Nursemaid to cock that Ana María.

'How is it,' I asked Mercedes, 'that you didn't tell me anything about this?'

I don't even know why I was so angry. Instead of answering she shrugged her shoulders and pointed her chin toward Jimmie and Alfonso. Better to worry about those two, she was trying to say. There was a lovely autumn sun shining on the square lighting up the crowd and the posters, pictures of Azaña, Stalin, Negrín, flowers flying through the air, the pavement strewn with colour. Alfonso looked around as if he wanted to swallow all the people, eat them and make them his.

'I'm not leaving,' he said.

I kept quiet and waited for the outburst, which soon followed.

'Where am I supposed to go?' he asked himself shaking his head back and forth. 'I can't ever go back to Italy. I'd have to live as an exile in France. How would you like to have that prospect in front of you? At least here I feel at home.'

Then Mercedes and I hugged him.

'Come on,' I said, putting a hand on his shoulder. 'Let's go talk to someone at headquarters.'

Up on the stage stood Azaña, Negrín, Martínez Barrio and la Pasionario – at least for the day they'd forgotten all their disagreements. You could see very well, even from a distance, that they were moved. Machado was even up there. What a great poet, don Antonio. I knew his poems by heart, as many of us did. Some nights out on the front I'd recite them for my buddies – even if Alfonso would really give me a hard time the next day. Machado was sick, but he hadn't wanted to miss that day, to miss the chance of being among the two hundred thousand listening to Dolores Ibarruri's speech: 'You can leave with your heads held high. You are history. You are legend!'

'*No pasarán,*' we cried. But instead . . .

Instead on October 30, the nationalists launched a week-long offensive on the Ebro. They started at dawn on the ramparts of the Sierra de Caballs, and then they attacked the mountains of

Sierra de Pandols where we had fought. Even Mariano wrote that things looked bad. The government kept saying 'Hold your ground, hold your ground.' As if it were that easy. Within two weeks the battle of Ebro was over. The first snows were already falling when Yagüe entered Rabarroya, and when Lister brought the last of our troops over the river. But the worst, my son, had yet to arrive.

I was busy travelling, going to the fronts to bring pay to the soldiers. They were starving in Barcelona now. There were a million refugees occupying the plazas, the porticos, the streets and everyone was just waiting for the last attack, the grand finale. I was in Barcelona when it started, because I had to bring the accounts to the command of my division. I wanted to spend the holidays with Mercedes but she disappeared on December 20, all of a sudden. Tramp. She left just like that without a warning. I knocked on her door day and night. I asked Ana María who knew nothing about nothing. The hospital told me that she had taken a month's leave and I had a nervous breakdown. I would have smashed everything, shot up all the nurses and doctors, but instead I just leaned against a lamp post and burst into desperate tears.

'Do you feel sick?' a lady asked me as she passed.

'Mind your own damn business,' I answered.

I couldn't take that war anymore. I couldn't take the life we'd been forced to live. Now it had even got Mercedes. I spent Christmas Eve at a shelter and then I was sent back to the front, to Balaguer in a sector that was already in retreat. I served as quartermaster with another three officers. They were sending entire companies right into the battle, just to buy some time. But for what? It was already late, too late to keep hoping. The enemy took Tarragona and then continued toward Barcelona. We caved all along the Catalonia front, abandoning our dead, our wounded, prisoners, planes, rifles, tanks. It was a bust. Run for your lives and focus on getting to France. I knew that I'd have to face exile again. On January 23, in Campdevànol, we received orders to destroy the archives and get a truck full of arms, papers and money – about two million pesetas – to the border crossing at Puigcerdà.

I confess. I didn't care about the orders. No one knew who was commanding who and I took advantage of the situation. There was only one thread of hope left, what if she'd gone home to her mother? What do you mean, she who? She, Mercedes. In the end, what difference did it make if I drove the supply truck to France via Port Bou? One border is the same as the next. So I took the road toward the Goubet hills, I got to Olot and hit the gas, east, toward Figueres. But I had to slow down almost immediately. At first I just saw scattered rows of people and then the procession expanded endlessly. All of Catalonia was on the run. There were tens of thousands of civilians and military, with their carts and mules, cars, trucks, invalids, soldiers with gaping wounds, entire families walking, bowing under the weight of their chests, trunks, wardrobes, dogs, sheep, bottles and mattresses – everyone watching the sky for bombers. Only some of them had shoes. The women were dressed in black as if in mourning, carrying their children in their arms and giant bundles of their things wrapped in colourful scarves dragging behind them. The worst thing was the terrible silence. It was the silence of ice covering streets. All you could hear was the distant bursts of muted cannon fire or the engines of planes getting closer. And then everyone would throw themselves into the fields, drop into the gutters and try to find shelter behind the trees.

There was a child alone in the middle of the intersection. People passed by him; he walked as if there were a vacuum around him.

'Where is your mother?' I asked, leaning out of the truck.

'In France,' he said.

'Your father?'

'Dead.'

'Get in,' I told him. 'Climb up in back with the others.'

I didn't get to Port Bou till the next morning. It was just starting to clear and you could see the lights of villages, icy and still on the hills. It was a cold, crystal-clear morning. The sea was calm and reflected the sky, echoing its limpid light. In the distance, however, up north, the horizon seemed to melt into a stew of black clouds. I parked near a bombed-out house and went alone, on foot, into town.

People were already out in little clusters on the street; they would pause here for an hour or so's rest before pushing forward the last kilometres to the border. It wasn't easy to locate someone who actually lived there.

'Mercedes Carraasco, the nurse? . . . Do you know where she lives?'

Mostly people answered 'no' absent-mindedly or turned their backs and kept walking. I thought it must be how I looked – the long beard, the ragged, dirty uniform. But it was really fear.

'Please, I'm begging you.' I was almost whimpering to a lady and she finally understood she had nothing to fear.

'Okay, wait here,' she said.

I sat on the pavement, a few steps from the beach. I kept my back to the sea, and I smoked and watched the people, looking for Mercedes. To my left, there was a promontory where you could see the outlines of a little cemetery with its white walls and rows of matching tombstones. Half an hour later, she was walking toward me, coming out of a little road leading from the main square. They had warned her, a man, a soldier was looking for her and here she was planted in front of me, staring at me. She was tense and nervous, there were bags under her eyes, her hair was falling out of its bun. I stood when I saw her but we didn't kiss.

'Hey,' she said.

'Hey,' I said. 'Where did you go?'

'Here,' she answered gesturing around her. 'Can't you see?'

'Why didn't you tell me you were leaving?'

She looked back at me as if I were just an obstacle between her and the view of the sea.

'Our agreement,' she said, 'was clear. Neither one of us owes the other one anything, don't you remember?'

'Yes, you're right,' I rushed to agree. 'But why don't you come with me now? I have a truck. You can bring your mother, if you like.'

She lowered her eyes. There might have been a tear caught in her eyelash, but I couldn't be sure.

'I can't,' she said.

Women – can't ever figure out what they're thinking. I cursed under my breath and then managed to ask her why not.

'Because I have a daughter,' she answered all in one breath.

I must have gone white, swallowed all of my spit, and then I was gasping like a male dog. I suddenly realised how little I knew that woman. And who knew what else she never told me.

But it didn't matter. I knew that I loved her and the thought of going on without her took my breath away; it strangled my heart.

'Bring her too,' I said.

Mercedes shook her head. There was the ever so slight shadow of a smile lightening the corners of her mouth.

'No,' she whispered. 'She's sick and I can't move her. Maybe, we'll join you when she gets better.'

'Will she get better?' I asked.

'Yes,' she murmured. 'I really think she will. But you should go on now before it gets too late. And send me news.'

It was useless to insist. I'd only met maybe one other woman, Pilar, who was that stubborn in my whole life. But we did kiss now. For a long time with our eyes closed and all the people around us watching. As slowly as I could I turned back toward my truck. After a few steps I called back, 'What's her name? What's your daughter's name?'

'María.'

I waved again and Mercedes finally smiled.

Chapter Sixteen

The moody February light came in through the windows, dripped down the walls, crawled up to the vaulted ceiling, came to stagnate sadly in the big reading room of the library. Benjamin was at his place, immersed in grey light, his hair more rumpled than usual – his only suit growing ever more threadbare. His movements were almost furtive as he read and reread the notes he'd taken in the little notebooks with black covers that he always carried with him. For years he'd been fishing those pearls from books, newspapers, conversations with friends and conversations on the train, recording it all with a maniacal fury and with a pride that often drove him to read his notes aloud to others as if they were part of some precious collections. There might be an obscure love poem from the eighteenth century or a passage from Balzac, a note about Simmel next to an article from a Viennese newspaper announcing the suspension of fuel service to Jews – which was just a suicidal economic loss to the fuel companies.

That February morning, though, Benjamin was studying the notebooks reserved for *Passagen-Werk*. Horkheimer had asked him for another précis of the work, and if Benjamin could write it in French then it would be presented to a rich businessman in New York who might provide a grant. But it was so difficult to concentrate on that when all he really wished to think about was the wretchedness and terror of the world that was crushing him. Hitler standing outside Prague, Barcelona fallen to Franco, half a million Spaniards on an ill-fated flight over the French border. It just kept getting harder to focus. And it would be useless to pretend that he wasn't still upset about the *Baudelaire* rejection. Every time his eyes fell on those notebooks it felt like a worm had got into his stomach and the taste of copper seemed to flood his throat. That was that, he would never be able to rewrite it. He was exhaling out his weariness when he realised that someone was standing behind him.

'You seem tired, Walter. Why don't we go get a coffee?'

That wide mouth, a nose pointed as a nail – it was Bataille. They had met in the library, where Bataille worked, several years earlier when Benjamin was a new exile looking for a home.

'Come on. It will do you good. Just a little break.'

Bataille had everything that Benjamin was attracted to. He was his opposite. He was self-possessed, open, young. Bataille would speak of *dépense*, of excess, to a man who considered himself fated never to squander himself – a good middle-class German Jew, educated in being reserved and behaving evenly. How could Benjamin not be fascinated by a man who – though under a pen name – had written an honest-to-God erotic master-piece like *Histoire de l'oeil*? Georges Bataille was like Walter's dark side, his negative magnetic pole. Whereas in many other ways the two men were peers, they shared the same kind of life, rippled with thousands of useless rituals and the same gratuitous yet profound urge to surround themselves with the veil of mystery.

Georges Bataille liked to pretend that the Collège de sociologie, which he founded along with Caillois and Leiris in 1937, was a kind of secret society. And Benjamin, who was a member, went along with that useless mystery. For years he never said a word about the meetings of the Collège held in cafés along the Left Bank gathering ethnologists, philosophers, sociologists, literary critics – all of them as disappointed by communism as by surrealism. Benjamin dived in and Bataille became one of his most frequent companions, although he never introduced him to his other friends. He kept it for himself, as with Scholem when they were young.

Now they sat in a bar on rue Vivienne, two coffees in front of them. Benjamin was gloomy and Bataille was using his smile like a shoehorn, trying to wedge his way into his friend's dark humour.

'So what's the matter?' he asked.

Walter snorted, rolled his neck and stared at the dirty rim of his coffee cup.

'Nothing,' he answered. 'It's just that I have to write a new proposal for *Passagen-Werk* and I don't know where to start . . . with everything that's been going on over these last months. There is all this information that I haven't quite organised in my head. Things that might change my perspective on all my work.'

'By new things, you mean Blanqui?'

'Blanqui.'

'You should include him.'

'You think?'

'I do, though it's clearly not the only thing bothering you.'

The sky turned angry and the clouds collected like skeins of filthy, coarse yarn. Bataille crossed his legs and smiled.

'We should go now,' he said.

Back in the library, Benjamin closed his eyes for a minute or two and then opened them reluctantly over the first pages of the first notes he took on the project. He was almost searching for the happiness of those days, when he'd only begun at that very same table in the Library. 'This work about the Parisian arcades,' he'd noted many years earlier, 'was started under a free blue and cloudless sky arching over walls decorated with leaves, all veiled with the secular dust of millions of sheets of paper, rustling in the fresh breeze of diligence, the breathlessness of the researcher, the zealous impetuousness of youth, the slow wind of curiosity. The sky painted in the colours of summer flooded in through the arches of the reading room of the National Library in Paris, spreading dreamy, opaque mantle.'

Benjamin turned the lamp on and flipped the pages slowly, one hand running through his hair. Sometimes he couldn't even make out his own handwriting, trying to decipher those minute lines, driven by a hand that seemed without reason or memory. Phrases, fragments, declarations of intent: 'Things that are deviations for others, are what define my project. I base my calculations of time differentials that for others might disrupt the overarching lines of research.' Or, 'Method for this project: literary collage. I don't have anything to say. I only have to show. I don't want to subtract from anything this precious and I won't appropriate any rich expressions of spirit. Scraps and rejects only — but not as an inventory, rather in a way that renders them the greatest possible justice — by using them.'

For years he'd been trying to compose a book made up exclusively of citations, braided together like a mosaic, ordered according to the most rigorous and painstaking design. When he was working on *German Baroque Drama*, he had collected over six hundred quotes and hung them on the wall of his study. 'My citations,' he wrote aphoristically in *One Way Street*, 'are like armed plunderers who burst out suddenly ripping assent from the idle reader.' These were words as emblems, images. He worked to rip them from their context, fragments of sentences, organising them around a centre that was his. Every sentence he wrote was written as if it were either the first observation of the world, or the last before catastrophe.

Would he finally manage to construct a book this way with *Passagen-Werk*? This wasn't the only thing worrying him. The Benjamin of ten years ago would have wanted to erect a 'great construction over a foundation made up of minuscule elements chosen with care and precision'. He would have wanted to illuminate the 'idea of a rendering that vibrates with the idea of happiness'. He would have wanted to begin such a historical exposition the same way Proust began the story of his life, 'With the awakening'. It would be like a field of rubble seen through the eyes of a survivor who wakes up wounded the day after the battle.

That field of rubble, we now know, was European culture. But that February morning in 1939, Benjamin couldn't find a trace of that awakening and rendering. The only thing that seemed to relate to his state of mind was the almost unknown book of Louis-August Blanqui that he had picked out of a forgotten pile in the library. At the end of his life in the prison of Fort du Taureau, the revolutionary Blanqui found himself without any desire to believe in his own impulses. Society had defeated him. Then, perhaps without realising it, Blanqui put forth a final accusation of time. 'Progress does not exist. What we call progress,' he wrote, 'is closed in every land, and disappears along with it. The very same drama, the very same scene on the same bleak stage is repeated everywhere and inevitably, noisy humanity, infatuated with its own bigness believing that it contains the university – it lives in the prison of its own immensity, trying to capture the entirety of the globe that it has carried for so long on its shoulders, the burden of its own pride. The monotony continues, the immobility of the external heavenly bodies. The universe repeats itself without end and stamps on its ground. Unperturbed eternity recites these same stories infinitely.'

Bataille was right. That accusation and its desolate surrendering, the desperation and solitude set Benjamin moving again. He lifted his glasses to his forehead and rubbed his eyes. He uncapped his pen, opened a new black notebook and began writing. Several hours later, when he lifted his gaze again, the rain had begun to tap against the window panes. Outside, the precocious winter night had almost cancelled out the sky.

Chapter Seventeen

Mother of hell. María. How old were you? Were you the daughter of Mercedes' husband, the fascist lawyer? And did Mercedes kill your father in cold blood? It was all too horrible and I couldn't believe it. But if not that, then what? A mess. The more I tried to wrap my mind around it the harder it all was to put it together. I cursed myself for not having thought of them then and there. These questions. How could I have left them all hanging, waiting for answers that would never come? Now I had to carry that tangle with me, as I drove the speed of a man walking toward the border.

The road was clogged, full of escaping people, of unleashed animals, families camped out on the banks of the road, the sick and wounded in wheelbarrows, broken carriages and cars run out of fuel just abandoned. We'd sit for hours only in order to advance a few metres and then kill the engine again. Never more than just a few metres. We just didn't move. Those French sons of bitches didn't want all these Reds in their house, and they'd shut the border. We waited there in the cold without anything to eat or drink. People passed us, faces sober, wrinkles black with dust. There were soldiers like me out there and then an automobile, flags waving, horn blasting a path through the crowd. Then an old man with a long beard stepped out into the middle of the road and lifted his rifle.

'No one gets through here. Not even Jesus Christ.'

'But it's the minister,' they told him.

'What do I care? If I can't get through then no one can.'

They finally convinced him to move, who knows how. It had grown late. The wind picked up and there were big black clouds tumbling through the sky. A woman with a child in her arms stood near me, her eyes glazed, she begged for help from everyone who passed.

'He has a fever. Can you please take care of him for me?'

I watched a man in a black suit and tie reach out his arms to take the child then shake his head sadly. The woman had already disappeared into the confusion. The man came over to me, looking around, his anger dark but controlled.

'He's dead,' he said. 'This child is dead.'

The cold got worse and then with nightfall the rain began. At first it just drizzled then came down in buckets with a strange kind of ferocity. It wasn't just night, it was a moonless night. There was wind and rain; it was one of those nights when the lord god king and Lucifer are facing off in a battle. On the cliffs below us, the sea blew giant sprays of foam up over the edge of the overhang where we were all gathered. I was lucky to be sheltered in my truck, but what about everyone else outside? It was like time had stopped, got sticky like jam, gone cold and motionless. Sometime around midnight I saw about twenty people coming toward us. Days before they had probably been elegant well turned out high-class people but now they were reduced like the rest of us. They walked slowly, sinking into the mud through the cars and carriages, the animals and asses, the fires and the fallen, under that rain and right into the north wind whipping the water violently. That elderly man . . . yes! It was really him. It was Machado – don Antonio, leaning heavily on the arms of his brother along with his old mother and mother-in-law. I leaped right out the truck.

'Don Antonio!' I screamed but he didn't hear me and I couldn't go too far from the truck where all the money and papers were. When I climbed back inside the rain had become relentless, the thunder was making the doors shake and then a burst of lightning scratched yellow and violet against the sky. The rain didn't let up for two days; it got heavier and then a little lighter. But I was stuck. I couldn't go forward toward the border or backward to Mercedes. If you knew what torture that was, my son. Until the French finally relented. They let the wounded in first, then the civilians, and then they finally let the military through on the condition that we surrender our weapons.

The border was two sentry boxes and a chain, as well as a little shack lit by a feeble lamp in the middle of the dark. A gendarmerie officer came over to my truck.

'Lieutenant,' he said. 'Park over there in the field and wait for orders.'

Orders? What orders? And from whom? I was hungry and thirsty; it had been days since I'd slept over three hours. I couldn't take this endless waiting any more. But I did have to wait – another night and into the next morning. I fell asleep instantly on the seat of the truck but it was a light, tortured sleep because I kept seeing Mercedes in Port Bou. I thought about her mysterious daughter and tried, senselessly, to come up with explanations. I saw Mariano running on the Sierra next to me, machine gun on his shoulder, and then the bloody face of the dead Dutchman. I kept seeing over and again the infinite procession of people streaming down the road in front of me and wondered whether they'd made it alive to France. The last memories of Spain I would carry with me were so sad.

At about noon, a colonel and a captain from the *Garde mobile* came to make a first selection. There were thousands of soldiers on that field. They'd ordered the troops onto trucks and sent them all to a nearby camp. The colonel ordered us officers to guard the supplies.

'What did he say?' a captain asked me. He was one of our men, a career officer. A tall guy with closely set eyes and tapering ears. I was one of the few who knew a smattering of French.

'Nothing,' I answered. 'He didn't say anything except to stay here and wait.'

'Maybe,' he said with a smile, 'they're planning on sending us back to Spain, putting us on a boat for Valencia so that we can go defend Madrid.'

'Like hell,' I said. 'I know these guys. You just wait and see what they have in store for us.'

He was a stubborn one. 'No. I mean there must be half a million of us; they can't possibly keep us all in France.'

Three days later, after they told us that we were going to be interned, I went looking for that captain. He'd disappeared. It was a sorry satisfaction to be right about this one. Then the colonel of the *Garde mobile* came through the crowd looking for me.

'Are you the one responsible for the truck? I have orders to confiscate your weapons.'

Now that was too much. Who did he think he was, the son of Napoleon? Both of us were wallowing in the mud even if he'd been fed and we all had to make do sharing whatever rations had been left over. Sure my side had lost, but he wasn't the one who beat us.

'I will only hand the weapons over,' I said very seriously, 'to a representative of my government, of the Republican government of Spain and no one else. Is that clear?'

He didn't answer. The next day he came back with a company of armed guards and they took the truck, the weapons and all the papers. At least I managed to salvage the money; I'd divvied it up the night before among all the high-ranking officers. Then they crammed us into military trains and brought us to the Argelès camp. 'Camp' in a manner of speaking. Kilometre after kilometre of open beach enclosed by barbed wire. There were fifty thousand of us in there, mostly men, but also women, children and the elderly, exposed night and day to the north wind that got tenaciously under your clothes. There was no bathroom. We had to dig holes in the sand with our bare hands, trying to get some privacy. We invented nests made out of branches and blankets. All the same it was too cold to even try to pick off the fleas. At noon, the French solders piled bread onto the edge of the street and left it there. That was it, our daily ration – bread – for lunch, breakfast and dinner. At first it was a stampede driven by terrible hunger, everyone crushing and stepping on the wounded and sick. Then we organised a distribution system. Just one hunk of bread each, but everyone got one. Still it was a nightmare. That's what I told a delegate from the Red Cross who came by.

'You don't even treat animals like this!' I shouted. 'Can't you see that there are wounded, mutilated people here, children, pregnant women? Scores of people die every night. Does the word humanity mean anything to you?'

He looked impotently at me. 'It is a true embarrassment. But I can't do anything by myself. I've asked for help.'

Help never came and we stayed there for another two weeks before they came to get us and bring us to Septfonds, a camp near Montauban. They called it a 'select camp', but in reality that's where they interned the undesirables, the most dangerous refugees, the most political. The only camps worse than this were Vernet and Fort Collioure.

We were a thousand officers in all when we climbed onto the train. I was already starting to feel bad after all that cold and deprivation, but my fever rose on the train. My teeth were chattering, my bones felt like they were shattering into a million pieces. I tossed under a blanket trying to find a little space on the ground to stretch out. I was shaking and cursing. It was a long trip, but when the train finally stopped in Caussade, we still had a long way to walk. The worst was what we saw when we stepped out, a battalion of Senegalese soldiers, armed with rifles and machetes and preparing to escort us. Their commander was a Frenchman. They circled the platform, screaming at us to start marching. I could barely stand. I thought I was going to die with every step. My buddies were carrying my bag but the black soldier on horseback who was guarding us didn't care. Every two or three steps he stuck his rifle into my back and pushed me until I fell to the ground like a dead man. Whoever helped me up after that was a good man. I'm not sure I can even say exactly what happened next. I heard someone running toward us from behind but it was as if his footsteps were coming from another world. I thought I heard the sound of someone being punched in the face and then I found myself two steps away from the soldier who was now sprawled on the ground. Over his yelling and screaming I suddenly thought I recognised a voice.

'Treat us like soldiers,' he was saying to the French officer, 'or else we'll be forced to defend ourselves and that'll be some bitter shit.'

I couldn't believe it was Mariano. But he was the only one who could have brought on a silence like that. Here in the middle of the country; you could even hear an ass bray.

'Look what you've got me into now,' he said smiling at me. 'I leave you alone for a minute and look at the trouble you get into.'

I smiled too and he picked me up and carried me on his shoulder. He had got into France with the last group to cross the border, the survivors of Ebro with Modesto and Lister's soldiers and now he was with me. Just in time. Just in time to discover that the Septfonds camp didn't exist anymore. We were going to have to build our own barracks. For now, there was just a fallow field, no trees or hedges, barbed wire everywhere and endless countryside beyond it. How many of us were there? Ten, maybe fifteen thousand. I don't know. All I know is that you couldn't move without stepping on another prisoner. Mariano pitched a tent and put me on the ground, wrapped a cover around me, and called one of our doctors to examine me. He said that I had bronchitis and needed medicine. They wouldn't give it to him. Mariano couldn't even get one of the French doctors to see me. It was raining now and water leaked into the tent across the top seam and along the ground. It rained, they told me, the whole week that I lay unconscious, almost dead, then a nurse gave me two aspirin and a carton of condensed milk. When I woke up again, I didn't remember where I was. I guess that's why I felt so happy.

'Did you have a nice sleep?' asked Mariano.

Chapter Eighteen

'Monsieur Benjhamèn, Monsieur Benjhamèn! There's a letter for you.'

The landlady. For some reason Madame Dubois only was permitted to mutilate his name and it didn't bother him. Although he was in a foul mood, the day had already gone wrong. The hot water had run out in the shower. The lift was out of service again which meant he'd have to climb the stairs. Still panting as he hit the ground floor, Benjamin saw Madame Dubois running toward him with the letter.

'It's from New York,' she explained. 'I thought it must be important.'

He nodded in agreement and gasped greedily for air. He opened it right away as Madame Dubois stood there watching him. His hands were shaking nervously in the dim light of the lobby. Just a moment of reading and he grew pale.

'Monsieur, don't you feel well?'

'Yes, quite. I'm fine, thank you,' he answered, trying to give some credible enthusiasm to his faint voice. He was gripped by anger and anxiety. He fluttered his hands in the air and then headed without reflection right over to his only refuge: his sister Dora's house. He saw splashes of sky peeking over the gutters on the roofs and little clusters of clouds moving slowly through the cold air. A crowd of people pushed past him on the street.

'What's wrong with you?' asked Dora the instant she opened the door.

His sister was feeling well for a change. Every so often the sickness that plagued her gave her a few days of respite. Walter silently removed his coat and sank down into the couch.

'What's the matter? Are you unwell? Can I get you something?'

'Don't torture me, Dora.'

That's what he always said when he wanted her to keep quiet. Couldn't she see that he needed to have some peace and quiet to think? He stood. His left knee popped a little making him wobble and then he went over to the window. Heavy drops of condensation were gathering on the glass and rolling toward the curtain. He pushed it aside in order to rest his forehead on the window pane and watch the sad pulse of life outside. It was a few moments before the commotion of thoughts in his head arranged themselves. What a stupid man he'd been. How could he have been so trusting? Just thinking about this mistake made his stomach ache like he'd been punched.

'So,' said Dora again. 'Are you going to say anything at all today?'

'I've been stupid. Terribly stupid,' he finally muttered without looking at her. Out on the street a couple were arguing in front of the flower shop on the corner. He rolled his brow against the cool wet window. 'Scholem was right, and so was Hannah.'

'Right about what, Walter? Are you going to tell me or is this an attempt to make me crazy?'

'About Horkheimer, Dora. He wrote today and says that the Institute is in serious trouble and "sometime in the near future" he may have to tell me that they will be unable to renew my research contract.'

'And what does that mean?'

'No more money, Dora. It means no more grant money.'

Finally he turned to look at her in that way of his, eyelids lowered, forehead wrinkling as if he were squinting to see something in the distance. She sat and started to worry the edge of the tablecloth. Her flowered dress heaved on her chest as she sobbed.

'What are you crying about?' scolded Walter. 'Stop that. It serves no purpose.'

'Why do you always treat me like this?'

'Like how?'

'Badly. As if I were a child. Mama was right.'

'Mama, mama. You don't really have to keep bringing her up. Let her rest in peace, at least in the grave. Don't you tell me that I'm treating you like a child.'

Before long he left, pulling the door shut and leaving her alone to cry, sitting there at the table, her face hidden in her hands. Then he came back, almost as if he were trying to find a better way of leaving her.

'Could you possibly lend me a few francs?' he asked.

Back out on the pavement he stopped dead. Left or right? He had no desire to go back home. What should he do? Continue his work on *Baudelaire* for the Institute? Perish the thought. Maybe if he stayed out long enough they would have time to fix the lift and he would save himself the climb up six flights of stairs. It would be better to walk around, stroll, very slowly, stopping often on a bench to catch his breath and look at details on the stucco façades. Quai Voltaire: he remembered he hadn't written to Scholem in a while and hadn't any further news about the possibility of emigrating to Palestine. Quai Malaquais: looking out over the balustrade at the mills in the Seinne and the murky water tugging at the bushes on the clay banks. Rue Mazarine, rue de l'Odéon: ducking into his friend Adrienne Monnier's bookstore to tell her the news, and pile books that he would never buy onto the counter. Back to Saint-Germaine where he recovered from the heat in Deux Magots, reading with a coffee in front of him. The tables weren't crowded and he didn't know anyone among the few people who were there. He had no choice but to surrender to his thoughts and ruminate on the dregs of his dreams.

The lift was fixed at home, but this wasn't enough to make life tolerable. Benjamin turned on the lamp, removed his coat and sat down at the desk. 'Dear Gerhard,' he began, 'your eyes didn't deceive you, nor did your humble servant think for a moment that they had. All the same, I didn't foresee a catastrophe . . . There is no time to lose. What kept me plugging along in earlier years was the hope of someday getting a position at the Institute under halfway dignified conditions. What I mean by halfway dignified is my minimal subsistence of 2400 francs. To sink below this level again would be hard for me to bear *à la longue*. For this, the charms exerted on me by this world are too weak to make it worthwhile and the rewards of posterity too uncertain.'

And again this idea burned in his head, this desire to bid it all farewell and good night. It was the evening of March 14, 1939. Two days later, when Benjamin left the house reluctantly to head to the library, Madame Dubois again came running toward him on the stairs.

'Good evening, Monsieur Benjhamèn, have you seen? Have you seen?'

'Seen what?' Benjamin sadly asked.

Madame Dubois handed him a copy of *Paris soir*.

'The *boches*,' she whispered with horror. 'The *boches* have occupied Prague.'

Chapter Nineteen

'I pass,' muttered Fränkel bleakly.

'I'll see you.'

Hans tucked his card into his palm and looked at Benjamin. It was his turn. It was a Saturday evening like many. Four exiles at Arthur Koestler's house playing poker and drinking wine purchased with some last bits of change. The little stove buzzed, muffling the noise from the street. Smoke curled up the beam of light coming from the lamp. Daphne was on the sofa drawing absentmindedly. Walter looked at Koestler's eyes, then moved his gaze down to the cigarette hanging hesitantly from his lips. He'd drawn three cards and then bet ten francs. He was bluffing. Not a doubt about it.

'I'll see you and raise you a hundred,' he answered.

Everyone looked up at him, mouths wide. Even Daphne stopped her pencil in the middle of the page and looked up at the players. A hundred francs. That table had never seen such a bet, and from Benjamin who struggled more than the rest of them to make a meal of dinner. You would have had to have known him since he was young not to be stupefied. Every so often he was overcome in the heat of the game and when it happened there was no escape. In the 1920s Benjamin would often go to the Zoppot casino. Fritz Rradt, who had sometimes gone with him, used to watch him become transported, separate from himself, it was a kind of surrender that Walter didn't concede to anything else in the world. He often lost, lost with a passion at roulette and *chemin-de-fer*. He'd play his last pfennig and Rradt would have to lend him the fare home. Now here in Paris, on rue Dombasle, there were four pairs of eyes on him and only the slightest quivering of his moustache that would betray him. Fränkel folded, but Koestler wasn't ready to give up.

'How many cards?' he asked.

'One, just one.'

Koestler sucked in a long breath of air, stubbed out his cigarette and turned to look at Daphne. Just a moment, an instant.

'All right. I'll see you,' he said.

'Pair of aces,' said Benjamin revealing his cards.

He could tell right away that it hadn't gone in his favour. The creases around Koestler's eyes relaxed and he struggled to keep a smile off his face.

'I believe three nines beat that.'

They did. They played another few hands and then everyone ended up on the couch except for Hans, who settled himself on the floor with a cushion and the bottle at his side.

'There will be no talk of war, tonight. Agreed?'

He said it though he knew it was a useless plea. For months now, every other discussion – books, films, women, theatre, trips made or only imagined – wound up pushed aside in favour of this war that would perhaps have a longer prologue than denouement. Austria, Czechoslovakia, and now it looked like it was Poland's turn.

'The French couldn't give a shit about Dansk,' Fränkel burst out. 'They'll let Hitler do whatever he wants and then they'll fix it all up with another Munich agreement. Could we have some wine over here?'

'I'll go get more,' said Daphne. 'I have half a bottle of the good stuff upstairs at my place.'

She stood and Koestler reached out to stroke her hand. She was so lovely and young.

'Come back soon,' he said, imitating her heavy English accent. She smiled. After Daphne had gone there was a moment of silence. The chatter gave way to the war, which filled the room, hard and inhospitable.

'There won't be a war over this, Fränkel,' Koestler said, lighting another cigarette. He was pacing now. 'But Hitler can't fight Russia and the west at the same time. That's crazy. What do you think, Walter?'

'What do I think? I think that I wouldn't be so sure. We might just be repeating it in order to convince ourselves that it's true. There won't be a war. There won't be a war.'

Benjamin shrugged and sank deeper into the couch.

'Whereas . . . ?' asked Hans.

'I don't know. I just know that the next war, whenever and wherever it is will be fought with gas bombs and other weapons that we can't even imagine. And I worry that that will be the end. The end of everything, I mean.'

Daphne came back with the bottle and a big toothy smile and found them in total silence, each absorbed in his own thoughts.

'What mirth,' she said.

No response. It was as if she hadn't even come into the room. Fränkel seized on the thread that Benjamin had left dangling like a funeral shroud.

'Maybe we need to get out of Europe,' he said, shaking his head. 'The problem is figuring out when to stop just thinking about it.'

'That moment has come for me,' said Benjamin with a smile as he stood. 'Excuse me, everyone. I'm very tired. Good night.'

He climbed the stairs struggling as always, his heart pounding and those strange little ants running up his arms. He panted as he fumbled trying to get the key in the lock of his door. Then he threw himself onto the bed, still dressed, hungry for sleep but knowing that it would be hard coming. He would have to think and rethink about that pair of aces and the hundred francs he lost without feeling like he could brush it off and then think about Fränkel and what he had said. It was a good question, you had to admit. But how and when could you know it was time to leave? The only thing he felt sure about was that his days in France were numbered. Even there, stretched out on his uncomfortable bed, he could feel time rifling through the days left in his pocket like a thief. But all that aside, even if he wanted to leave, how could he?

It wouldn't be long before Benjamin lost his German citizenship too. The Gestapo finally got to him over an article he published in *Das Wort*, the paper that Brecht edited and that was published in Russia. The article was enough to make him a stateless person; to deliver him into what Koestler would later call the 'scum of the earth'. From that point on, he had to rely on his French papers, which legitimised him as a *réfugié*. He continued to try for French naturalisation with the support of Adrienne Monnier – though it was ultimately futile. He waited for months on end, letting the angel decide his fate. The Angel of History. 'I live waiting constantly for that unlucky missive,' wrote Benjamin in April. For the first time in many years he was seriously considering a move to New York or Palestine – if only for a period. But by that point it wasn't easy anymore and perhaps it was even too late. The immigration network aside, in order to get to the States, Benjamin would have to win a visa beyond the quota, the sort of visa that the consulate would only grant with the sponsorship of the Institute or some American university. But how much hope could he invest in Horkheimer's interest? Could he believe that he would try to help him win a professorship? And, as if these doubts weren't enough to dissuade him – or because there were no other options – he began studying English along with Hannah Arendt. Though reluctantly, he began to accept the possibility that he might have to separate from *Angelus Novus* in order to collect the money he'd need for his trip to the United States. He entrusted the job of selling it to his old acquaintance Ernst Morgenroth who had already moved overseas.

In the meantime he kept writing letter after letter to Scholem, to Gretel Adorno, to Horkheimer, to Ernst Morgenroth's father. They were agitated letters, scrupulously describing the smallest details of his predicaments. He anxiously enquired as to what his friends were doing to help his cause, and he recounted details of the enervating queues at the prefect's office and outside the American consulate, and of his useless encounter with Alexandre Koyré from whom he asked help, of tourist visas and official forms, of how the threat of war was growing in France and the anti-Semitism was sharpening its fangs, the difficulty he had paying his rent on rue Dombasle, the new ordinances against foreigners, and of how alone he felt. Somehow in the middle of the tempest, Benjamin managed to dredge up the concentration he needed to finish a revision of the much-contested *Baudelaire*, and the new version was received very well in New York. Friends like Hannah Arendt and Adrienne Monnier, who stayed by his side during those three months in 1939, could hardly believe that such a desperate man could work as if the whole world had suddenly disappeared around him, dropped away into the purest empty silence. It seemed that his angel, his Angelus Novus, was standing at his side, protecting him from the ruins around him. And yet those ruins just kept mounting.

In late May, Hannah Arendt decided to write to Scholem, 'I am very concerned about Benjamin,' she confided. 'I attempted to find some income for him here and failed miserably. By the same token I grow increasingly convinced of the importance of getting him the tranquillity he needs to pursue his work. I have the impression that his work has undergone a change, down to the smallest details of his style. Everything he writes is so much more definitive and less hesitant. I'm often struck with the notion that he is just coming to a turning point and it would be dreadful if he had to stop now.'

But Scholem either didn't want to or couldn't respond to this explicit appeal. 'I wonder if you should try to get to the United States, if it is still possible,' he wrote to Benjamin, 'Perhaps this would be the better solution for you.'

He meant to say that Palestine was no longer an option. But

it wasn't going any better on the other front. The wooden benches and grey tiles of the waiting room in the American consulate had become as familiar to Walter as his table in the library – and yet he had little interest in the United States.

In early August, a hot August that wrapped Paris in a suffocating heatwave, his chest pains grew worse. Doctor Abrami, who had agreed to see him for half his usual fee, gave a stony diagnosis: cardiac congestion and weakness. He would have to start being very careful. He would have to stop smoking and avoid exerting himself and not worry. Benjamin smiled bitterly.

'If only that were up to me,' he said as he left.

He wasn't the only one being tossed about by history, which was now prancing forward nervously. On August 23, Benjamin wasn't the only person who opened the newspaper and blanched. That day, millions of people throughout Europe read with icy hearts the news that Germany and Russia had signed a non-aggression treaty. Koestler was travelling with Daphne in the south of France and he smacked himself on the head. 'There is no death,' he wrote, 'sadder or more definitive than the death of an illusion.' He helplessly tried to explain it to Daphne; 'She couldn't understand why a thirty-five-year-old man should make such a scene at the funeral of his illusions, for she belongs to a generation who never had any.'

By the next morning, the news had moved from the third page to the first. Sitting on the bottom step in rue Dombasle, Benjamin read of Ribbentrop's rush visit to Russia, the Hitler–Stalin pact and of the notorious paragraph three of the treaty that gave Germany carte blanche in Poland. The Red Army troops sang *Horst Wessel Lied* and a swastika blew over the

Moscow airport. 'The spirit of the time,' he would write to Scholem, 'has planted certain signs in the barren landscape of these past few days, that have unmistakable significance for old Bedouins like us.'

He finished reading and folded the *Paris soir* carefully, handing it back to Madame Dubois.

'Are you going out, monsieur?'

'I have changed my mind,' he answered.

A week later the Luftwaffe attacked Polish air bases while the Führer's armoured divisions moved into Warsaw from the north and south. On September 3, France and Great Britain declared war on Germany, but it was as if Paris didn't notice. 'War arrived without much fanfare,' Hans Sahl would write many years later in his memoir. 'It had been predicted too many times already and when it came it was as if it was trying to say, let me prove that I'm true. Men pull their uniforms from their closets, trim their nails and cover their mouths as they yawn. The sky over Paris darkens and at night the clubs use flashlights.' That was all. Nothing happened for months and months on the Maginot line. The real war began on the internal front, first against the French communists and socialists, and then against the foreigners and émigrés, against the *sales métèques*. There wasn't time enough to distinguish friend from enemy. It didn't matter who was an anti-fascist and who was a persecuted Jew – they were paying for their political views with exile. It didn't matter that the Gestapo had seized passports from many Germans and they couldn't possibly belong to Hitler's fifth column. Their origins made them suspect. And among the *ressortissants*, no one ever thought of fleeing 'hospitable' France. People often surrendered, believing that their arrest was a mistake that would be cleared up in a matter of time. Not one among them imagined that they had just stepped foot into one of the most merciless shredding machines of history.

PART THREE

Chapter Twenty

What was I saying . . . Oh, yes! I was telling you about Septfonds, 'camp' in a manner a speaking. It wasn't really ready until the end of March after the worst of the cold had passed. We built row upon row of barracks in that marsh – rather, frames with roofs, and then just one wall made out of wood scraps. The rest was open air – leaving us bare to the good graces of the rain, snow and north wind. I always wondered whether it was stupidity or meanness that made them order them built that way. How much would three more walls have cost? But those were our orders. Take them or leave them.

In the beginning there were still some among us who hung on to the fantasy that the French were going to bring us to welcome centres and then send us off to arrange our lives in peace, the way they'd done with the evacuees of Aragon the year before. But now, after Hitler took Prague on April 1, and Madrid fell, we had to resign ourselves to the obvious. We must have been twenty or thirty thousand men in all. We were prisoners in a concentration camp and there was no hope of things getting better. Mud and filth and cold and hunger. We were allowed a trickle of dirty water from tubes down at the end of the camp to wash with for one hour a day. Lunch and dinner was bread and a plate of unsalted rice. Lucky for us, war had got us used to misery. Now the war had ended, and ended badly. Even if we wanted to, we couldn't go back to Spain.

I had lost about twenty or twenty-five pounds. I only survived that pneumonia because I was young. Every morning when we woke, Mariano would look me up and down from his wet straw pallet and smile.

'You know what, Laureano, you look good, slender. You've lost some weight.'

'And you're that much less of a wreck than me.'

I don't have the slightest idea where we found the energy to joke. It seemed like a century had passed since the last time Mercedes and I . . . but it had only been a couple of months. There was always the war, but war was better than that slow incipient miserly death, where you get eaten up little by little over days and weeks. The only news of invasion that we ever got in the camp was the attack of the fleas, or dysentery or the *Garde mobile* that came into the camp some nights to search a barrack leaving us out in the cold for hours waiting. Or the commander would wake up one morning and decide that everyone should line up in front of their barrack to salute the flag. It's not that we had anything against those three colours, but considering how they treated us – tease and humiliate us and then tell us to stand at attention. Well, let's just say that didn't go down well. There's only so much a man can swallow.

Mariano and I were the chiefs and we organised everyone properly.

'Attention!' cried the lieutenant as the flag went up the pole.

And all of us in barrack 36 stood as if nothing was going on.

'Attention!' he repeated.

We didn't leave anything out: whispering, chattering, some guys chewed on their fingernails, others whistled. So they suspended the little bit of rice that they gave us and closed us all up in the hippodrome, the rectangle of barbed wire, about five square metres in all, right in front of the commander's tent. They left us there for days and days with no blankets out in the cold and rain – tough luck for us.

But it didn't end there. As far as the French were concerned, the refugees were not only Reds and contagious subversives but we were a dead weight, an expense, and that really made them angry. You get to them through their wallets, that's how. So in the middle of May, the French police flooded the camp with spies trying to convince us to go home – that a Spanish jail would be preferable to living like a starving refugee. But that didn't work. So then they sent in an officer's commission that tried to convince us to volunteer in Africa – the Foreign Legion was waiting for us.

'It's either the Foreign Legion or we send you right back to Spain,' they threatened.

All that effort netted them about thirty volunteers. So they sent in the CTE, the Spanish Workers Association, which was led by our men but commanded by one of theirs. But even though we weren't organised we knew what they wanted; cheap labour, slave labour, to compete with French workers – and we opposed that. A few guys signed up and they were beaten and taken down by the CTE leaders of Montauban. In the end the *Garde mobile* stormed our barracks trying to take us by force but we resisted and we protested and hid whoever they'd come in after. With all this, the nights were busy. When I did get the chance to sleep, I barely had time to conjure up an image or two of my Mercedes – she was usually naked with her face in the pillows and I was behind her – before crashing. I hardly ever had the strength to make a little deposit in the bottom of my socks. I thought about her and wondered whether María had got better and whether she was getting the letters I sent every week. That's how I spent the summer. And at least we were philosophical about it all. We even laughed sometimes, as if it were all a farce gone wrong – a play we'd been forced to act out. Then Hitler invaded Poland and the music changed; it got really dismal.

Chapter Twenty-one

He saw the first poster when he was coming out of the métro. It was plastered on the wall of a building at the corner of Carrefour and Saint-Germaine des Prés. There was another on rue de l'Odéon. They were enormous white posters with brilliant red lettering. From the other side of the street, Benjamin squinted his eyes and tried to read but couldn't make anything out from so far away. There was something, a sixth sense, a faint presentiment telling him that this poster was a harbinger of something – it was the gate through which the war was introducing itself. Walter stood on the pavement, melting in the sun. As always he was unsure whether he should pretend it was nothing or cross the street. A group of French people who seemed to be discussing the poster convinced him with their eyes that it would be better to leave and avoid any problems.

'Well, it's about time. I can't take these damn *boches* any more,' yelled a red-faced man, the hem of his white shirt hanging out of his trousers.

Prudence. The man was being prudent with all his hollering – better not to leave his back open to cowardice. Benjamin kept on walking down the street, moving more slowly now and wobbling a little more. He stole glances at shop windows and stopped often to catch his breath in the hot, motionless air. Far away, beyond the square, on rue de Vaugirard, he saw a convoy of military trucks. Fortunately, rue de l'Odéon was a friendly street. Adrienne Monnier's bookshop was at number seven. Adrienne was a writer and editor who collected many French and foreign intellectuals around her. Across from her, at number twelve, there was Shakespeare & Company, Sylvia Beach's bookshop, another writer, slim and austere, who had come to Paris from Baltimore only to find herself at the heart of the European and American avant-garde. In 1922 she had published a cerebral novel by an almost unknown Irishman named James Joyce. A little further down the street, at the end, in number eighteen, lived the photographer Gisèle Freund, an independent and volatile lady with sharp eyes and high cheekbones like an Indian. Walter and she frequently went on car-trips through the Loire together and would talk late into the night about books and photography. Twice a week, in those days, Gisèle and Benjamin would meet at the Deux Magots to play chess.

Of all his friends, only Helen Hessel lived quite a distance from rue de l'Odéon, in rue de Grenelle. Helen was married to Franz Hessel, who had worked with Walter on a Proust translation in the 1920s. Helen, Adrienne, Sylvia and Gisèle were Benjamin's four muses – four women who respected him and looked after him in France. They were attracted to his manners and fragility, to the naïve way he moved through life, to his bright blue eyes, and the way his brain processed ideas never giving the impression that the way he thought was in any way out of the ordinary.

Pale and rumpled, bags under his eyes hanging down to his cheeks as if he'd spent a night tossing in bad dreams, Walter ducked into the Maison des Amis des Livres with a great sigh of relief. He found Adrienne standing on a stepladder organising the books on the highest shelves.

'Good morning,' she said without turning around, 'I'll be right there.'

'It's me, Adrienne,' Benjamin announced himself; he was still huffing.

'Walter, what are you doing here?'

Adrienne abandoned the books and rushed off the ladder, her round puffy face long with surprise.

'Didn't you see the posters? It's utterly insane to be walking around as if nothing's happened?'

'*Those* posters, the white and red ones? Yes I saw them, but I didn't read them. Why? What do they say?'

'Sit down now.'

Adrienne was so stern that she almost frightened Benjamin.

'Meanwhile,' she said, 'can I get you something to drink. I'm going to call Gisèle, then I'll close up and we can go to lunch. I'll explain it all to you then, okay? Of course, you'll be my guest.'

Sitting behind the counter, his hand crossed over his black bag on his lap, Benjamin nodded. He had only wanted to catch his breath, rest, carve out a corner of life where it would be possible to exist as little as possible. Where could he go to disappear and avoid the blows that were coming his way? What was in store for him now? As Adrienne fussed in her office, Walter stared and waited for the desire to live to come back to him. Nothing. It didn't work. He wearily watched his friend put the books away and lower the gate over the shopfront. It was with reluctance that he decided to stand and follow her. His eyes were downcast and the sun was punishing on his shoulders. But he saw the poster, stuck to the wall of the theatre, still gleaming with wet glue.

'Adrienne,' he called to her, as he read: 'NOTICE TO ALL GERMAN *RESSORTISSANTS* FROM DANZICA AND SAAR AND TO ALL FOREIGNERS OF UNDETERMINED NATIONALITY OF GERMAN ORIGIN UNDER FIFTY YEARS OLD.'

The poster was talking to him. His turn had come; they were going to intern him. He was to report to the Colombes stadium with a blanket, personal hygiene items and food for two days. The order was signed by the Military Governor of Paris.

'I can't believe it,' he said once he'd finished reading. He was pale and struggled to breath. He looked like a dead man emerged from the grave to haunt the living. Adrienne took him under the arm and supported him as they walked to the restaurant.

'You'll see,' she comforted him. 'It will all work out.'

'Of course,' answered Benjamin with barely any voice. 'It must be a mistake.'

But it wasn't and Gisèle was the one who told him that. She was trying to shake him up, make the blood come back into his face. She was already at the brasserie, waiting for them at a table, her eyes gleaming, tense, and flitting around the room.

'It's not a joke, Walter, they mean it this time.'

'Would the ladies and gentleman like to order now,' interrupted an elderly bent waiter with a deep crease in his forehead.

'Wine, of course,' said Adrienne Monnier. 'And I'll have a filet, rare, thank you.'

'That will be fine for me too,' said Gisèle in a rush. She was trembling and didn't care what she ate.

'And for the gentleman?'

Ordering was a large undertaking. Walter read the menu, then he read it again. Then he asked about the soup of the day. He was sweating, lost among all the options. The waiter was standing over him, explaining and growing ever more bent and more wrinkled.

'Fish? Do you have fresh fish? Or, perhaps I should have meat too. No. Just bring me the sole, but only if it's fresh.'

Benjamin suddenly seemed peculiarly imperturbable. His breath returned to normal and even the tightness in his chest had passed. He drank a little wine and stared at Gisèle, holding his glass aloft.

'As you know,' he explained as if he were giving a lesson, 'I am no longer a German citizen, but a refugee. I am a Jew and an anti-Nazi. They can't want to shut me up. Surely there must be an error.'

Gisèle struggled to remain calm. She wanted to convince him, explain things the way they were but she also knew how hard-headed he could be once he made up his mind about something. Old Benjamin would do exactly as he pleased. Period. She sighed, almost ready to acknowledge defeat.

'But don't you see that for the French, anyone with a *boche* accent is an enemy now? Daladier knows that and he's exploiting the situation. However, it is better to show up at the stadium than risk ending up in jail which frankly doesn't seem like a heartening prospect.'

Benjamin huffed and pinned his eyes to the point of his knife. He kept his gaze there obstinately until he saw the reflection of the waiter passing – and he called him over.

'Excuse me. I changed my mind. Can I order a filet instead?'

133

'Rare or well done?'

'I'm not sure.'

He hesitated again, embarrassed, and toyed with the unlit cigarette in his hands. Then he looked around the room as if someone else at another table or something on the wall might provide an answer.

'I'm sorry,' he eventually muttered. 'I've reconsidered. Pretend I said nothing. I'll take the fish.'

Gisèle shook her head. She didn't know whether to laugh or get angry. Adrienne reached out her hand and rested it on Benjamin's shoulder.

'This is only a temporary thing,' she said gently. 'There will be a committee there to sort out the friendly Germans from the Nazis and it will only take a couple of days.'

The fish wasn't bad. But as he ate, Walter's eyes kept drifting over the plates of steak, garnished with steaming potatoes.

'I can't believe this,' he suddenly said. 'I have to work. I have an important piece to finish and they want to shut me up. *Here*, no less, in the land of Voltaire and Montesquieu . . .'

'Stop it. I've had enough philosophy,' exploded Gisèle. 'Do you read the papers or not? Think about what would happen if France were to fall into German hands. Now why are you staring at my plate? Do you want to trade? Go on, take it. It doesn't matter to me. Better that than let you ruin my lunch.'

'Thank you. Thank you very much,' whispered Benjamin, switching their plates. He seemed shaken by her outburst, almost won over. 'Please don't get mad. I'm begging you. Just tell me what to do.'

Now they both smiled.

'Report to the stadium and then we'll get some people involved and you will be out in a couple of days.'

And Benjamin just nodded. As he ate the meat he allowed himself to mull over his thoughts.

'I was right the first time,' he eventually announced with some displeasure. 'The fish was better. This steak doesn't have any flavour, does it?'

Chapter Twenty-two

Thousands, tens of thousands, armed with blankets and enough provisions for a few days at the most. They were Jewish refugees, anti-Nazis in exile, tourists taken by surprise and veterans of the Spanish Civil War. There might have been among them some agent of Hitler's who'd carelessly let himself be caught. They were wearing summer shoes and clothes and all were hoping that the *Commission de criblage* would review their papers quickly and send them home before nightfall. Instead, the day was consumed and darkness wrapped the stadium.

Benjamin had packed a toothbrush, a nightgown, two baguettes and cheese in his black bag. In the inside pockets he'd also put his notebooks and Montaigne's essays, and letters from Valéry and Romains sponsoring him for French citizenship as well as letters from Adrienne Monnier and Max Horkheimer lauding the high value of his work as well as his devotion to France. From the early morning of that first unendurable day, Walter sat on the stairs of the stadium waiting to be able to present the letters to someone. He'd been there for hours, his briefcase on his lap, watching the September sky shine like an enamel blade beyond the barbed wire. He was thinking of his life raining down on him in slow motion like in a gloomy silent film. And slowly his mind had become grey and dense like an empty blackboard, like a sky without any trace of blue. When night fell he hardly noticed everyone else bustling about trying to gather a little straw to sleep on. There was even quite a bit of shoving as people tried to secure themselves a space under the covered part of the stadium. Walter just sat where he was, his back hunched over in his fraying suit, his eyes half-closed and his brow furrowed as if he were trying to see something in the distance. That's how he was when Max Aron saw him.

Max was about twenty years old and had a rebellious shock of blond hair falling over his forehead and a ferocious will to live. That first evening he was, like everyone else, concentrating on getting himself a little bit of dry straw and he worried about food and water. How long would they be in this stadium? But then a motionless old man caught his eye, a perfect rock in the middle of the crowd, solemn and dignified amidst the mayhem. He didn't look a day under sixty. Max thought he must have misread the poster and reported by mistake. He went to sleep but then the next morning as he was trying to work out his kinks, he saw the old man again in exactly the same place as if he hadn't moved all night long. Poor old man. Had he eaten anything or managed to sleep at all? Max jumped up, brushed his trousers off with his hands and asked. At which point old Benjamin stood and attempted a bow.

'I welcome your concern, Mr Aron. Thank God I feel fine at the moment and don't need anything. I thank you again.'

He sat back down and then stood suddenly, mortified.

'Pardon me. I neglected to introduce myself. I am Doctor Walter Benjamin of Berlin.'

The sky was a filthy clamour and it didn't seem obvious that the sun would ever come out. A heavy dampness rose from the field, the smell of hay, rotting grass and dirty, sticky people.

'Would you allow me to ask just one question, Mr Aron?'

Benjamin didn't stand up this time but spoke with such gentility that Max almost thought it was affected.

'You'll forgive the, shall we say, intimate nature of the question,' and he lowered his voice, 'but where does one go to address his private needs?'

The young man held back a smile and pointed toward a gathering of men on the side of the platform.

'It's over there, you see? Just some buckets, copper buckets. We'll have to make do, adapt ourselves a bit.'

'Thank you,' replied Benjamin but he didn't move a muscle.

He was inscrutable from the outside. But he was a wreck inside. He cursed the world and all of its misfortunes – to have to piss there in front of everyone. If he forced himself he might even manage to do it, but to relieve himself – no, it was out of the question. And yet this wrenching in his gut was making him paler with every tug. He shut his eyes and dismissed outright the idea of sitting on a pail. He decided to stay right where he was. This all, *la via cruces*, couldn't possibly last much longer. Hopefully they would call him soon. Perhaps they were going in alphabetical order and he would be among the first allowed to leave. He settled his case on his lap and waited. He waited until nine o'clock when the stadium speaker turned on and began playing a military march. *Now*, they would start calling people. The steady rumble of conversation ceased

and thousands of people looked expectantly up at the platform. But that voice, the voice they'd been waiting for, came
crackling and whistling through the speaker. The announcement was that from this point, they should all consider themselves prisoners. This was a measure that had been taken
for their own protection and that they would be shortly
transported elsewhere.

Shortly lasted ten days. Which were spent walking around
the racetrack, dozing on rancid straw, gossiping on the stairs
and asking each other one or two thousand times why they were
there, and when and how they might be released. They ate pâté
three times a day, fishing with their fingers in the tins and then
spreading it on bread with their fingers. The pâté got gummy
in their hair and stuck to their faces and gradually worked its
way into every available pore. There wasn't much water, so
cleaning was a challenge too – just a single pail for every fifteen
people and one was grateful for that.

Benjamin spent the day reading Montaigne and talking to
Max about Kant and Baudelaire; or strolling, hands clasped
behind his back, his eyes roving around the field, composing
petitions in his mind in which he complained about this treat-
ment. He assumed that he would be released as soon as possible.
At least he had a friend in Max, who brought him pâté, fetched
water for him, held a cover up in front of a pail when Benjamin
finally resolved to take care of his private business, and freshen-
ing his pallet when he could with new straw.

'Thank you, Mr Aron,' he said each time, bowing.

Then, fortunately, he also found Sahl. It was the afternoon
of the fourth or fifth day and it seemed about to rain so people
began crushing toward the shelter of the box seats. Max was

pushing and elbowing a path and old Benjamin was following, his briefcase hugged to his chest.

'Excuse me, excuse me,' he repeated. 'Do you mind leaving me a bit of space?' No one listened, they just pushed and screamed. He turned sideways to slide through and a hand grabbed his shoulder and pulled. He was turning in surprise when he heard his name.

'Benjamin! Is it really you?'

He almost wept upon seeing a familiar face in that inferno. Sahl stared at him uncertainly, a faint smile hesitating on his face. Could this really be his friend Benjamin, this man with the bristling hair, long beard, hollow cheeks, a face that was all teeth and nose. And on top of that, one could never really be sure how to approach Benjamin. There was always the risk he would start acting peculiarly. He had a mania for mystery, for example. There are some situations of course that might send even the most stable person over the edge. But now Walter let himself be hugged and hard – he didn't even shrink from Sahl's filthy hair.

'I know I shouldn't say this,' he whispered in his ear, 'but I'm so very happy to see you.'

He couldn't tell if Sahl heard him because in that same moment a long rumble of thunder seemed to crack the black sky and the rain came right after falling in buckets. The downpour lasted an hour or two, beating on the copper roof, filling the field with mud and puddles, flooding the stands, carrying off every little bit of straw. The downpour became a mist, almost a fog, and then became a slow chilly rain, forcing everyone to stay amassed and crushed under the overhang, trying uselessly to nap through the storm. At dawn the western sky seemed to break and a little blue poked through. At eight o'clock on the dot, the guards, mostly elderly reservists, braved the throng in order to dispense the bread and pâté. Max wrangled enough for three and carried it over to his companions tucked safely under his jacket.

'Thank you, Mr Aron,' said Benjamin.

'From now on,' whispered Sahl seriously, 'we have to make sure they don't separate us.'

There were all together the morning when a second announcement came over the speakers following the usual military march. This time it explained that they would be transferred throughout the day to volunteer labour camps all over France. There would be a roll call and then they should board the trucks parked out in the square.

The stadium filled with whistles, screams and hollering. Voluntary labour camps? And they had the nerve to say it was for the refugees' own protection.

'French bastards,' spat Max. 'They're treating us all like spies, like criminals.'

Abrahamski, a hulking Pole who'd come with Max to the stadium, was in a blind rage. Like everyone else, he wanted to know what had become of the famous *criblage*. Weren't they planning to pick out the Nazis from the refugees? Not a word more had ever been said about it.

Benjamin shook his head and breathed heavily in the dense, humid air.

'Keep calm, Mr Abrahamski,' he slowly said. 'It would only be a farce if there were a *criblage*. You know very well that even with the best intentions in the world it's impossible to review the cases of thousands of people.'

The truth was, Sahl would write many years later, that France hadn't been prepared for that war. The decision to intern the refugees was made at the last minute. To make matters worse, the French military was incapable of 'identifying any kind of German opposition. For the readers of *Action Française* there was no difference between the Germans who opposed Hitler and the ones who supported him. You needed to fight back together.' Koestler was even harsher. 'During the first months of war,' he wrote in his novel, 'it became a deliberate policy of the Minister of Information to feed the public terrifying tales of crimes committed by foreigners (this was long before the psychosis about secret agents even started). He depicted a situation in which the government was locked in a heroic duel against the dragon named *sale métèque*. One needed to remember that almost three-and-a-half million foreigners were living in France, which was almost ten per cent of the total population. The foreigners were an even better fall guy than the half-million Jews in Germany. French xenophobia wasn't anything but a local variant of Ersatz, of German anti-Semitism.'

So that mid-September morning, the tens of thousands of men interned in Colombes stadium had no choice but to wait. Name after name after name hissed out of the speaker. The sky was destroyed and the field overturned from the storm. Benjamin and his friends' names were called well after noon and, filing between two rows of soldiers, they boarded a black, flat-bed truck. If someone didn't move fast enough, hampered by luggage or blankets, they got a powerful whack on the back from the *flics* – the police.

There were ten rows of benches to each truck; one foot soldier with a raised bayonet positioned at the front and back and each corner. The trucks caravanned through the almost deserted *quais*, down the Louvre and the Tuileries. At the Gare d'Austerliz there was a long freight train parked on tracks waiting for the prisoners. They were divided into groups of fifty and loaded into the trains. It was so dark inside the wagon cars that they couldn't see each other's faces, couldn't tell who was a friend. Walter tried. He peered between the slats, trying to figure out where they were being brought, but the train sped through the stations too quickly to read the names of any of the towns. They travelled for hours. They were sweating, parched, and their legs ached from standing, until at last they arrived at the Nevers station – the whistle blaring loudly enough to cover up the hollering and cursing.

Walter recognised the name. It was a little city in the Loire. He may even have visited once over the winter with Gisèle. The air was bright and cool out in the open and the sun was setting behind a row of poplar trees growing along a little canal. About ten men and women standing by the stationmaster's hut stared grimly at them as they tumbled out of the train. Benjamin thought they would have lynched them if they could and the thought got stuck in his throat. He took off his tie, shut his eyes and focused on breathing. When he opened his eyes again the train had left and there was a queue in the square of three or four hundred prisoners. Max took his arm and told him not to worry.

'Just be strong for a little longer,' said Sahl comfortingly. 'We're almost there.'

Hell if they were. The guards forced them all into a long single file, poking some of the resistant prisoners with their bayonets.

'Forward march!' cried a captain finally.

'Give me your bag. I'll carry it.'

'I thank you heartily, Mr Aron,' said Benjamin.

They started out down the road toward Paris, a single stretch of asphalt cutting through the green countryside, the vineyards, the deserted villages where the shutters were all drawn – a long black ribbon winding toward the saddest sunset. After two hours of walking in total darkness they found themselves at the castle of Vernuche, a low, wide building with a steep tiled roof, one square tower on either side.

Benjamin had difficulty on the walk. He often gasped for breath and tried to stop and rest but the guards tormented him. Twice he was on the verge of fainting, but Max pulled him upright and made him drink. Old Benjamin stayed the course. They were like a prophet and his guide, an old wise man escorted by a young disciple up to the temple. And then almost at the top of the hill, the prophet starts feeling a quivering and his legs go so weak they collapse under him, and he tumbles into the dark.

'My heart,' he whispered.

After that, Max, Abrahamski and Sahl carried him to the castle.

'I'm fine now, thank you,' he said with a bow. He climbed up the stairs, followed the dark and empty corridors to the dark and empty rooms where they would stay. There was no light, no beds, no seats, tables, or even hooks to hang something. Max spread the blanket on the ground and Benjamin fell instantly asleep and didn't move again except to occasionally toss in a dream.

Chapter Twenty-three

He dragged himself from sleep as if from a viscous desert, a desolate inferno of thoughts. The wobbling light coming in through the window outlined the shadowy figures in the room, it was a tableau of unreal perspectives, and Benjamin, eyelids still heavy, suddenly recognised the tenuousness of his future.

'Already? What time is it,' he asked, tapping at a painful rib between the buttons of his shirt.

Sergeant Guizot woke them at six o'clock on the nose, screaming like the devil and poking each one with his bayonet. Within half an hour they were gathering in the courtyard standing in front of an empty booth. An icy hint of storm swept the clouds in the sky, promising certain betrayal. Squeezed between Sahl, Max and Abrahamski, Walter stared at the gravel on the ground. He was worried. Occasionally he turned around to look incredulously at the castle of Vernuche, with its ivy-covered walls and slate roof, the tiles uneven in the light. His companions were stamping their feet to keep warm. When he turned around again, he saw Hans Fittko a few rows behind them. He was standing straight as a rail, defying the wind and the French with a stony face. Even his hair, carefully combed and pomaded, stood out in the midst of all the messy heads. Benjamin nodded at him and smiled. Then he lowered his eyes, turned back around and snuggled, trembling, into his coat.

The camp commander had climbed up onto the booth and stood clearing his throat. He was short, thin, and French to the last. He wore the moustache of a miserly aristocrat, and the longer he spoke the more evident it became that he didn't know what to say. He seemed disconcerted, at least as much so as the three hundred men who'd been ripped from their exile and dragged like prisoners to an empty castle surrounded by barbed wire and foot soldiers.

'So why are they keeping us in camps?' Benjamin asked himself under his breath.

'They're going to put us to hard labour,' answered Sahl. 'You'll see, building roads, repairing bridges. We're prisoners. Prisoners of war, remember that.'

'It's just not possible. We're German Jews, persecuted, we're victims of Hitler. It's not logical; it doesn't make sense.'

'Silence!' cried a corporal from the ranks.

Benjamin fell instantly silent. He watched the commander who was still speaking, his breath gathering in little puffs of vapour. But Benjamin couldn't concentrate on the words. He wanted some time to himself, to sit and rest, but when the speech was over, he had to line up to see the doctor. The wind carried the scent of damp countryside and the river that ran beyond the road. But his nostrils seemed to tingle rather with the odour of his own past: his father's smell, tea and pastries in the living room of the house on Nettelbeckstrasse, his school companions on the steps of the college. He was there, but he wasn't there, even as, half-naked, he pulled Doctor Abrami's diagnosis from his briefcase to show.

'It's my heart, you see.'

'Okay. Excused from work,' he was at last told.

That's how life in the camp began. It was a disaster at first. Nothing worked. It was six days before they had straw to sleep on, and before a basic kitchen was set up, and before blankets were distributed. And it wasn't the soldiers taking care of these things; it was the prisoners. 'Not even in jail,' commented Sahl sardonically over thirty years later, 'did those men forget they were Germans.' The discipline, the orderliness, the gumption was a sharp contrast to the inefficiency of the French. The inmates established a cleaning rota for the bunks and built a kind of latrine, found the straw and blankets, fashioned mugs and procured jars with evaporated milk. They also organised courses on the difference between Freud and Jung, between Trotsky and Lenin. In no time, from nothing they built a community, from chaos and anxiety, they made a society. A leader emerged in the form of a man who had been a supervisor in big warehouses where he'd learned to give orders and organise his personnel. No one knew where he'd come from, just that he was the right person for the job in the right moment. A stamp collector set up a post office; a painter who was a gourmand became head chef. Even Benjamin started giving lessons, hanging his head in that way of his, walking as he spoke. He was paid for his lectures, one button or three Gauloises. But that wasn't the only kind of money circulating in the camp. Sahl wrote his poetry in a little notebook a soldier had smuggled in, and sold it for three nails and a pencil.

Of course, getting by wasn't easy. You had to adapt yourself, be quick and flexible. Benjamin wasn't really the type. He was methodical, in love with his rituals, a systematic man, catapulted into a situation that escaped him and upended all logic. Walter lived in details, and from the minutia he'd always been able to fabricate a world. Here at the camp, the days wove together into a series of absurd details that even the needle of his mind would never manage to thread. 'He didn't know how to adapt,' Lisa Fittko would say years later. 'I think that old Benjamin could only face a cup of boiling tea after he'd formulated some kind of theory about the cup.'

Benjamin had always taken life in small bits, and now life was taking its revenge. He was confronted with the problem of procuring bread and a blanket for himself, of finding shelter from the cold or the rain. And still he was stunned, disoriented, as if he'd lost the compass he'd used up until then. Fortunately he had his friends. Hans Fittko taught him to sew and helped him negotiate the price of his courses and rounded up food for him. Max Aron, his young disciple, hung a potato sack off a spiral staircase creating a lean-to where Benjamin spread his straw pallet. It was that privacy that saved him. Because the worst part of the camp as far as he was concerned was the closeness of the small rooms. He was never alone, and was exposed to every sound and the stench of the other prisoners.

At noon they'd all go down to eat in the courtyard, gathering under the half shelter of a corrugated iron sheet. The days of pâté were gone. Now they ate onions or a glutinous broth with scraps of meat or potatoes floating in it. Other prisoners came from a nearby camp that still didn't have a kitchen to eat under their roof. Kesten was among them. With his high forehead and heavy brow he seemed desperately in search of someone to speak with. He approached Walter.

'Do you remember me, Doctor Benjamin? I'm Hermann Kesten, the writer. Do you remember? You even reviewed one of my novels.'

Old Benjamin stared at him, searching his memory. He certainly did remember him. It must have been around 1929. At the time he'd liked the irreverent approach that Kesten had toward his protagonist Josef Bar. He looked him over as he tried to fish a potato from his bowl.

'Those were other times,' he said.

'Right,' said Kesten, staring at the line of black on Benjamin's neck. 'How absurd. War finally broke out against Hitler and we're locked up here, unable to do anything, not even write.'

Was this perhaps what was really torturing Benjamin? One evening he and Sahl stood watching sheep graze lazily on the other side of the barbed wire. It was almost sunset, a storm of swallows swooped through the sky.

'You know what I'd like,' Walter said. 'To be able to just sit at a café and pass the day scratching my belly.'

Sahl nodded and looked at the darkening sky. The ground was being swept smooth by a gusty wind.

'No. I don't believe you,' he finally said, rupturing the silence. 'Instead of sitting there doing nothing, you'd start working on something. You'd write.'

Walter reflected and smiled. 'Maybe you're right. I wouldn't be able to do nothing. One always needs to have something to think about. It's the same here. You know what I've decided? I'm going to stop smoking. If I want to survive, I have to concentrate on something difficult.'

Survive. It was easy to say. Back in Paris, Helen, Gisèle, Sylvia and Adrienne were all keeping busy. It was already October and they still hadn't figured out where to bring their friend's case. They were constantly coming and going from the Sûreté, the Préfecture and all the other military stations. They wrote long hopeful letters asking him if he needed cigarettes, chocolate, a sweater. But he read between the lines and saw they were discouraged.

But old Benjamin withstood it all. He had a few books, his friends, his lectures, a pencil and a pad for his notes. He even participated in a performance they mounted one Sunday morning for the soldiers and prisoners. He recited the chorus from 'The Voice of the Granary', and then an actor read several of Sahl's poems. When the great room of the castle filled with the verses of *Elegy for 1939*, composed the day the war broke out, three hundred bearded, ragged men wiped their eyes. Sahl ran to the bathroom because he couldn't bear the sobbing that his own words had provoked. There was a man already there, who'd fled the room shortly before.

'What good is it? What is this for?' Sahl nervously asked. 'Songs, poems, the commander doesn't know a word of German and he's a criminal. He couldn't care less about the Geneva Convention. Do you know what he's done? He sold us to a factory, five francs for each of us a day. They're sending us out to work tomorrow – to pave an airfield.'

After that, life in the camp grew more difficult. Every morning at six, Benjamin watched his companions, chilled to the bone, as they headed out to the airport under the watch of four indolent soldiers. It was an hour-long walk and they were all still wearing the summer clothes they'd worn that day to the

Colombes stadium – all of them in tatters now, too lightweight to protect them from the stinging autumn wind and rain that so often accompanied them. When they returned at night they were stinking and bone-tired, their shoes in pieces. They cursed the work, their destiny, the lack of food and the idiocies and incompetence of the French.

'They didn't even give me a shovel,' complained Abrahamski. 'They made me dig with my hands.'

'If I had known, I would have given you my shovel,' said Hans Fittko, shaking his head forlornly. 'They had me dig a hole two metres deep and then ordered me to fill it back up with the same dirt.'

That's how it was. And sometimes worse. The papers didn't always make it there and they were forced to live off the *bobards*, the gossip – the *boches* have broken through the Maginot line, they are already at the gates of Paris, or not, that the Allies were about to launch an offensive . . . There they were, slowly swallowing time, hunger, cold, exhaustion, asking themselves why and for how much longer, waiting for letters that never came, fanning little flames of hope – and thinking about how the few real Nazi prisoners were protected by the Red Cross and treated with kid gloves. Whereas they, anti-Nazis by choice and conviction, were being treated like human waste, the scum of the earth.

Apart from the declared Nazis, there were two other prisoners who forged a comfortable life for themselves. They were filmmakers and had proposed a film called *Vive la France!* to the commander. In order to do the research, they would have to go to the library in Nevers. Certainly it was a long trudge, every day for three hours, but they were willing to make the sacrifice. The commander was moved and gave them special armbands so that they could leave whenever they wanted. They came back at night, half-drunk, still tasting the delicacies of *cuisine française*. They were welcomed into the enclosure by the curses of their fellow prisoners. But the real torture started at bedtime when they would talk out loud about the dishes they'd sampled in all the local restaurants. Benjamin would shake in his little shelter, his empty stomach grumbled and he plotted how he could get an armband too. It became his obsession. He plotted about it for days and then one evening took Sahl by the elbow and dragged him into a corner.

'It's about the armband,' he whispered. 'No, don't laugh. I have a plan.' He wanted to propose a literary magazine to the commander. 'Of the highest level, naturally. A journal for the camp. It would be for the intellectuals but then we can use it to show the French who we really are, these people they've locked up here as enemies of the state. Come to me tomorrow at four,' he concluded, looking furtively around. 'We'll have the first editorial meeting.'

The next day, under the stairway, hidden behind a sack of potatoes, five of them gathered. There was Sahl and Benjamin, Max Aron (who'd become a personal secretary by now), Hans Fittko and another prisoner Sahl didn't know. They were all kneeling on the ground, heads together, sipping thimbles of aquavit bought off a soldier.

'My friends,' began Benjamin. 'The important thing is the armband. It is a matter of survival. Only those who get an armband will make it out of this camp alive.'

He was very serious and spoke with the sombre tone of someone defending a philosophical thesis from unjust, calumnious attacks. The armband had been transformed for him into the symbol of survival itself. It was the detail that became his new point of departure. The armband could become the foundation of an entire new world.

'Now, what are some of your ideas for the first issue?'

They suggested articles about books being read in the camp, a statistical chart of the prisoners, representing the many different social levels of the émigrés. Max Aron proposed an article about the Sunday-morning performance. Sahl chose a theme he knew would be received well.

'I would like to write,' he said, 'about how a society is born from nothing. A kind of sociology of the camp, beginning with building a latrine and arriving at the cultural superstructure we are now constructing with this journal.'

'Good, very good,' said Benjamin as he took notes on his pad.

After that they met twice a week, drinking aquavit from a thimble and reading aloud the articles that were being developed on the back of envelopes. But the journal was never published and they never got the armband. November came instead. The first snow fell. The courtyard of the camp was transformed into a giant icy swamp and no one spoke of going home. Walter's letters grew more frequent and more desperate. Adrienne Monnier wrote that she'd gone to Benjamin Crémieux, but that the best person to talk to would be Henri Hoppenot, director of European Affairs to the Foreign Minister. In the meantime, Horkheimer had brought on Georges Scelle and Maurice Halbwachs in the States. On November 6, Helen Hessel told him she had a meeting in Tours with Jules Romains who promised he'd write to Henri Membré, secretary of the

French PEN Club to have him intervene on Benjamin's behalf. In the end it finally seemed that things were moving. They just had to keep trying and hope that their efforts didn't damage his case. But Benjamin wouldn't be the first to go home. Kesten came to lunch one day in the middle of a biblical storm, hail beating heartily against the roof.

'Good day, Doctor Benjamin,' he yelled.

You could read in his face that he was very pleased but was trying not to show it so that he wouldn't upset everyone left behind.

'They're letting you go,' Walter said gravely as he looked him in the eyes. It wasn't a question. Thunder shook the earth and cracked the sky.

'It's true,' said Kesten. 'I leave tomorrow. Our friends at the PEN Club managed to secure my release.'

Walter's face lit up and a gloomy blue flashed in his eyes. Wasn't the PEN Club agitating on his behalf too? This was the right path. Perhaps it was too early to lose hope.

But his salvation didn't come only from there. On November 17, Gisèle Freund wrote him a short postcard. '*Dear friend,*' it went, '*I just received a telephone call from our friend Hoppenot telling me that your case was decided yesterday by the Commission de criblage. You are free and we anxiously await your arrival. I hope that your commander receives word immediately. It is definitive! So you must remain calm and brave. With affection, Gisèle.*'

His friends embraced him. Max even seemed to cry, hiding his face against the wall.

'If you see Lisa, tell her I'm well,' whispered Hans Fittko in his ear.

That night old Benjamin tossed and turned under his blanket.

When he fell asleep he dreamed of walking with Doctor Abrami down into a large cave where there were many people sleeping on beds. There was one lovely woman, she moved quickly like a flash. Walter saw her, but not with his eyes. He watched her with his mind as she pulled up the blanket. The dream might have lasted several minutes, but Walter knew he wouldn't be able to sleep anymore. He put on his glasses, stood and went to the window. He stood there for hours looking at the pale sky, the fading stars peeking out from behind the clouds. Then the night got soft, the clouds began to redden and blanch, a flock of kites lifted suddenly into flight spinning in wide circles over the castle and the camp.

Chapter Twenty-four

Only nine hours? That's all it takes to get to Mexico from Italy. How about that. In my day, a trip like that would have taken at least two weeks. But this is better. The time you save, you can spend listening to my stories. There you have it. For once, for at least once in your life, you can listen to someone who can tell you a whole story from beginning to end. Lucky you, to have stumbled upon me. We don't have much longer to go before we get to Benjamin. Be patient. Where were we? Oh yes. We were in the Septfonds camp. I already told you about that. Except that when the war broke out it went from bad to worse in days.

You didn't need to be a fortune-teller to figure out what the Germans had in mind but the officers in that camp couldn't see the forest for the trees. How surprised they seemed by the idea that after Poland, Germany would set her sights on France. No, war was the only thing they seemed clear on. Their war; our fault. They reduced our rations even further. The discipline got stricter. General Gamelin came in person and threatened to send us back to Spain if we didn't enlist. It was his sticking point – the Legion, and for many it started to seem better than the hunger we were suffering in the camp. Luckily Mariano had his ideas clear. One morning after the raising of the flag, and after we here harangued about volunteering, he raised his hand and stepped forward. He'd got thin and looked tired, but he still had that gleam in his eyes and those pupils that fixed on you like magnets.

'We want to fight the Germans,' he explained in the middle of a great silence. 'But with dignity. Not as mercenaries.'

Mariano talked and I translated. Everyone was looking at us. I could barely speak but I kept going, trying to focus and not make any mistakes.

'Let us join the French army,' he went on. 'We'll have the same duties, of course, but also the same rights, equal to you French. Then, yes, we'll fight.'

They didn't listen. The commander just looked at us hatefully, he was almost smiling with disgust. 'That's enough. Fall back into line.'

It was evident they didn't know us. They thought the fear of returning to Spain, the hunger they were inflicting on us, would have driven us to choose dignity. But, of the twenty thousand soldiers, only fifty joined the Legion. They had to backtrack, invent another strategy to dismantle the camp. Work brigades: made up of Spaniards and commanded by the French. But they wanted us to disarm landmines. It was better, but all of the promises that they made lasted just until we got to the famous Maginot line.

We headed out at the beginning of November, crowded like animals into the freight cars, transported for days and days going from one region to another until we got to the Sarre-Union station in Mosella. It was late at night, there was a fog coming down on the tracks and over the low grey buildings. The shadow of a smokestack melted into the sky. They made us get out in silence. The darkness was dense and the air smelled of gas. A dog howled in the distance beyond a bridge and behind a blot of black fortifications.

'They sure planned this one well,' muttered Mariano.

'Why?' I asked as they herded us onto trucks.

'Make us arrive dead tired in the middle of the night. Now they're going to separate us and we won't even be able to protest.'

As always he was right. The truck headed up a secondary road and travelled two hours on over the bumps until we arrived at an isolated farm in the middle of a field. There was a barn with a little bit of straw spread on the ground.

'Get out here,' they said. 'This is a war zone. From now on there will be no smoking or building fires.'

Mariano elbowed me awake at dawn. The wind was scratching at the wall like a file. It was a dull relentless sound.

'Come with me,' he said.

Under that filthy barely lit sky, I saw an immense courtyard, barbed wire all around it, and a sentinel posted at every twenty metres. Mariano stared at the grim scene, his jaw clenched. He was in a chilly rage.

'You see?' he said. 'We're prisoners. And there are only a hundred of us here. Now the rebels of Septfonds are scattered all over France.'

I didn't answer. What was there to say? I looked at the other men who were straggling into the courtyard. They were dressed in dark grey uniforms, disorderly, gesturing and talking loudly. This time I elbowed Mariano.

'Spaniards,' I said quickly. 'These other guys are Spanish, too.'

'Bullshit,' he answered.

But it was true. Actually, it seemed . . . I looked and then looked harder. Who did I see, but Alfonso, the Italian. Yes! It was really him. I was so happy I didn't hear myself.

'It's Alfonso,' I said. Or maybe I yelled.

'Are you out of your mind?' Mariano said.

'Maybe,' I answered and called over to our friend, waving broadly and shouting. Alfonso finally saw me. He stiffened for a moment and then nodded and casually separated out from the group, walking over to us, one finger planted against his nose. We understood. We should keep it down.

'I'm known as Andrés now,' he said in a muffled voice. 'Andrés Del Campo. Is that clear?'

What an asshole. In the middle of the Babel on the border, he'd passed for a Spaniard so that instead of exile, he'd gone to the camp at Argelès and in May they'd sent him to work in Marne, and now finally to the front.

'Do you remember Sepúlveda? He's here too, in another company.'

'So we've got a royal flush,' I said with a smile.

The truth was that there wasn't much to smile about. That same morning an official interpreter rounded us all up in the yard and explained where we were – between Sarralbe and Sarreguemines, just a few kilometres south of the Maginot line. We were one of six Spanish companies serving the 125th regiment of sappers.

'But are we soldiers in the French army or not?'

The voice, the one perforating the cold like a knife, belonged, as always, to Mariano. He was still in his position in the third row, hands in his pockets, his collar up. From there he was challenging the officer, who was standing on a low wall.

'Yes, of course,' muttered the lieutenant, tapping his whip on his boot.

'Then,' Mariano said calmly, 'take away this barbed wire immediately. And I mean immediately. Get it?'

Now it's going to get good, I thought. In fact the little officer turned lilac then blue and his moustache twittered nervously.

'That's not up for discussion,' he said. 'You've been arrested and whoever is not in agreement should step forward.'

It wasn't a single person who stepped forward, but two, then three, then all of us together. We surrounded that son of a bitch, that cardboard *guappo*, who was now practically peeing himself. He wilted. In the end they took the barbed wire away, so at least we could move around. But the French made us pay. They put us to work like slaves, building barricades and trenches against tanks in the middle of the desolate plain. They barely fed us. It was so bad we had to go looking for potatoes and carrots in nearby fields, and steal the dry bread they fed the horses. I don't remember our commander's name. I just remember the nickname we gave him. We called him The Seal because he was fat and walked with his gut sticking out. He wasn't just fat, he was mean and he had a beef with us Spaniards, with the Republicans. They must have worked hard to dig this guy up. It would have been difficult to find a bigger son of a bitch. He had us spitting our own teeth. The winter was bitter up there, the temperature often dropped to thirty-five below zero, and there we were digging in dirt that was as hard as ice, living on bird rations. We'd be sent to isolation if we stood up for a minute to rest our kidneys.

The other companies had it bad too. When we saw Sepúlveda he'd been reduced to skin and bones and had no colour at all. It had been months since he'd last been able to pee on any church steps. But this wasn't what made him mad.

'The trenches of Aragon were better. It was better on the Ebro,' he went around muttering. 'I'm hungry like the ninth circle of Dante's *Inferno*, that's what I am. And I'd kill these French bastards, these good-for-nothing officers, sons of whores.'

One bitterly cold evening around the middle of February, when the few thoughts that we might have had left were frozen solid, we were all talking at the low brick wall between our two companies. Alfonso, Mariano and I were all in agreement, but what could we do? Sepúlveda smiled and lit up like he'd had a vision.

'I know,' he said. 'It's just that I'm not a good organiser.'

He fell silent and pulled on the last bit of cigarette that had been passed through eight hands.

'What?' I asked.

'Let's strike,' he said. 'We'll hold a hunger strike. Considering how little they give us to eat as it is . . .'

No sooner said than done. The next week we refused our rations and went on like that for almost two days. Finally a colonel came, a state-level big cheese. He arrived like a bull, tough, charging in head first. What were we thinking? Staging a hunger strike in the army? It was crazy stuff. And then we were stealing food from the horses as well. But he was a good man, the old colonel, I have to say. He didn't know anything about our conditions and when we explained what had been going on he was shocked.

'I can't believe it,' he said falling heavily back in his chair.

'What you're telling me is unworthy of France and unworthy of her army. Give me a little time and I'll see what I can do.'

He was true to his word. An old-fashioned man of honour. Three days later we were served chicken and loads of bread, then they held a soccer match between all of the troops in the sector. It had been years since Mariano and I even touched a ball, but we joined a team. We won, you know. Alfonso played defence, and I was centrefield. Mariano was a forward. Sepúlveda watched and advised our coach, a Basque captain who'd played in the B league when he was younger. That was living. If it hadn't been for the work on the barricades and the occasional burst of cannon fire from the Krauts, you wouldn't have said that we were at war. If only Mercedes were with me; that would have been the best. But that peculiar period of revelry didn't last long. The *drôle de guerre* was about to end.

Chapter Twenty-five

Benjamin returned to Paris on November 25, 1939. It was a humid day. There was the promise of a storm in the air; black, webby clouds raced across the sky. A wan light hovered over the rain-sprinkled streets. He knocked on his sister's front door, barely touching the wood with his knuckles. It didn't occur to him to use the doorbell.

'Walter!' Dora exclaimed, putting her hands to her face.

'What's wrong? Am I a ghost?'

He was – more or less. He'd lost at least twenty-five pounds, his eyes were deep sockets under his shaggy eyebrows, the skin on his face was loose and his shoulders were drowning in his shirt. As for his state of mind – it was better left unsaid. 'You can well imagine,' he wrote to Horkheimer a few days later, 'what the constant racket and the impossibility of being alone even for an hour must have cost me over time.' He felt extraordinarily tired, extenuated to the point of having to pause every three or four minutes along the road because he couldn't walk any more. It was his heart, though he didn't tell Horkheimer this. The three months of hardship in Nevers had weakened it even more. Old Benjamin was an invalid.

'Myocarditis,' declared Doctor Abrami. 'You must not worry so much. Take advantage of the truce. Stop smoking. Only walk when necessary.'

This was the real killer. He'd made an art of walking, roaming Paris. It was his way of understanding things and now he was reduced to panting after just a few steps, heart pounding through his chest and his vision clouding over. It was a nemesis, a curse. All that aside, even Paris seemed sickly. Benjamin found it greyer, darker; the shutters were drawn and people used flashlights and candles. The sound of sirens ran amuck in the darkness and there were armed sentries on every major intersection.

That was the war for old Benjamin, an undoing that hovered at his back like a shadow, a silent, empty self-annihilation. The thread of his days was as precarious and as sticky as before; he seemed to be waiting every hour for life to take another direction. As soon as he rose in the morning he felt the day slipping away, losing itself in the cold early darkness of winter. The house on rue Dombasle was poorly heated so he stayed in bed most of the time. The first month, he only went out when it was strictly necessary – to thank Adrienne and his other friends, to shop, pay bills, unblock his bank account and apply for a library card. Then, in early January he saw his ex-wife, Dora. She was on her way back to London and she stopped in Paris to see him and ask him again to come away with her.

'Maybe just for a while, until you regain your health.'

'It's better that I don't. Thank you for the invitation though.'

They walked across the Ile St-Louis arm in arm, fending off the pitch of the howling wind through the winding streets and aiming for the open spaces over the river. Suddenly Benjamin stopped and leaned against the balustrade of Ponte Louis-Philippe. Here it was again. He could barely breathe. He gasped for air, letting the rain drench his face.

'What's the matter? Are you sick?'

'No no, I'm fine,' he gasped. 'I'm just a little weak still and I tire quickly. That's all. Perhaps we can go to that café?'

They sat down; Walter like a broom, stiff and pale, looking out over the Ile de le Cité and Notre-Dame through the rain-stippled windows. Dora rested her face on her hands and looked at him worriedly.

'See? You should come to London. It would do you good. You could rest, eat properly, visit Stefan, work.'

He inhaled deeply, sucking at the air, then shook his head and brushed back a grey lock of hair.

'I said no already. It isn't possible for me. The only place I can work is here in Paris. In just a few days they will issue me a library card and I have to finish my work at all costs.'

'You wouldn't even do it for Stefan? He really needs to see you.'

'Dora, you know I'm a bad father.'

It was dark when they left the café. The rain had stopped and the wind was cleaning the sky. Under the early evening starlight, Paris dripped as though buckets of water had just been emptied on it. The few cars left on the street made fleeting shots of light that lasted a few minutes and hung in the damp air.

'We'll see each other soon,' said Dora.

Walter stood in front of her, his head down, tapping at his feet with the tip of his umbrella.

'Yes, soon,' he confirmed.

They looked at each other. A happy silence fell. And then their smiles stretched into the obtuse, scattered expressions of people who don't know what else to say to each other. Dora gave him a quick kiss, just two lips fleeting on his cheek.

'You're a stubborn mule,' she murmured.

Walter watched her disappear behind the glass door of the hotel, wiggling her fingers at him. He lingered for a few moments on the pavement and then headed off again, leaning on his umbrella. His shoulders sloped and he walked uncertainly as if he weren't passing through very familiar streets and squares, but rather in a dangerous, strange place. He walked through time, in his own past.

At home he lay down without undressing. He fell into a stony sleep and in the morning he woke in a cold sweat, shaping bitter words without meaning. Was it really his rumpled face reflecting back at him from the mirror? He stared at it, closed his eyes, and stared again. He looked away when he started to fear that there was someone else looking back through the mirror. He shook himself and began to clean up. All those lies, he thought. He'd told them to Dora and then repeated them to himself. It would be, he knew, certain disaster to go to London. But staying in Paris was difficult as well. So he had settled down to study some English with Hannah Arendt. And he had written to Horkheimer a few days earlier asking for advice. Should he stay or go? And would Horkheimer even be willing to prepare the affidavit for him?

The letter had turned out a little whiney, possibly even servile in his clumsy attempt to be proud. 'It goes without saying,' he wrote, 'that your advice will carry the most weight for me in this situation. For I would not like my arrival in America to cause difficulties of a material nature, introducing a discordant element into our friendship. That friendship at the moment constitutes for me not only the sole support of my material existence, but also almost the only moral support I have at my disposal.' And further, 'Please be as explicit as possible in informing me of your own opinion, namely whether I should stay in France or join you in America. It is really important to me that you consider this request in detail and that you are aware that it does not constitute an attempt on my part to shun my responsibility to what I must unhappily call "my destiny". On the contrary, the only purpose of this request is to allow me to come to a decision in full cognisance of the situation.'

Decisions did not come easily to Benjamin. But even if he were to decide he wanted to leave, it wouldn't necessarily be easy. As a *ressortissant*, a stateless foreigner, a Jew, it would be problematic to leave Paris without a permit. Getting a visa for the United States would mean going through a network of queues, sponsors, documents – far beyond his capabilities. So all that was left to him was to concentrate on his work. On January 11, his library card was renewed. This was his lot. And as always when circumstances took him by the hand, they also alleviated him of choice, allowing him some peace of mind. He found an icy serenity in the middle of an old world falling to pieces. The armoured divisions meanwhile gunned their motors at his borders.

Chapter Twenty-six

They met on the stairs in the middle of the afternoon. The elevator was broken again and Benjamin was sliding slowly down, leaning on the banister. Koestler passed him at a run and then stopped suddenly. He'd got back from the prison camp two days earlier; he was thin as a rail, and his face still marked with hunger.

'Walter, is it really you?' he asked turning.

'It would seem so,' said Benjamin with a half-smile. 'I'm so pleased to see you free. Are you still you?'

'More or less,' answered Koestler with a grimace. 'But I'm well, at least I'm better than I was a few days ago. I'm in a hurry. Will you walk with me to Madame Suchet? We'll chat as we walk and get some wine and cheese so that tonight we can celebrate.'

'I really . . .'

'Come on. It's not every day that you run into a man who's just come out of Vernet.'

That name didn't ring any bells for Benjamin but he realised he couldn't refuse.

'Okay,' he decided, 'but let's walk slowly. You see I'm not in the best shape.'

The rain had stopped early that morning after an overcast, damp week. The January sky over rue de Vaugirard hung low, colourless and glowing with light. There were clouds but they were invisible and the sun was filtered through them making a beam of light here and there. They walked from bright spots into shadows. Koestler walked ahead, awkward, hands in his pockets, a cigarette stuck between his lips.

'It was rough, right? Unbelievable. For years France has been denouncing the Nazi camps as blights on European civilisation and then the first thing they think of doing is to imitate them.'

He was indignant, shaking his head and flapping his elbows in order to avoid extracting his hands from his pockets and exposing them to the cold.

'And it's not as if they put Fascists in there. No sir,' he continued after a pause. 'They put the soldiers of the Spanish Civil War in there alongside German and Italian refugees and those who have nothing to do with anything but are Hungarian, neutral like me. I have nothing more to say about democracy in France.'

Benjamin just nodded. After walking on for a bit, he managed to mention Vernuche. Just a few words because he didn't like to think about those three months anymore, or of Sahl and all the others left there to rot. But Koestler still needed to vent, to recount the horrors he'd escaped. He walked and talked, smoking one cigarette after the other. He hardly looked at Benjamin, the roads, the passing cars; his head was a tumble of racing images. They'd held him in a stadium too, but he'd been in Roland Garros, the tennis stadium, then they'd transferred him to Le Vernet, near Ariège, about four kilometres from the border of the Pyrenees. It was a punishment camp if you thought about it. He could still see the barbed wire and trenches all around, the rocky soil that turned to mud when it rained and icy clumps when it was cold. The barracks there had been built the year before by Spanish refugees using jerry-rigged wooden planks. There were two hundred men crammed into each barrack, forced to sleep five across on wooden planks two and a half metres wide. In December, the temperature dropped to twenty below zero but there was neither heat nor blankets in the barracks. There was no mess hall for meals, no tables, chairs, spoons or forks. There was no soap to clean with. The work was back-breaking. The food was disgusting. The guards beat and whipped you or put you in the hole, eight days minimum, no food or drink then after a while bread and water.

'The agony,' he said sadly, 'is that there are still two thousand people there. Good people. I met an Italian name Leo who'd already spent nine years in a Fascist jail. And a Hungarian poet who'd already served three years of hard labour at Seghedino. Then two Spanish soldiers – this was their reward after all those years of fighting Franco. I'm only here because my English friends moved heaven and earth to get me out. What hope do the rest of them have?'

They'd arrived across the street from Madame Suchet's shop, but neither of them moved. They both looked at the ground, lost in thought, hunched into their collars. Then Benjamin took Koestler's arm and pulled him gently through the middle of a convoy of trucks filled with soldiers, and around the puddles on the pavement. Madame Suchet was alone, perched among her cheeses.

'We'd like some Borgogna,' said Koestler, 'and a nice piece of Camembert. Make sure it's perfectly ripe, stinky but not over done.'

'Cher monsieur, I can only give you 350 grams but I will have to charge you ten times the official price. What can I do? If you report me, I know, I'll go to jail, but if I were to stick to the government rates I'd have to close the shop right now. Blame it on the damn war.'

'Fine, we'll take 350 grams. What news does your husband send from the front?'

'Sorry to be crude, but his backside is full of haemorrhoids because of the disgusting food they make him eat. He asks me to buy him medicine. They don't even provide that in the army. Then the newspapers tell stories about how wonderful life is at the front. The truth is that France should mind her own business. What do we care really about Poland?'

Koestler was about to answer, but he felt Benjamin pulling on his sleeve.

'Please leave it be. Pay and let's go,' he whispered between his teeth. He spoke in German and faced the lady with a little smile pasted onto his mouth.

'French brains are full of shit,' Koestler said when they left. 'You know the worst torture. The worst nightmare? The minute they release me, I run to the police station to renew my papers. They send me here and there, five or six offices and then I get to a clerk who is stamping my papers and he realises that I am Hungarian and that I have just come from Vernet. "In that case, I can't stamp these," he says.

'"What does that mean?" I say. It means there's nothing to do about it. If he knew that I am a well-known journalist and a citizen of a neutral state . . . but no. It's *Eloignement* for me. You know what that is? Expulsion. But there's a war and it's hard to expel someone so they've invented this *régime de sursis*, which consists in refusing to renew visas and then conceding only short extensions – the *sursis*. They gave me twenty-four hours, and now five days. I don't know how much longer this can go on. Every time, I have to stand for hours at the police station. French bastards.'

'What's important is that you're free now,' said Benjamin in an effort to console him, 'and can you slow down? I fear I'm out of breath.'

'It already feels like we're walking in a funeral procession.'

The road was quieter now, as if petrified by the evening. The shutters on the houses were already drawn as they rounded the corner back onto rue Dombasle. They walked side by side, lost under the blackening sky. They looked just like two friends – two friends experiencing the same inexplicable defeat.

Chapter Twenty-seven

They were his footsteps echoing through the atrium and carrying breathlessly up the stairs. He ran along the corridor, past the rooms filled with index cards and came to a hesitant stop at the door to the reading room. Benjamin heard every one of his footsteps, listened to them float through the silence. It was the first time he'd set foot in the library in four months. He'd imagined it as a homecoming but instead he felt like a stranger as he walked among the tables, under the vaulted ceilings. There were hardly any readers there, the clerks were all hidden in their offices and there was an icy silence. Discouraged, he leaned on the desk, holding his new library card in hand. He read it and reread it as he waited for someone to appear to fetch his books: '*Numéro 3454, BenjaminWalter, Titres: Docteur en philosophie, critique littéraire. Adresse: 8, rue Dombasle.*' They'd even got his address wrong.

That's when he heard the applause and saw the clerks emerging in a line from the stacks at the other end of the room. Georges Bataille came over to him with a smile.

'Welcome,' he said. 'Welcome home.'

Louvet from the photostat room opened two bottles of wine

he'd taken from his father's cellar. Madame Grenelle from the loan desk had baked pastries.

'Now you are safe back with us,' said Bataille comfortingly and sentimentally. In a daze Benjamin ate pastries, shook hands and tried to find the words to thank everyone, although deep down he just felt that old weariness, that sense of resignation – like a person who only glances or smiles shyly at the world. Then Bataille took him by the arm and led him to his desk.

'Work well,' he told him with a hug.

From then on, that desk became the Maginot line of Benjamin, that room with its columns and tiles; it was from here that he pushed back the assaults of the world. 'Leave while there's still time,' his friends said. Scholem wrote from Jerusalem. Adorno, Horkheimer, even Brecht told him to leave: 'Go to Portugal, Cuba, the United States, get to Marseille and take the first boat out.'

'What about a visa and money?' he answered. And so he stayed. He came in to work in the early afternoon, turned on the art nouveau table lamp and lost himself in his reading as the light painted his face with amber reflections. For many days he was undecided whether to keep working on *Baudelaire* or to start a new essay on Rousseau and Gide for the Institute. 'My hesitation,' he wrote to Gretel Adorno, 'is the fear of having to abandon the Baudelaire once I will have begun writing the sequel. The sequel will be a work of monumental breadth and it would be a delicate matter to have to start and stop again and again. This is, however, the risk I would have to take. I am constantly reminded of it by the gas mask in my small room – the mask looks to me like a disconcerting replica of the skulls with which studious monks decorated their cells.'

Never before would he have liked more to put the Gracián motto into practice: 'Seek to enlist time on your side in all things.' He'd copied it out into a notebook over twenty years earlier. But time pressed on him heavy and consumed his thoughts. 'Every line that I might publish,' he wrote to Scholem, 'is a victory seized from the powers of darkness, for how uncertain is the future we've been promised.' And so he doubled his efforts, pretending that his time unfurled endlessly and would be made up of mornings spent reading in bed and long afternoons at the library. He had to pretend because he knew that time was caught up in other circles and isn't always as steady and empty as it seems – that it doesn't only move forward infinitely. But Benjamin was not good at pretending. By virtue of thinking about it so much, instead of writing about Gide or Baudelaire, he ended up writing about time and history.

'War,' he wrote to Gretel Adorno, 'and everything it brings with it, has convinced me to put down in writing several ideas that I can safely say I've been holding inside of me for at least twenty years, keeping them all for myself.' Now that someone seemed to have signed a death warrant on his world, these ideas welled up and took form. He wrote in a fever, as often happened to him, starting with a triviality, an image, a crumb that would be transformed into dense phrases and revelations, perfect sequences of words. He wrote these eighteen ideas on the back of his notebook, filling the margins with his minuscule cramped calligraphy, transported by the urgency of each reconsideration and refinement. He wrote as if he were finally putting Marxism and Messianism together, bound in a final terrible defence against obtuse faith in progress, against the senselessness of history. He wrote with gleeful irony, crossing boundaries between theology, philosophy and literature, as if in these dark times every mode should be called upon to participate in salvation.

All February and March he spent in the library, rubbing history the wrong way. Then in the evening he'd dictate his notes to his sister. Every now and then, Dora would lift her eyes from the typewriter and stare out the window at the closed shutter and sigh with hunger and tiredness. Then she'd look at him.

'That's enough for now, Walter. My eyes hurt.'

'Just a little more,' he pleaded and he'd start reading again.

'There is a painting by Klee named *Angelus Novus*,' he said one evening, dictating what would become one of his most famous passages, 'it shows an angel looking as though he is about to move away from something he is fixedly contemplating. His eyes are staring, his mouth is open, his wings are spread. This is how one pictures the Angel of History. His face is turned toward the past. Where we perceive a chain of events, he sees one single catastrophe which keeps piling wreckage and hurls it in front of his feet.'

'You said *killing*?'

'I said *piling*, Dora, *piling*. One single catastrophe that keeps piling wreckage and hurls it in front of his feet. The angel would like to stay, awaken the dead, and make whole what has been smashed. But a storm is blowing in from Paradise; it has got caught in his wings with such a violence that the angel can no longer close them. The storm irresistibly propels him into the future to which his back is turned, while the pile of debris before him grows skyward. This storm is what we call progress.'

'I'm not sure I entirely understand that, Walter.'

'I'll explain later, Dora. Let's eat something now.'

'Bread and salad without dressing. I'm out of oil and I haven't been able to find any for two days.'

Dora disappeared into the kitchen. Walter sank into the armchair and closed his eyes to ruminate. The future. Hope? Outside the rain fell silently on the dark streets.

'It's ready. Come eat.'

'Wait, Dora. Write this down before I forget.'

'Can't it wait? I'm hungry.'

'Just a minute more. Type. It's noted that Jews are prohibited from investigating the future. The Torah and prayer rituals teach memory. This liberates Jews from any fascination with the future, and keeps them from becoming succubae to fortune-tellers. But that doesn't mean that the future becomes a homogenous, empty state. Because every second of time offers a little door through which the Messiah could come. Now I'm done.'

'The sound of Walter's voice when he dictated to me is still in my ears,' Dora would tell Scholem several years later. It was a collected, melodious voice, surefooted, presenting one argument after another without ever tiring. It was the voice of a prophet, serene and bursting with a sureness that could never be shaken. It was the voice of a man who looked at defeat and saw only the verification of his prophecy. Who would undertake the reordering of the world's catastrophic burden 'in a whale'. *Tikkum olam*, say the scriptures.

These themes weren't born for publication, at least that's what Benjamin claimed. But deep down he wanted all of his friends to read them and to discuss them with the lucidity of someone who from a hilltop understands the battlefield better than those who are fighting. In early May, he wrote about the themes to his friend Stephan Lackner in the States. 'I've finished a little essay on the concept of history. It's not inspired by this new war but rather by the whole experience of my generation, among those perhaps most severely crippled by history. You might ask if history wasn't forged through the cunning synthesis of two Nietszchean concepts: the good European and the last man. What comes out of that is the last European man. All of us are struggling not to be the last European man.'

Chapter Twenty-eight

You know what Mariano said? We were taking a shower after crushing the fourth company three to zero. I'd even made a goal off my head in the second half after Alfonso gave me the perfect pass from the right.

'It won't last,' he said, drying himself off. 'This carefree feeling won't last.'

Mariano always knew everything. And in fact as the weather got better we started to hear the Germans from the opposite shore. By early April they were hammering us, and every day the Junkers flew overhead. We used to call them *los Ramones* when we were in Spain. We heard them before the French did because we'd learned their engines. It brought the mood down. It wasn't that I was scared; it was just that the more they bombed the more I thought of Barcelona and Mercedes. It was like torture, a stabbing pain, an old scar that suddenly started hurting. I knew that in order to stay alive in the middle of the trenches and cannon fire I had to not think of it. I had to pretend that I'd never met her but instead I slept at night with my teeth clenched and my jaw tense going over and over my memories.

During the day I cursed myself for not even having a photo of her. I was scared I'd forget the curves of her body, the green lights in her eyes. I was so worried that I'd have nothing left of Mercedes in the end, just some powdery dust, nothing else, not a damn. I talked about her to Alfonso one evening. We were out in the dark walking in the courtyard. There wasn't much time left before curfew and we were the only ones out.

'I wonder how Mercedes is,' I said in a whisper, as if only for my ears.

But he'd heard. He lit a butt in the cup of his hand and looked up at the thick blanket of stars in the black sky.

'Have you heard anything of Ana María?'

I'd almost forgotten he'd left someone behind too, and that the both of us were dragging around our bundles of sadness.

'No,' I said. 'I haven't heard a thing.'

Then Alfonso took a picture from his wallet, lighting with the flickering match. It was a photo of him and Ana María standing in a café in the port of Barcelona. In the background, almost hidden behind a wall, was Mercedes, smiling – at me, I was sure. It was as if that smile could fly through time and space and conquer the years; it could leap across the Pyrenees and the Vosque mountains to find me here at the ends of the earth in the trenches of a war that didn't really belong to me. But instead of minding my own business and thinking about how much I missed that smile, I started lecturing Alfonso.

'You have to forget about her,' I said seriously. 'You need to forget that she exists. A man in war who can't shed useless memories is a dead man walking.' I don't have the slightest idea why I said that. It would have been better if I'd shut up or lectured myself with those stupid words. Alfonso looked at me, astonished. Laughing might have been too much, he must have thought. So he just smiled.

'So, should I write it down?' he asked. After a moment he added, 'You know there's a saying in Italy, *have your picture painted by someone who doesn't know you.*'

I didn't say anything. Soon we were worrying about the war and had entirely different things to think about. Two days later we were all sent to work on the Maginot line at Sarreguemines, a few metres from the German trenches. That's when the bullets were really whistling by our ears. Each day was worse than the one before. And that's how we ended up once again unloading cases of bullets in Forbach and then in Longwy on the border of France, Luxembourg and Belgium. We had covered over 200 kilometres by foot. We marched by day and stopped before dark fell to work. The good part about this phase, we thought, was that for the first time in six months we would be seeing civilians – men and mostly women. Up to now we'd been so cut off, because all the villages along the Maginot line had been evacuated months before. But when we got to Sarre-Union we found that people hid from us as soon as they saw us. Even the shopkeepers – if they were willing to sell us something – kept their heads down and were gruff. The infamy of the Red Spaniards preceded us. No one talked to us at all. What could we expect of the women. They turned and ran or spied on us through the shutters as if we were strange animals. The beauty of it was that by that point humiliation was our daily bread and we laughed it off, joked about it like children. Sepúlveda was happier than the rest of us. He sneered and teased us. But he had something on his mind. He broke away from the group and headed down an alley, and I knew. He'd seen the church spires from a distance. He returned a few minutes later, a victory fist in the air and a smile on his face.

'Mission accomplished. Long live Bakunin,' he said.

But there was no peace on our road. In just a few days they moved us several times through the whole sector. In Sarrelouis they had us flattening a road between two forts and later they sent us to Thionville to unload trains, dig ditches, build a dam in order to flood the camps, to blow up bridges. And then one fine day, Mr Hitler decided that the time had come to invade.

PART FOUR

PART FOUR

Chapter Twenty-nine

The invasion started on Friday, May 10. Guderian armoured cars moved down the Maginot Line, navigating the hair-raising hills and valleys of the Ardennes Forest. Sedan was evacuated on the fourteenth. Stuka dive-bombers hit Rotterdam. On the fifteenth the queen of Holland and her government flew to London. The Germans crossed the Meuse at Sedan. No war had ever moved so fast. The French army was taken by surprise and retreated in spurts. But the enemies advanced even more quickly, mounting new attacks in less time than it would have taken to figure out new positions. 'This battlefield,' wrote Marc Bloch at the time, 'saw the meeting of two adversaries from two apparently different epochs of human civilisation.' It was lances against rifles as in the colonial days; but this time, it was the French army on the side of the savages.

All they knew in Paris was that everything was going fine – at least until Tuesday. The newspapers and radios reported several German victories around Maastricht and Allied advances through the Ardennes. The brutal wake-up call for the French came that day in Sedan – it didn't open their eyes but rather plunged them into the midst of a confused, horrifying nightmare. Benjamin lived through it by fishing in the arid streams of his 'profound calm', scrupulously repeating the ritual part of every day, clinging to any kind of order in the middle of disaster. He always put his right foot first when he stepped out his door. He used the same route, over the same pavements; he placed his pen on the desk with the point always facing precisely to the right. Before going to sleep, he never neglected to put his glasses on the book that he had just closed and set on the nightstand. But he knew that the tanks could destroy even these rituals. He knew it with certainty when he heard the funereal voice of Prime Minister Reynaud at Adrienne Monnier's house: 'Because of a grave error that will not go unpunished, the bridges over the Meuse were not destroyed and German artillery penetrated our front using that route.'

He was at Georges Bataille's house the day the news came that General Gamelin's order had been 'Die, but don't retreat.' Though the same day the army pulled back along the Asine River. Paris was in danger but no one admitted it – perhaps in order to keep hope alive. Benjamin didn't hide from it. He needed more time or else he needed that damned visa. Just a few days earlier he'd written to Adorno explaining all of the obstacles he encountered at the American consulate. And now he was waiting for some kind of news from New York as the earth boiled under his feet. Sitting at the Deux Magots, on the way to the library, or walking slowly over the Seine – he saw the muddy cars of refugees flooding in from the north: mattresses strapped to the tops, bicycles tied to fenders. They moved through Paris like animals running from fire. He heard the talk in the city, the rumours: Gamelin killed himself; the paratroopers have landed in place de la Madeleine; three children died in Belleville after eating poison chocolates that the Germans handed out; Arras has been seized by paratroopers who descended in the night with flaming torches. Tired and feeling insecure, he read in his landlady's *Paris soir* that Gamelin was no longer chief commander of the army. Weygand, a seventy-year-old general had been installed in his place. Pétain, who was over eighty-four, had been called back from Spain to come on as the government's new minister of defence. The posters reappeared on the streets: 'SECOND WARNING TO THE RESSORTISSANTS.' This time they were casting the ultimate net. The order called for everyone to be sent to a concentration camp: men under seventy-five, women, invalids, the sick – torn from their beds only to die a few days later behind barbed wire.

Old Benjamin saw those posters in the afternoon on his way to the library and changed course immediately. He passed by the Louvre, crossed back over the Seine and Saint-Germain disappearing back down rue de l'Odéon in search of one of the few friends he had left in Paris. He walked as fast as he could, shoulders hunched, lurching forward with his head down – every bit the picture of someone who wants to defend himself, react to injustice, but instead sits curled up, blocked by impotence. He burst through the door of the bookshop, his heart in pieces, his breath stuttering through his teeth.

'Not again, Adrienne?' he said with what little breath he had left. 'If they take me again, it's all over.'

They called Hoppenot at the parliament, Henri Membré at the PEN Club; they wrote a joint letter to Saint-John Perse who was a diplomat now. Benjamin had met him several years before when he'd translated his *Anabase*. Couldn't he help?

'Go home now,' said Adrienne, walking him to the door. 'It will all work out. Wait. I'll pay for your taxi.'

It was spring out. The sun was moving toward sunset, speckling the building fronts with sad orange, making the edges of things stand out, reddening the trim of the few scattered cotton puffs in the sky. Then it was dark and in the space of a thought, Walter was struggling to climb the stairs to his apartment, where he would pace like a soul in agony around the room. By now the heating didn't work anymore, the hot water was barely a memory. The foreigners were all in camps somewhere, the majority of the French men were drafted, no one paid rent anymore, and the landlords had long since stopped worrying about maintenance. Benjamin was practically alone in the building, now that even Koestler had disappeared without a trace after miraculously evading the last round-up. Life on rue Dombasle seemed to consume itself, as if the rigor mortis of the war was standing behind its own avant-guard, the saboteurs, into the innermost part of its prey, and now there was hardly any more need for combat. In fact, it seemed as if one of those saboteurs had got into the pantry and demolished the provisions. Benjamin looked thoughtfully at the shelf where a crust of bread decomposed under a layer of mould. Then, without looking out onto the street, he shut the blinds, lit a candle and lay down on the bed, thinking about the crucifix. Would Saint-John Perse, Membré and Hoppenot be able to save him from another internment? His heart surely wouldn't last a second time. And now, with the invasion of France, going to a camp meant walking right into the arms of the Gestapo. It would be better to die at home, on that very bed perhaps, and with a full tummy – better still.

All twisted inside, Walter tried to reread an old Simenon, one of the ones he'd always loved best, but his eyes slid over the lines like he was slipping on ice. An hour later he blew out the candle and began to wait out the great silence. Like a scent it carried up from the dark street and from the dust accumulated under the furniture, distilled in the lamplight and blending with other silences, dripping from damp patches on the wall, wrapping around him as he tossed in the covers and worming through the slats in the shutters to capture the first secretions of dark, the first purities of the coming day. He skipped washing up, as he often did, and ran to Adrienne's bookshop as soon as it opened the next day. He felt as lost as those he saw on the metro, sharing that gloomy glint of fear in their eyes.

Whether it was the work of Saint-John Perse or Hoppenot, Benjamin was among the few who were saved from the camps. It was a privilege reserved to three or four at the most.

'Thank you, Adrienne,' he whispered seriously, lowering his head in a bow. That was all he said, but how could one know the thoughts that pass through a man's head when he's just been told his meeting with death has been postponed.

'Unfortunately,' said Adrienne, with downcast eyes, 'Hoppenot says there's nothing that can be done for Dora and Hannah. They have to report to the Vélodrome d'Hiver, and then we'll see.'

Dora was weeping as she walked with her brother to the metro. It was just past noon and a light breeze ruffled the trees along the boulevard. The sun had just a hint of sobriety as it rolled off the red roofs. There were formations of soldiers marching all around them.

'Stop crying, please. They'll arrest us.'

'Does it matter?' answered Dora. 'Could that be worse than what's happening to me?'

'Be quiet,' growled Walter. 'I was in the camp too and now I'm free. I'm sure they'll release you as soon as you tell them about your illness.'

Dora's bag didn't weigh much at all, yet a sudden tightness in his chest forced him to stop on the stairs. 'I'll be there in a minute. Go ahead and buy your ticket.'

By the time they arrived at the gate, he'd decided to stop lying to her. He kissed her quickly and then watched her leave, disappearing into the crowd of other passengers in the dimly lit hallway. Another brick of his world crumbled; the last member of his family, gone. Benjamin inhaled deeply when he got back out onto the street; the wind was gusting around him. He was overcome by an unease that seemed to come to him from a distant point in time, that slipped through the years like an old eel returning to its birthplace to die. He walked aimlessly down rue de Vaugirard, contemplating that trickle of sadness without looking up at the streets, the squares, the people and the soldiers whose paths he crossed. Suddenly, the idea of going home – of climbing all those stairs only in order to find himself in that same deteriorating squalor – seemed awful. He decided to go back to the library. There among his books and notebooks full of notes for *Passagen-Werk*, he felt safer. He was a ship-wrecked man clinging to a sodden plank – his salvation. But in his work he could still cry out for help; release a scream that would carry forward into the edge of the future.

Abbéville, Boulogne, the Germans arrived at the English Channel while the French and English fought them back at

Dunkerque. The voice of Reynaud dangled again from the radio like a funeral banner: 'If a miracle is the only thing that can save France, then I believe in that miracle. France cannot fall.'

It was raining now. Raining over the people descending on the stations, on the buses and taxis parked in lots, on the Parisians obsessed with the paratroopers and with Hitler's Fifth Column. It rained on the millions of French men and women travelling by foot, by car, on rickety carriages under the Stuka bombers. Their tents and mattresses occupied the roads; roads out of town were blocked; military action was paralysed – a mud slick covered what remained of France. It was still raining on June 3, when the Luftwaffe bombed Paris at dawn. Benjamin had just fallen asleep, but was awakened by a muted drone in the sky – like thunder – the scattered anti-airfire and then the first sounds, distant explosions in the north. He looked out the window at the sky; the grey clouds twisted around the chaos brought on by the planes of his countrymen. They swooped and grazed, then hooked and banked. Though muffled by distance, the sound of the falling bombs was unbearable, inhuman – as savage as the death they brought to the bodies they fell on.

He didn't have time to grab his gas mask and go down to the street because the bombing didn't last long. It left behind the stench of burnt flesh, fumes and gunpowder wafting through his open window and curling around with the sirens of the ambulances and firefighters. He sat for a long time in the middle of his bed, motionless, ruffled, looking out the window with bulging eyes at the columns of smoke rising over the rooftops and at the sky cracking open to let through the blue, and what struck him as an inopportune ray of sunlight. Then he heard Madame Dubois calling to him.

'Are you all right, Monsieur Benjhamèn? It's me. Is everything okay?'

'Yes,' answered Benjamin. Then he realised that hardly a breath had passed his lips and she couldn't have possibly heard him. 'Yes, everything is fine,' he repeated, forcing himself to shout.

'There's a lady here. She says she's your sister.'

Dora! Could it be? He opened the door and almost didn't recognise her. She seemed made of skin, her body was like a sparrow and her hair hung in heavy clumps around her face. Her cheeks were hollow and she was trembling all over, sobbing in splintered gasps like when she was a little girl. There she was looking at him and hiding behind Madame Dubois as if she were frightened of him, and should apologise for wriggling her way back into his life.

'Come on. Stop crying,' mumbled Walter as he hugged her.

'I'm leaving now,' said Madame Dubois. 'I am going to my aunt's house in Périgueux. I'm afraid that I don't trust the *boches* and neither should you.'

It was a while before Dora calmed down. Walter made her lie on the bed and he offered her water and uneasily stroked her hair for what seemed an eternity. Finally, staring at a spot on the ceiling, Dora was able to tell him about Gurs. It was a camp near Oloron in the Pyrenees. After a week in the Vélodrome d'Hiver, they'd been packed into trains for a never-ending journey. They were tired and starving and hadn't a drop of water to drink. Everyone was shocked when they finally got there. Gurs was already famous. It was where they kept the undesirables: the officers of the Spanish Republican army, the insurgents and communists, the most politically active exiled anti-Nazis. They called it Inferno. And the more that Dora spoke the more Walter felt like he was listening to Koestler again – speaking of the barracks at Vernet, cold and flea-ridden, the same punishments, the same hunger, the same inhumanity. Only that as Dora spoke she did not grow indignant as Koestler had, but wept, trembled, gestured and confused names and dates. Walter understood that she'd seen Lisa Fittko and Hannah Arendt from a distance but that she'd never spoken to them. She ended up being visited by a medical lieutenant who must have been a Jew, and he sent her home.

'You see? I told you they'd send you home once they saw you were sick.'

But he'd hardly believed it himself. After so many prison stories – but no one had escaped easily. He stood up and began pacing the room, his hands clasped behind him. At last he sat at the desk. A halo of dusty sun illuminating the books piled carefully on the corner.

'You're here now,' he said. 'You can rest.'

'Rest, yes . . . Your landlady is right. We should leave. We must escape Paris.'

His sister was an idiot, stupid and stubborn. Walter stood again, planted his fists on the table.

'Won't you understand,' he cried, 'that I must finish my work. It's the most important thing in the world to me. I must stay here and that's all there is to it.'

Then he saw her curled up against the wall weeping. He saw a weak woman, ill and terrified. His anger subsided and he lowered his voice.

'And,' he added more gently. 'I have to wait for a visa. If Horkheimer sends papers and money here and I've already left?

Just a few more days. Then we can perhaps leave together. Calm down. Let's go get something to eat.'

She sighed and made a clumsy attempt at a smile.

'You can't go out like this,' he said. 'Clean yourself up. Mother always said that your hair was like a bird's nest.'

That afternoon, Walter was back in the library. No one said a word about the bombing. But he borrowed money from Bataille and kept busy going back and forth between his table and the photostat counter, spreading out all of his notes for *Passagen-Werk* that Dora hadn't had time to type before ending up at Gurs. Louvet noticed Benjamin's grim expression and his splotched, dirty unshaven face. His tie was loose around his neck, and he was on edge.

'Could you possibly work a little faster?' he asked.

'We close in five minutes,' Louvet patiently explained. 'I can finish it all up for you tomorrow. Don't worry.'

'Can you please at least do these twenty pages?'

It wasn't that Benjamin was really in a rush; he hadn't decided to leave yet. It was just that he had the vague feeling that he wouldn't be able to wait too much longer. The anxiety and craving had hit him the moment he'd come into that almost empty room. In the seat next to his place, he'd seen Asja bent over an enormous folio edition. At least he thought it was her, and his heart stuck in his throat. The same helmet of dark hair, the green eyes and careless sensual air that had stopped him like a fish on a hook on Capri fifteen years before. And that then led him to Riga and Moscow, pulled forward by the throbbing in his trousers. Asja, Asja Lacis. Of course it wasn't her. Asja was dead – or if she was lucky she was surviving Stalin's prison. That girl poring over an ancient book right after a bombing and in the middle of an invasion wasn't her, but just seeing her there, right next to his place was enough to trigger a flood of visions, memories, emerging from the darkest corners of his mind. Asja leaning against a white wall at Faraglioni on Capri, rigid and irritated when he came too soon in her hand. Asja only ever looked at him once with fascination for just a moment in the café in Riga as he discussed Kant with his friend Bernhard. In sad, muddy Moscow, wrapped in light February snow, when she told him to leave while he begged her to love him without a scrap of pride. Seeing this woman was too much, despite the fifteen years that had passed. It was too much because he was tired and he didn't want to remember. Benjamin was startled, moved, ashamed, full of regret and embarrassment – feelings that would rinse off the bitter sensation that had been tenaciously clinging to him – like one of the signs he saw predicting the future. Yes, perhaps that's what it was. The girl was a sign; death showing herself, letting him know she was waiting for him. So he was in a great rush and didn't notice that the time had come to leave.

It wasn't dark yet outside. The rain had just started to fall, scattered cars swept over the wet roads. A bicycle bell ringing right behind him startled him. A dark mass passed and shoved at his black bag. The man carrying a girl on the crossbar of his bike sent him to hell with a hand gesture.

'Pay attention, grandpa.'

Dora was waiting for him at his house, sitting in front of the typewriter. There was a pile of papers on the table that Walter had left for her to copy.

'How do you feel?' he asked coming in.

He didn't imagine she would actually respond. He left his bag on the chair and ran to the bathroom.

'I feel better,' she finally said, 'but I'm still tired. I wasn't able to type. You could have waited until tomorrow to ask.'

'I know, you're right, but it was urgent,' he apologised unconvincingly. He wiped his hands and looked out the door. 'That means I have to do it.'

Dora, wrapped in her dressing gown, stood. She looked down at the street and the sad colourless sky. Was now the right moment to tell him? The air was still; the rain was falling soft and monotonous.

'Listen,' she decided. 'Emma wrote to me. You remember her, don't you? Emma Cohn, my friend from school? She's taken refuge down south in Lourdes. She says that it's better than most places; the people are hospitable. They're used to pilgrims.'

Benjamin didn't answer. He slowly tapped a finger, trying to beat down his anger.

Chapter Thirty

The invasion started on May 10, a Friday. The armoured divisions arrived with the paratroopers and their planes. Sure, we'd had a test run in Spain but we'd never seen so much equipment and so many weapons, and we'd never seen a war move as fast as that. The Krauts blasted through the holes in the Maginot Line; they crossed Holland and five days later were crossing the Meuse. We'd already realised that something wasn't right with the French army. There were hundreds of abandoned cannons in the Alsatian forests. Entire regiments passed by, drifting; they came to the front line but didn't know what to do. The situation stunk; it seemed like no one really wanted to fight. We didn't even want to fight. They had us wandering along the border for several days, not a camp in sight. Then we doubled back to build anti-tank trenches in the Ardennes. As if they had any purpose at that point. Actually the German paratroopers ended up hiding in them to attack our retreating troops from behind. We had to work at night because all day long those Stuka dive-bombers fried us; they made a joke out of the ones we'd seen back in Spain. Towns, little villages – the planes left nothing standing. Then the tanks moved in to occupy the territory. And we were running. Then one morning we sort of stumbled onto their side of the line. The Krauts moved fast. They had already crossed the Meuse and were already thirty kilometres to our south. Lucky for us our new captain, a count from Grenoble, managed to organise a manoeuvre so that we could double back and get in contact with our guys again. But by then, it was like in Catalonia a year and a half before – we got out by the skin of our teeth, but more hectically, in the middle of utter chaos, a Babel of orders and counter-orders that basically ended up saying the same thing: run south.

We covered thirty, forty kilometres a day, never stopping. One evening we got to the city our command had designated, and the Germans had already caught up. So the next morning we formed a delegation to negotiate with the battalion commander. We wanted weapons to defend ourselves in case the Germans mounted a surprise attack. There were four of us: Alfonso, Mariano, me and Sepúlveda, the four musketeers, along with a Communist Party captain and the former secretary of the socialist Estremadura. We made a good argument but the commander sent us to hell with a stream of cusses. We couldn't tell if he was angry or just taken by surprise. We were on our way out the door, heads hanging, when the Marseillaise came crackling over the radio and then the voice of Prime Minister Reynaud came on, speaking in the same tone of voice you'd use to recite *Miserere nobis*. 'Because of a grave error that will not go unpunished, the bridges over the Meuse were not destroyed and German artillery penetrated our front using that route.'

'Fucking bastards. French cowards,' burst out Sepúlveda as soon as we left. 'They don't trust us. *They* don't trust us.'

I believe that we were in Montmédy. Rows of dusty trucks, carriages, ambulances, soldiers looking for their companies, scattered houses still burning from the bombing the day before.

'The truth,' said Mariano slowly, 'is that it would fry their asses to see us fighting; they run without firing a single useful shot.'

We found weapons ourselves. It was easy. They were scattered everywhere, just abandoned. Our captain, the count, told us to just make sure and hide them when we got back to the camp at night. Can you beat that? We also found three machine guns and positioned them at the rear of our formation. To cover our back. But a company of Senegalese troops met us and told us to hand over the arms. They threatened to shoot us if we didn't obey. So we put our guns in position and screamed back at them. We were there for half an hour, fingers on the triggers, staring each other down. Then the captain intervened. We were allowed to hold on to the weapons but we had to hide them in the carriage until the next morning and it went on like that.

At the end of May we were at Bar-le-Duc. The Germans were still dropping bombs on the city and shooting at the escaping civilians and military. We didn't stop to think; we started putting out fires and carrying the wounded to the ambulances, burying hundreds of dead and all of that while they were bombing us. The French suffered a lot of losses and we only lost four Spaniards. We already knew the German planes and we already knew how and when to take cover, while the French just started running around like crazy people in the wide open. Of course the Krauts got them. Our company was almost intact when we got to Toul. But what good did that do? It was obvious that we were around the corner from the grand finale. What could we do? There were those who felt that we should keep trying to get weapons to fight with in order to show everyone that the Spanish were ready to fight off the Stukas but were being held back by idiots. Others thought that wouldn't do any good. And we'd just end up like trapped mice. It was better to follow through with the retreat and then we'd see.

I was waiting for Mariano to pipe up, finger in his curls — but he kept to himself, sitting up against an old wall, smoking, eyes closed. I shot him looks and tried to figure out what he wanted so that I could help, but he just leaned on that wall. Of course he had something to say once all the discussion was over and we were all sitting there in a death grip of silence. Son of a bitch.

'You can do what you want,' he said without standing. 'All I know is that it's suicide to keep pulling back like this. But if we dressed as civilians and went in small groups we could probably get back to the Spanish border.'

And so that's how the four of us, Alfonso, Mariano, me and Sepúlveda ended up walking away from the Germans, heading south, then east, then south again — to Vital, then Neufchâteau, east to Epinal. We stayed off the main roads and cut through a lot of fields. We went through abandoned villages looking for something to eat, but it had all been sacked already — the fields, granaries, wine cellars. We couldn't even find drinking water because they'd severed the pipes. It was like wandering in the desert, as if death had already set her sights on us and it was futile to try to escape. There is a limit to what a human being can take. We were still only in the outskirts of Rambersvillers in the middle of June, and we were exhausted. We'd been walking for weeks, we'd covered thousands of kilometres and it was all as good as useless because the Germans invaded France like a tidal wave that was just going to drown us all. We set up camp that night in an abandoned farm near a forest on the top of a hill. It was the first time in two months that we could have got a little sleep. But none of us managed to sleep.

'You know something,' said Alfonso at a certain point. 'It would almost be better if the Germans caught us. That way it would be over and done with.'

'And what about Ana María?' I answered.

He didn't respond. Our thoughts were swallowed by silence.

Chapter Thirty-one

'Would you mind buying me another croissant?'

They were practically the only customers in that café on rue Saint-Augustin. Georges Bataille waved to summon the waiter and then tucked his hand back between his crossed legs.

'It comes down to this,' he concluded as he stretched. 'I rather think that you should leave.'

'It's easy to say,' muttered Benjamin. 'But where would I go? I don't have any papers or money.'

'You don't understand. Does your life mean that little to you. Just think what will happen when the Germans get here.'

Walter swallowed his melancholy with every new mouthful of croissant. He looked out at the street and the cars and the people – it all seemed to have been reduced to a single, muddy grey colour, and he shook his head.

'Anyway,' he said.

Sometimes truth can be touched. It's all in an image, a landscape, an atmosphere, a specific smell, in the flavour of a cigarette or croissant. Now Benjamin seemed to perceive his destiny as he stared at the sadness of Paris dripping off the café windows.

He tried to escape it, to fend off with his last impotent defences.

'And what of my work?' he asked. 'My notes, my books? I can hardly carry it all with me and nothing matters more to me in the world.'

'There's a way to resolve this,' consoled Bataille. 'You can leave some things with me. I know where to hide it so that it will be safe and when the war is over you can have it all back intact. Is that all right?'

He didn't say yes and he didn't say no; Benjamin just lowered his eyes, scratched the arm of his chair with a finger. Bataille could see him debating it all in his head – he was like a fish hanging on a hook and it would be useless to force the matter.

'Let's go,' he said. 'It's late; I have to go back to the library. Think about it more calmly and then let me know.'

They walked slowly and without talking back up rue Saint-Augustin. Benjamin had his hands behind his back. The sun low and pale cast a deadening light. It was June already, though it didn't look like it. There was a little crowd gathered in front of a radio shop on the corner of rue de Richelieu. The mood was sombre. Bataille stood on tiptoe to see over the heads of the rest of the group.

'What's happening?' he asked.

'Reynaud,' answered a blond woman in a smartly tailored blue suit. 'Reynaud is on the radio.'

She'd barely turned back around before the old speaker hanging off the shop awning started emitting a scratchy version of the *Marseillaise*. Even the traffic on the street came to a stop when the speech started, as if an angel had passed over and silenced the crowd. The Weygan Line had fallen. The Germans had crossed the Somme, the Bresle and the Aisnes and occupied Reims and Rouen. Then Reynaud announced that Italy had joined the war. Many women in the crowd were crying silently. The men too – with that same dignified anguish. And Reynaud spoke: '*Que le Français se resserrent fraternellement autour del leur patrie blessée.*'

This tremulous voice, a voice that had once sparkled with life, and these tears, were the last gesture of unity in a fallen nation, thought Walter.

'Okay,' he said to Bataille as the crowd quickly dispersed. An urgent wind crept along the building façades before getting to the Tuileries where it ruffled the leaves of the chestnut trees.

It was dark by the time he got to Dora's. 'Let's go to Lourdes,' he said, eyes lowered and head shaking with the difficulty. 'We'll leave as soon as I can round up the papers.'

She was standing in front of a boiling pot in the kitchen. She set the mixing spoon on the edge of the counter and looked at her brother. She couldn't hide her satisfied smile.

'My bag is ready.'

That was all that needed to be said, and then Benjamin was back out on the road in the deep dark of after-curfew. He walked home with his head lowered. He was trying to assemble his thoughts but all around him the rustling silence of the night was like the wind in a flag, and to the north there were sirens, and the footfall of soldiers on patrol, shutters slamming closed, car engines heading south. He turned onto rue de Vaugirard and realised that his head had filled up with fears, and he wished he weren't there any more. If only he could end it, disappear, put a full stop to the exhaustion of this jinxed life. He was breathing hard when he got to rue Dombasle. He opened the front door, climbed the stairs and then rested on a step before putting the key in the lock. The attack only lasted a few seconds but it was sharper and more intense than usual. He searched his pockets for a heart pill and swallowed it dry in the dark. Half an hour later his breathing was back to normal, his head felt lighter but he still didn't sleep well. Dozing in fits and starts; he woke often feeling that heaviness on his sternum. His teeth were clenched and he was sweating and it went on like that until the first light started to break – a light whose colour could best be described as somewhere between faded black and dirty grey. He woke, ruefully rinsed his face, quickly dressed and gathered his documents. He left the house at eight on the dot walking under a mist so fine it evaporated before ever hitting the ground. There was no one about except for the soldiers with their grim expressions bouncing down the street in the military convoys that lorded over the city. The bookshop on rue de l'Odéon was closed and Adrienne hadn't arrived yet. Benjamin waited for her in the shelter of a doorway, pacing with one hand on his back and the other swinging his umbrella back and forth. When he saw her round the corner he waved, attempting to smile and look calm. But Adrienne quickened her step and held her hat fast to her head.

'More trouble?' she asked as she drew closer. Benjamin lowered his eyes and offered her shelter under his umbrella.

'I'll explain,' he said as he helped her lift the gate.

It was dark inside and the smell of old paper seemed to cling to the walls. Adrienne opened the blinds and a veil of dust danced into the air.

'Can you see what a mess it is? No one comes anymore and I don't know why I keep opening the shop. But sit now and do tell me what's happening.'

'I've decided to leave,' confessed Benjamin, letting himself fall into a chair. 'And if it isn't too much to ask, I need help getting travelling papers.'

Adrienne's watery gaze settled kindly on him. It was obvious that Walter had to leave but she was sorry. What was she going to do all alone in this France that had been invaded by Germans? She was so unprepared and fragile.

'Are you sure,' she said. 'Are you sure you want to leave? It's not going to be any easier down south. At least Paris is big; it's the ideal place to hide – the Nazis will never find you here.'

'Adrienne, you don't know the Germans as I do.'

A bitter smile and a hint of irony dressed his words. But on the inside, old Benjamin just felt terribly, terribly serious. He felt an ancient pain and the most vague, imprecise something well up in his ice blue eyes. In the meantime he was turning over a book by Stendhal that had been left on the counter.

'So,' he muttered, 'would you mind calling that minister?'

Before the end of the morning, Hoppenot promised to round up travelling papers for two to Lourdes for the next day.

'Done.' Adrienne set the telephone in the receiver and smiled. Now there was everything else to think of. She opened a drawer and pulled out a roll of francs and put them on the table.

'I'll make coffee,' she said, disappearing into her office.

She came back to find old Benjamin sitting still in the same chair, a cigarette in his mouth, hands clasped over his stomach, staring at the money on the counter. The sound of the cups clinking together on the tray startled him.

'I can't accept this,' he said. 'I really can't.'

It was almost dark outside; the rain pounded softly on the windows, but it was still too early to turn on the lights. Adrienne set the tray on a pile of books that were about to be sent out and sat on her chair.

'Please, Walter,' she said in the dim light. 'Don't be so proud. That money is your only chance of getting out of this horrible situation alive. Take it for me. At least I'll feel reassured.'

Benjamin looked at her and gripped the hot cup in his hands. He nodded a little between one sip and the next.

'So,' he concluded, 'since we happen to be here, could I have a copy of *The Red and the Black*? I'd like to reread it but my copy's been missing for years.'

Twenty-four hours later the Germans crossed the Seine and occupied Pontoise. In his last radio address, Reynaud launched a desperate appeal to Roosevelt. Benjamin spent the morning preparing his bags. He packed two bags with notes, books, excerpts, magazine and newspaper clippings to leave at his sister's house. To carry, he packed his briefcase with his *Themes* on history; a copy of *Passagen-Werk*; support letters from Valéry, Horkheimer and Romains; an X-ray and a certificate from Doctor Abrami; two or three books; the gas mask; and a toothbrush and two shirts. Lastly, he put the manuscript of *Passagen-Werk* and Paul Klee's *Angelus Novus* wrapped in newspaper into a blue bag, which he delivered to Bataille. The library was deserted and the rainy light of day barely made it through the large skylights.

'I'm depending on you,' he whispered breathlessly. 'These are the most important things in the world to me.'

'You've already told me, Walter, don't worry. I'll put them where no one will ever think to look for them, not even the SS. More importantly, take care of yourself and be careful. Good luck.'

Bataille was hugging him as he spoke, and had his chin on Benjamin's shoulder, trying to hide his emotions. He was sure he'd never see him again.

'Until the next time,' said Benjamin. Then it was a matter of running around in the frightened, rain-soaked city, fighting the tide of time as he procured two sets of travel papers and then brought his bags over to Dora's house. Finally, he breathlessly knocked on his doctor's door.

'Sorry to bother you. But could you prescribe a sleeping pill for me? I haven't been able to sleep for some time. Or, something for my asthma – I don't know, maybe some Morphium tablets.'

He could tell that Abrami had guessed what was going on in his head the instant he answered. And the doctor was weighing the effects of the advancing German army on the exhausted man sitting before him.

'It's not a good remedy,' he said, 'for the affliction of your countrymen.'

'Please,' begged old Benjamin.

Abrami sighed as he wrote out the prescription: one Morphium tablet, in the evening, as needed.

'Think hard,' he said, 'before abusing the drug.'

Out on the street, walking through the drizzle, under the low-hanging, moody sky, Benjamin felt the sadness of the world decomposing in front of his eyes. He barely made it to the pharmacy and then back home and then to Dora's; then they raced to the station, getting there just as the Germans were occupying the outskirts of Paris.

His bag was heavy and Walter had to stop several times along the way to rest his lungs. Surrounding Dora and him on the road were thousands of old Citroëns and Peugeots loaded down with trunks, boxes, gas canisters, dressers, dogs, cats, bottles and mattresses filing in a neat procession south.

'What did you bring all those papers for?' asked Dora in annoyance. 'You could have left them with Bataille or Adrienne. Can't you see we won't make it? We're late. Let's go.'

'You don't understand,' replied Benjamin. 'You don't understand anything.' He shook his head unhappily.

A few dim lights, barely visible against the still grey background, illuminated the station. Most of the trains were stopped on the tracks. Walter and Dora just barely managed to squeeze into a wagon that was overflowing with people and household items before the whistle blew. Everyone breathed a collective sigh of relief. It was the last train out of Paris. As darkness fell and the train ran past Orléans and Tours, Benjamin pressed his face against the window streaming with raindrops. He could see the river of people escaping under that torrential rain, which drenched their tents and mattresses. He saw the fire trucks of Maubeuge, and recognised the pharmacist from Soissons. He saw horse-drawn carriages and children pulling their elderly parents in rickshaws. He saw tourist buses with the writing PARIS LA NUIT on the side, and people clinging to the baggage racks. He saw exhausted children and desperate mothers. He watched France escaping in the mud, reduced to a single, incomprehensible wreck. He pulled his papers from his pocket and turned them over in his hands, looking with satisfaction at the black and red stamps and the prefect's signature. Then Dora's voice came buzzing in his head like an irritating fly.

'Are you listening to me or not?'

'No, Dora. I'm not listening. I'm sorry. I'm tired.'

He leaned back in his seat and turned to look outside again. Before his eyes closed in sleep, he made out a row of pine trees along a river in a distant city, the spire of a cathedral pointing like a finger at the silver-grey sky, twisting in the storm.

Chapter Thirty-two

Alfonso and I were the first to wake up. It must have been five in the morning. It was a transitional time of day, the night sky was shrouded by the fog that clung to the walls of the courtyard and farm — the walls that were still standing, and the sun slowly sending its first rays down. It was quiet all around us. Though we could hear the occasional shots of a cannon in the distance. Mariano and Sepúlveda looked like they had just finally succumbed to morning sleep. Alfonso and I exchanged a glance and understood each other instantly. We had no more desire to escape. In that moment all we could feel was a tremendous, almost animal-like hunger. So we went out into the field to gather some potatoes and then came back to the courtyard to start a fire so we could boil them up. Standing by the barn, we could see the forests and fields, a straight and dusty road that extended out and then got lost in the hills. We were peeling the potatoes when we saw a white cloud and heard a motorcycle engine. Within seconds, barely time to say Ave Maria, there were two Germans standing in front of us. They climbed off their bike screaming bloody murder, *Hands up! Face the wall!* I'd spent the last two years of my life fighting. I'd fought on the Ebro and in Aragon. But standing there in front of those two Krauts and you couldn't have put a needle up my ass I was so scared. I started shivering in my teeth and it went down my neck in waves that moved all the way down my legs. One of them put the barrel of his rifle on my back and I felt like I was melting. I still remember that feeling. I thought of my mother and of Mercedes, who I would never see again, of Uncle Adolfo, and about the old socialist in the port, the day my father took me to the merry-go-round and I fell off the blue horse. It was all just a flash and then that son of a bitch whacked me on the arm with the butt of his rifle to make me drop the knife I was still holding.

Those two Germans were laughing at our fear. They laughed and that's what fucked them. Because they lifted their heads and sort of pulled back, just enough. I can't remember hearing the shots. I just know that when I turned around I saw this ridiculous hole in the Kraut's face, right under his helmet, and I saw that frozen smile. The other one was on the ground next to him. I looked up to the window above and there was Sepúlveda and Mariano, smiling and waving down at us.

'You shit yourself, huh, Laureano?'

'Fuck you,' I spat, and slid to the ground.

'Come on,' said Alfonso. 'We have to get out of here,' and he touched my shoulder.

I was almost crying as I curled up against the wall, while my three buddies moved around, surefooted, collecting the Germans' weapons and disabling the motorcycle.

'Get up, Laureano!' yelled Alfonso.

'Don't forget the potatoes,' said Mariano.

And so we set off, heading through Morlange to Bruyèyes.

We really did feel like escaping now. I would have done anything never to have to face a Nazi armed to the teeth ever again. Hunger was better; exhaustion was better, and the thought of Mercedes pushed me on like a train engine. We walked at a breakneck pace through the hills, ignoring the stomach cramps, the German patrols, and all those kilometres we still had left to cover. We were moving like warriors now. Mariano out in front, leading, the three of us behind. We looked for sheltered paths, walked at night and hid during the day. We swam across the Moselle south of Saint-Amé at night. It was useless to remember Ebro and the rest – that was all history.

'You never bathe twice in the same river,' I said, just to say it once we'd got across. We were drenched and heaving.

'Funny joke,' said Sepúlveda icily. 'But enough of that. Let's just concentrate on walking.'

And we walked. I still remember those towns even if we only saw them from a distance. Luxelle-Bains, Vesoul, then Besançon, Louhans, Chauffailless. I don't remember where we were when we heard about Pétain begging the Krauts for an armistice. An old farmer told us about it. He had an open debt on the Germans from twenty years before. If we hadn't met him, I wouldn't be here talking to you today. He saved us. First because he gave us meat, wine and fresh fruit. Then, because he told us that the town was split over handing foreigners over to the Krauts. We gorged ourselves, and realised that we weren't going to be able to trust either the gendarmerie or the French army.

'It's better that way,' I spluttered.

'Better like hell,' said Mariano.

From that point on we had to keep from meeting anyone along the way. We ate roots and drank from rivers or abandoned wells. Sometimes we'd steal carrots and tomatoes from gardens. One foot after the other, we headed south. We were shadows, crossing France like ghosts, like shades – the invisibles. Good thing because the Germans took thousands of Spaniards back to Mauthasen. They were kept in concentration camps throughout France, camps that had already been filled to the brim by Pétain and his cronies. Maybe because we'd fought alongside the French army, my fellow Spaniards thought they'd be safe under the Geneva Convention, instead they were tossed like bones to the dogs.

We always played straight with each other, and yet somehow, I don't know how, midway through July when we reached Limoux, about twenty kilometres south of Carcassonne, we realised that something wasn't right between us. There was a strange tension. If you asked Mariano how he was, he didn't answer. Or he'd tell me to walk faster and I'd tell him to shove it. So it was. We realised what the problem was one evening standing on the edge of a stream in the middle of a cane field. I had been pushing toward the sea in order to get to Port Bou and Mercedes. But he was aiming west, to cross the border near Pamplona and get back to Asturias.

'We still have friends there, support,' he said tossing stones into the water.

It was just before sunset. There was a yellowish glow on the western horizon and to the east, by the sea, the sky was a life-less, cold blue.

'More support than Mercedes . . .' I stuttered, but he ignored me.

'If things go well,' he continued, 'we could even get back into the fight.'

The stone went plop. I didn't say anything and he resented my silence.

'I never would have thought it of you . . .' he said sadly to himself. 'One hair on a pussy and you lose your head. Isn't that so?'

What the hell did he want from me? Instead of answering, I turned to look at the others. You could see that Alfonso agreed with me and felt like he was on thin ice. He wanted to go back to Barcelona and find Ana María, but he couldn't tell Mariano that, considering how riled up Mariano was likely to get. Sepúlveda was leaning against a tree and plucking leaves off the branches.

'What do you say?' asked Alfonso under his breath.

He slid to the ground and scratched his head.

'I'm going with Mariano,' he finally croaked.

We split up half an hour later, exchanging hugs and kisses. Alfonso and I cut across the field heading east and the other two went toward Foix. I never saw them again.

I learned years later that Sepúlveda had made it to Chile. Mariano was executed by Franco's men in 1943. He'd become one of the leaders of the guerrilla fighters in Asturias. An old buddy of ours from Gijón sold him out. Someone who'd fought by our sides in '34. Maybe he did it for money, or to get out of jail – but he told them where Mariano was and what he was doing. They came for him early in the morning where he was staying in a farm near Sama. An entire unit to take one man. They beat him to a pulp first, then they put him up against a wall and shot him as he stood there on his own two feet, no blindfold, in cold blood. I doubt they even buried him; there was never any tomb. Oh, my son. I can't even count the friends

I've lost along the way, but Mariano, well, he was different. The day I found out what happened to him was the day that I really started to know what it felt like to be alone. I haven't slept well since then. I often wake when it's still dark out, dripping with sweat from some dream. Maybe it's not about Mariano, or even about that war. Maybe it's this city. I've been here for so many years that I couldn't even imagine living somewhere else. But I have to admit that it's as if the noise of the cars, the old Indians sitting on their rugs with their wares, the smog, the volcanoes, the police raiding the kiosks, dogs running wild on the streets, the taco and carnitas stalls. Each day that passes I realise that the people who seem much older than me are younger and that there are more names crossed out with a black mark in my address book than living people. What can you do? I have to be philosophical. Oh God, you're right. That man. Your philosopher.

Chapter Thirty-three

By now Benjamin could sense a headache long before it ever got to him, when it was still a swaddled hint, the faintest pressure on his temples, growing more and more intolerable. He started to sense one coming on when he woke at the station in Anoulême, drifting in his seat, breathing the almost solid air in which there was mixed the breath and sweat of passengers all crammed together into one car. It got worse as they moved from one city to the next, suspended on a thread of stilted, dull light. By early afternoon in Pau, the headache had become a beast bearing down on his neck; he could hardly talk from the pain. He found a little respite when they finally got to Lourdes – going through the endless military checkpoints at the station, and then the queue at the welcome centre. They were at last assigned a room, but there was still the boulevard to walk, dragging their bags among scores of shops, their displays full of Madonna figurines and terracotta renditions of the miracle, and a flood of wandering pilgrims and lost-looking refugees.

As soon as they got to the inn, he abandoned his black bag and threw himself onto the bed without even looking around the room – two cots side by side, white sheets, a sink dark with lime, flowered wallpaper on the walls. He felt weak now, worn down. The pain wasn't only pounding in his head but seemed to have attached itself to his stomach, twisting. He felt like throwing up.

'Close the blinds, Dora.'

'Do you want me to get you something to drink or eat?' asked Dora.

'No,' he groaned, 'I just want a little peace.'

He stayed where he was, whimpering and panting, alone in the shadows, stretched out with his eyes closed, trying to ward off the torture, begging pity from a god he didn't believe in – only to feel ashamed a moment later. He struggled to his feet and vomited a thin stream of acid specked with bread and cheese from breakfast into the sink. Purged, exhausted, a fetid taste in his mouth, his face creased. But once he lay down again he could feel the pain lifting slowly, like a long tide pulling out to sea. Sleep came suddenly, with no warning, almost depriving him of being able to enjoy his liberation from the ache. He slept so deeply that he didn't hear Dora return and the next morning he hardly noticed her rising and going out to the bathroom, then coming back and getting dressed.

'How do you feel?' she gently asked.

'Better,' he answered. 'I feel better, thank you. I know my head-aches. You have to give them time, let them run their course, or else they'll persecute you for a week.'

A quiet light filtered in the window, striking the objects in the room at a slant, sculpting them with almost agonising preci-sion. The room was modest, unadorned, but looked out over a garden of hibiscus and wisteria. The bathroom was downstairs, and they shared it with the nine other rooms. It was next to a dining room and a little parlour furnished with faded armchairs clustered around a radio. This was where Benjamin spent his first day in Lourdes, listening to Reynaud's speech, his last, in which he refused England's offer to unite the two empires. Walter immediately understood that this was a surrender. Pétain took Reynaud's place and the next day the old marshal's weak voice rippled out from the radio, coughing and whispering the words that Benjamin had never wanted to hear. 'It is with a broken heart,' he said, 'that I must inform you all that the fighting must end.'

'*Fallait en finir*,' agreed the innkeeper, Madame Toussaint.

Benjamin stared at her. She was an elderly lady with green eyes and white hair that she wore gathered low on the nape of her neck. She wasn't sad, but rather seemed relieved that the war was at last over. Like many other French, she didn't seem to grasp the gravity of what was happening. 'Sparrows,' Koestler would later write, 'sparrows twittering on the telephone wires – the same wires that were transmitting the telegraphed order to kill them.' But Benjamin could see his future as if he were reading it in a book, a children's book full of drawings and figures, like one from his collection that he'd entirely lost track of. He saw himself walking down a road stinking of candle wax and prayer, joining others at a queue in a soup kitchen hoping for something to eat, a piece of bread, writing letters that grew increasingly anguished as he waited for a visa to go to the United States, or even travel papers for Marseille, where he might be able to climb onto a ship that would carry him to safety.

'We're stuck here in Lourdes,' he whispered, 'like in a labyrinth.'

And so it was. But not even Benjamin realised that the armistice that Radio Paris was announcing, *Horst Wessel Lied*, foresaw the delivery of all the anti-Nazi refugees identified by the Gestapo to the Germans. After June 22, any kind of movement for men and women like Benjamin would be overseen by the authorities. From that point onward they would have to avoid the welcome centres in order not to fall into that web of horrors. They had to hide, move like wolves – starving and cautious, in a furious attempt to escape. Walter moved through that trap like a sleepwalker. Sometimes he was so overcome by resignation and laziness that he'd spend whole days in bed reading and worrying about the fate of his abandoned manuscripts. The sky outside was a fierce blue and a ruinous heat rose from the streets, weighing down gestures and words. Only during the long, diaphanous June twilights, after the eight o'clock curfew, when the moon was shining like crumpled soapstone behind the bell tower, would Benjamin manage to write the letters in which he tried to recapture hope that they would ever find a way out of the labyrinth – or else he'd just express his desperation. 'I can say,' he wrote to Gretel Adorno, a few days after his forty-eighth birthday, 'that I predicted everything but was unable to protect anything.' In the meantime, over the month of July, France was split in two and old Pétain claimed to be directing a national revolution. Adorno and Horkheimer were trying to get him a visa for the United States. They called on the National Refugee Service; they appealed to Scholem for help; they tried to get him an assignment in Havana or Santo Domingo to get him out of that place. But it all seemed hopeless. The doors of the labyrinth closed back on him every time Benjamin got a whiff of freedom.

'I told you not to trust Adorno.'

It was the beginning of August by then. The dark, sticky heat died a slow death in their room. Dora came in to find him still in bed, reading, glum and sad, exactly how she'd left him earlier in the afternoon.

'Aren't you going to eat dinner?' she asked, peeking through the door. He muttered that he didn't feel up to it. She shot him a look of rage and compassion.

'I'm leaving,' she suddenly said with an unforeseen decisiveness. 'I'm going to the countryside with Emma. She has friends there who will hide us in an old house.'

She waited for him to respond, but he didn't even look up from his book. Dora opened the closet and pulled out her suitcase. Then she moved to turn on the light. At which point she finally resolved to finish her sentence.

'You're coming too,' she whispered, sure what his reaction would be. And she was right when he did answer, immediately, dripping with anger and resentment.

'How else can I explain,' he almost shouted. 'I am waiting for a visa to go to the United States.'

'You have been waiting for a year. I told you never to count on Adorno.'

Dora's voice was like a drill, an indefatigable drain on the brain. And the way she was taking aim at the Institute was twice as cutting as it raised doubts that Walter didn't want to entertain. It was over an hour before Benjamin's anger quieted and he was able to see his sister again as she was, weak and frightened, looking for support from her brother that he didn't know how to give. The spectral silence of the deserted night street rose out of the freshness of the end of the day. Walter stood and held out exactly half of the money that Adrienne had given him.

'Good luck,' he said.

'Please come with me.'

'No, Dora. I have to get to Marseille. We'll meet up again soon. Don't worry, a month at the most.'

There were tears in the corners of their eyes, but they both forced them back, out of fear of sadness. Once she left, Benjamin went over to the window and looked out, inhaling the perfume of the wisteria that was winding up the drainpipe – he looked out on nightfall that was coming in on tiptoe, like a collapsing agreement. Now he was really alone. The bells outside struck eight thirty. It was time. The moment in which he was almost transported by his desire to disappear even deeper into this trap. He wanted to write to someone in order to sweep away a little of the solitude. He wrote to Adorno. He sat down on the bed and began, 'The complete uncertainty about what the next day, even the next hour, may bring has dominated my life for weeks now. I am condemned to read every newspaper as if it were a summons served on me in particular, to hear the voice of fateful tidings in every radio broadcast.'

The only sound in the room was the scratching of Benjamin's fountain pen over the paper, the sound of thoughts falling into place in his head. It was already deep night outside. Benjamin took a breath and continued, 'My attempt to reach Marseille, in order to put my case at the consulate there, was a wasted effort. For some time now it has been impossible for foreign nationals to obtain a permit for a change of residence. Thus I remain dependent on what all of you are doing for me from abroad. I hope it's clear to you that I am keeping calm despite the difficult circumstances. I've not wavered on this. I can't hide however that the situation has grown dangerous. I think very few people will manage to get out of this.'

He fell asleep late. The darkness was already diluted and he slept fitfully, tossing and grinding his teeth. He woke exhausted before dawn and lay awake for a very long time with his eyes closed, thinking and rethinking about what awaited him. At last he decided to get up and go out. Settled in at the table of a bar, a coffee in front of him, he nervously leafed through the *Paris soir*, Marseille edition. He read of the actors and society people filling the beaches of the Riviera. A new decree from the Vichy government required swimsuits to cover down to the knee: 'No more shorts. No more French women cross-dressing as men!' wrote the journalist enthusiastically. '*La Révolution nationale marche*.'

When he rose, dismayed, Walter struggled to grasp the slender thread of hope still left to him. He headed reluctantly out into the pounding sun and went to the post office. He went more out of a sense of duty than conviction, but there was a surprise waiting for him. Juliane Favez, the secretary of the Institute in Geneva, had forwarded him a telegram from Pollack in New York: '*Please tell Benjamin to get to Marseille right away. There should be a visa for America waiting for him there.*'

He could hardly believe it. He turned the paper over in his hands, one thought after another tumbling through his head. It was done. He hadn't been wrong to count on Horkheimer and Adorno. He wished he could show the telegram to Dora, and run to get travel papers for Marseille, and go to the station. But instead, he had to return to the café and order a chamomile tea and choke down a heart pill, so frightened he was by the shivering that felt like it would take him down. A shiver that seemed to be made of memories come looking for him that should have stayed instead in the trenches of the past. Calmer now, he squinted into the bright light and watched two women teeter past on their high heels and then disappear around the corner. He smiled when he looked at the telegram on the table under the ashtray. It was August 4, and he thought all his problems had been resolved in a moment.

But he was wrong. It would be days and days before he could get confirmation from the American consulate in Marseille and to convince the military command in Lourdes to grant him a travel permit. It was days of telegrams and going back and forth between offices. Now that his request for a pass had put him back into the open, he lived in terror of being arrested and sent back into the mouth of the Gestapo. But he kept that fear to himself, speaking with people as little as possible and leaving his room only when necessary. He wrote careful, disconsolate letters. On August 9, he wrote to Hannah Arendt at her old address in Paris, hoping it would get to her even if she was still in Gurs. 'Time,' he wrote, 'is so oppressive, it would be better for my mood to suspend the life of my body and spirit.' He told her he was reading *The Red and the Black* and that he was in agony thinking about his manuscripts and that he possibly had a visa for the States waiting for him at the consulate in Marseille, but that he was still waiting for confirmation in order to secure his travel permit and leave.

Marseille finally sent that confirmation on the seventeenth. Three days after that Benjamin left on the midnight train — though he had to get to the station at eight in order to make curfew. Those were four long hours, waiting on the platform, then hunched in the car, his legs folding under him, and his head getting heavier and heavier. Every so often a patrol would pass.

'Papers?'

His heart raced when he displayed his papers even as he reminded himself that he had nothing to fear. And yet as soon as he saw the hats and uniforms, his breath grew painful and his palms wet. His lips trembled. He was a wreck by the time the lights of the pavement started moving along the window and he could feel the tracks clanging under his feet. The dark of night cancelled out the landscape. He sat there, his bag squeezed between his legs and his forehead pressed to the side of the car. As for his eyes, he couldn't seem to choose between the darkness outside and the pounding behind his eyelids. He couldn't sleep because he kept being wakened by a strange, tickling sensation, like ice on his stomach; it was a feeling Walter recognised by going back to his childhood, remembering how the hunchback from the nursery rhymes chased him beneath the covers. There was no mistaking it now either; it was fear.

Chapter Thirty-four

No, not yet. I didn't meet your philosopher then. It was July when I got to Port Bou but I didn't see Benjamin until the end of September, over two months later. I stumbled over him one night in the middle of the Pyrenees. He was trying to sneak across the border but it wasn't easy then. When I did it the first time in July, right after the armistice, it hadn't occurred to anyone to watch the mountains. Pétain deployed French troops there later, and then the Gestapo came and the Spanish border control. But we didn't meet a soul. We left Port-Vendres at night. It still wasn't dawn when we got to the top of a hill and saw the sea. The town was darker than the sky that was slowly turning violet over by the horizon and there were lights dangling in the blackness.

'We don't have far to go,' I said. 'That must be Port Bou down there.'

'Down there . . .' muttered Alfonso, indicating toward the horizon with his chin, 'is my home too.'

You did forget – you just didn't think about the fact that Alfonso was Italian. No one was forcing him to go back to Spain, to Franco's Spain, I mean. He was in love, really deeply in drooling love.

'You'll go back soon,' I said trying to comfort him. 'Hopefully with Ana María.'

But he sucked his lower lip between his teeth and didn't answer. He practically didn't open his mouth for the whole time we were hidden. Almost a day. The village was dark, but we still couldn't go prancing around there like two tourists, so we waited until nightfall. The sun set behind us, a crumb of red like an apple, its warmth tickling our backs. It filled the mountains with a soft clean light that extended across the sea and the sky, lighting the edges of the clouds and the houses of Port Bou, a stain in the dark at the bottom of the hill. Spain. This was my home, this sky, this light, this perfume of sage and rosemary, cow shit, sea and burnt wood. By the first houses of the village, before the train tracks, the rubble of war was still everywhere, in the squares and the flowerbeds. We were lucky to find Mercedes' house in the dark, picking out addresses from the narrow and empty street corners. When I knocked on the door, my heart was leaping crazily in my chest.

'Who's there?' came the voice of an old lady.

'My name is Laureano. Is Mercedes there?'

'It's late; come back tomorrow.'

'Please, I'm begging you.'

I don't know how long the silence lasted but it seemed endless to me. We were about to turn the whole show around and go back to the mountains for the night when the door opened. Mercedes. Not even the time to say how d'you do and she was crying, just standing there crying. No hugs or kisses. She should have been happy to see me again after all this time, but instead her tears were flowing like a river. Emotion is fine, but in this world, you have to laugh too, be happy. Isn't that so? Women, bless them. But I still don't know what goes through their heads and I'm seventy-eight years old.

'Come now. Why are you crying?' I asked, pressing her to me.

'You're like two ghosts,' she said, her words broken by sobs.

That wasn't hard to believe. I could only imagine what I must have looked like in a mirror after all those months – a rag. Thirty pounds less meat on my bones, a long beard, sunken eyes with the bags under them hanging down to my feet. Mercedes was run-down too. Her eyes were red and circled with melancholy, her nose had got sharper, and her blue dress couldn't conceal the deep pits around her collarbones. Her mother, on the other hand, doña Pepa, was a big lady, fat as a pillow. You could see that she took care of things. The three of us were still in the doorway and she was already in the kitchen cooking.

'Come on. It's ready,' we heard her call.

Bacon, cheese, bread, wine – and all of us sitting there in silence, like a funeral. It's always like that when there are too many questions. Your tongue dissolves. Or, when there is only one real answer; that's too scary. Even doña Pepa was quiet. She poured the wine without saying a word, and walked around the kitchen as if she were sliding on a carpet.

'Your daughter?' I said, looking at the wine in my glass. I had to ask.

A smile, that's all. Just one of her smiles. And I sighed in relief.

'María is well. She's sleeping now,' she answered.

There would be time to ask everything else later. Once the silence has been broken, a good man knows how to keep it. Alfonso, his mouth full, began, 'Do you have any news of Ana María?'

I shot him a look that would incinerate a bull.

A grey cloud of unhappiness passed briefly over Mercedes' face, gathering in her eyes and burst out like a storm.

'You'd be better off if you just forgot about her.'

Alfonso turned red; he coughed, drank some wine and coughed again. Some cheese had gone into his windpipe and he was gasping for air. His eyes bulged in his purple face like a drowning man.

'Why?' he asked in a high-pitched, almost falsetto voice.

Mercedes thought for a minute before telling him and then sighed in frustration.

'Because she goes with a killer now, a fascist – one of the ones who went around after the war shooting people,' she spat out all at once. 'They came with a truck and rounded up whoever they could and put them in a row against a wall and then shot them. Laughing like madmen. Bastards, fascists, sons of bitches. They still come around. And she goes with the worst of them – the secretary of Figueres Party. Did you realise who you were fucking?'

'Mercedes! Your language,' scolded doña Pepa.

That was it. And this time the silence was good. What was there to say to Alfonso? I stood and put a hand on his shoulder, squeezing it gently.

'Can we stay here tonight?' I asked without looking up at their faces.

Mercedes nodded. She stood and disappeared behind a door. A few moments later, there was a flash of her crossing the corridor, a bundle in her arms. Her mother pulled a straw pallet from the closet and laid it out on the ground in the kitchen. How were we going to sleep? Mercedes alone, or Alfonso on the pallet and me with Mercedes? I was blushing like a boy, and felt like I'd never had sex before. I was as nervous as if my entire future were being decided there. But the anxiety didn't last. Mercedes poked her head back into the kitchen and looked at Alfonso.

'That mattress doesn't look comfortable, but it is. We'll talk tomorrow. Good night.'

Then she looked at me and said nothing. She just held out her hand and smiled.

'Good night,' mumbled doña Pepa.

I couldn't believe it. Today it might seem normal for a girl to bring you to her bed while her mother mutters good night. But back then, my son, it was a whole different ball game. Still a little stunned, I followed her, followed her perfume, her shoulders – so skinny her dress was falling off – and that ass I hadn't forgotten.

'Here we are,' she said.

Four bare walls, two chairs, a dresser and a big old walnut bed. I could see a depression in the mattress where María had been sleeping.

'Undress,' whispered Mercedes.

There was a bit of war cry in that invitation. I took off my clothes and lay down next to her. Her hand was between my legs and her tongue was exploring my neck. Then what? That's it. The last thing I remember was my body relaxing, like a boat coming into the harbour. I must have disconnected, told her that was enough and let the tiredness of the past year and a half collapse around me, and it was a moment really. I slept without realising it. What a feeling.

Chapter Thirty-five

Standing, or rather leaning against the door of his car on the train, Benjamin looked out on the docks and warehouses, the poor quarters, the periphery, the pitched battle of the telegraph poles and the Agaves, the barbed wire and the palms, the steps and stinky alleys against the green hills. Then there was Marseille, with its odour of closure and brine, gas, piss and ink, its archways, stairs, bridges and balconies along the alleys. Coming out of the station of Saint-Charles, the sun was already setting. From the top of the square, Walter narrowed his eyes and shaded them with his hand against the setting sun. He looked out over the stretch of roofs, mountains, Notre-Dame de la Garde on the hill, the bridge that the train crossed. The blue below the Canebière and then the old port and the sea. The flat-bed boats slid under the iron drawbridge; the masts of the boats seemed to brush the façades of the old houses. Benjamin stopped for a moment to inhale the mistral carrying the germ of August. Then he picked up his black bag, adjusted his glasses and set off.

'Let's go,' he said to himself out loud.

A dark girl on the train had already warned him: 'It's useless to look for a room. All the inns and hotels are full. It's like the whole world decided to meet up in Marseille.'

So what was he to do then? The girl conspiratorially told him about a refugee centre where you didn't have to show papers or ask questions. The city had put it up in an old school over by La Joliette. Benjamin was now walking, hunched over, practically limping, and looking for the school. He descended into the fray of Canebière and then almost down to the quai des Belges in the old port that had been destroyed in the Great War. In the Corsican quarter, he sat down to rest on the edge of a fountain, heaving for air, his bag on his knee. It was ten years since he'd seen it for the first time, and Marseille still struck him; it was as spare, still and naked as an African city. But those alleys, ports, and boulevards forcing your gaze out to sea, were very much a part of Europe. The Europe of refugees and of all the nations, of people flocking from concentration camps, lost soldiers and deserters, people stranded without their family, papers or money, whom the neutral countries had pushed out like a plague. People like Benjamin were ultimately lucky because they hadn't died yet in a concentration camp or cattle car. Marseille was the last refuge for a shattered continent, the end of the line for an exodus that fed right into a trap. The trap of waiting without hope for ships that would never leave, where you could go crazy trying to get visas, money, permits, and trying to escape the Gestapo; the night patrol and the police ready to pluck any suspicious-looking man from the crowd.

Benjamin breathed, stood up and began to climb a steep stairway. He paused on each step to catch his breath, look out over the stalls and empty piers in the quai de la Joliette, and the beams of light coming from the Coniche lighthouse, its islands barely visible in the faint twilight. He got to the school when it was still light enough out to see the straw pallets spread haphazardly over the floor, the hundreds of men and women crowded into the room, and to smell the bitter, unbearable odour that clung to the walls. They gave him a baked tomato on bread in the refectory and then turned off the lights. 'Better than nothing,' he thought as he stretched out on an empty cot and arranged his bag under his head. This was his last thought as he sank helplessly into a deep, dreamless sleep. When he woke the next morning, he was bruised but rested.

By eight he was sitting in the glassed-in terrace of the Café de la Rotonde, at the head of cours Belsunce. His black bag was on the table in front of him along with the remains of his morning coffee. It was still cold outside as the mistral wrapped around the city, whirling down streets and across squares, full of brine and bits of paper. The café was already full of smoke, a gallery of every different kind of European face and language. Every so often you could make out a word, 'Oran . . . Portugal . . . Cuban visa . . . in transit . . . Martinique . . .' At first he liked being alone there, observing like a *flâneur* the people on the Canebière weighed down by their belongings, the crumbling façades of the houses, and light cutting obliquely through the damp air, making the pavements glisten. But then the voices from the neighbouring tables, the cities and places whirling around him, began to compose an atlas of defeat. He slid into an almost liquid discomfort, into solitude so unrelenting that just in order to talk to someone he ordered a croissant from the waiter.

'Do you have a coupon?' replied the man irritably.

'What coupon?'

'You just got here, right?' The old man sitting next to Benjamin drew near, leaning imperceptibly on his seat and just turning his face slightly from where it was resting on his closed fist.

'There's been rationing in force for a while here,' he explained. 'You need a coupon for everything. May I? Carl van Erde.'

His face was serious and traced by wrinkles; blue eyes and long white hair parted neatly down the middle. Benjamin noticed it when he bowed and extended his hand in introduction.

'It's my pleasure,' he said, nodding, and making a gesture of standing. 'I'm Doctor Benjamin, Walter Benjamin.'

'I imagine that this is your real name. Well this is your first mistake. It's better to avoid your name unless all your papers are in order.'

'My papers are in order,' protested old Benjamin. 'I even have a visa for the United States.'

'Are you sure they're in order? No one can ever be sure. Tell me. Do you have a visitor's permit?'

Perhaps it was his deep calm voice that made him nostalgic. Walter didn't feel angry at the way this old stranger butted into his life. He offered the man a strange, perplexed look. And then van Erde's face collapsed into the patient, bemused expression that one might save for children or idiots.

'You have to get a visitor's permit,' he explained, 'to stay here in Marseille. You have to report to the prefect's office in place Baret. Unless you get one it's useless to try to escape with just your visas.'

'Visas? Isn't one enough?'

'Forgive me for saying this, but you don't know very much, do you. And yet, you're lucky if you already have a visa for the United States. Now all you need is an exit visa and a travel permit.'

Benjamin narrowed his eyes and looked at van Erde, then he looked outside again beyond the window. A cloud cast a dark shadow over the buildings. He looked at the old man again, stunned. He didn't believe him and couldn't believe him. He'd thought that he was at the end of a *via cruces*, and now this man was spoiling everything.

'I'll explain it all to you,' offered van Erde. 'But would you treat me to a coffee. I'm short. Very sorry.'

Walter counted out the coins and then signalled for the waiter. Van Erde drank his coffee and stretched out in his chair, launching at last into a long explanation. He seemed happy now, as if the complicated discussion would save him from quite a lot of solitude.

'In order to get to the United States you have to get to Portugal – and get through Spain, right? You'll need a transit.'

'What's that?'

'Didn't they explain *anything* to you, my son? We're the plague. Any country that we pass through wants to ensure that we won't be stopping there, that we'll leave right away. The most important thing to get is a Portuguese visa, but you have to have a ticket on a ship to New York in order to get one. If they do give it to you, then you have to report to the Spanish consulate and get a Spanish transit. All of this costs money. I don't even know why I'm bothering telling you all of this. In the end, you'll still need an exit visa from France which is very difficult to get.'

Outside it had suddenly started to rain. It was one of those quick angry storms that sometimes happen in the Marseille summers. Long tears of water beat against the windows; people out on the street hid in doorways. The chatter inside the café stopped for an instant. It wasn't the best moment to talk, but Benjamin didn't realise that until too late.

'Exit visa?' he shouted – eyes turned his way from every table in the room. 'But why?' he added in a lower voice. 'The French have to keep people from leaving?'

Van Erde sighed and shook his head. 'Watch out,' he said. 'I believe you're German, right? You know that the people in charge now are the Germans. They control everything and they want to control whoever leaves this continent.'

Ten minutes later the downpour stopped as suddenly as it had started. The sky opened back up, and the sun was already drying the water gathered on the pavement. The café was thick with the smell of dampness and people clustered together.

'Or,' said the old man slowly, picking the conversation back up, 'even with all the visas, then it's not a given that you will be able to leave, that you'll find any way at all to get to Lisbon or to America.'

'What do I do?' asked Benjamin.

After not talking, his words came out husky. He cleared his throat but didn't continue. He waited for the old man to finish licking his spoon and look back up at him.

'What?' he repeated.

'So,' said van Erde, 'you need time and a lot of it. And you mustn't get discouraged. Me, for example, I had a contract to go teach in Mexico and with the contract there was a visa and a transit too. It took a month to get the exit visa and in the meantime the transit expired, and without the transit I lost everything else. Now I am waiting for the contract to be renewed so that I can start over.'

Now it was his turn to look outside and he didn't like what he saw at all. A car with a cross stencilled on the side panel was slowly descending toward Canebière. The first one in Marseille. There was a driver and two men in uniform looking out. One of the men was tapping his glove against the window and smiling.

'Hurry,' whispered van Erde. 'Bring your papers to the prefect. You see there's not much time left.'

At place Baret they sent him to the office for foreign nationals in rue Louvois. There wasn't much of a queue there, just two or three people pacing in the waiting room. Before stamping Benjamin's visitor's permit, good for a month, the clerk asked Benjamin what he was doing in Marseille.

'I have to leave,' said old Benjamin. His husky voice betrayed his agitation, 'and I need time to put some of my affairs in order.'

'Okay,' said the clerk and then stamped the paper at the bottom, signed it and passed it back. 'Good luck, Monsieur Benjhamèn,' he said with a half-smile.

Walter didn't get angry this time. Instead he felt almost happy. He tucked the paper into his bag and went back out onto the street. It was just past noon. On the opposite pavement the clerk for *Transport maritimes* was writing names and departure dates for ships on a blackboard. There was a queue of people right behind him. Benjamin headed in that direction, toward the quai des Belges where scattered seagulls sat in the sun. His happiness from a few minutes before had already passed. He sat on a step and stared at the water, the boats bobbing in the harbour, their rudders almost touching, streaming to the breeze.

Where had he ended up? In an enormous open-air concentration camp, surrounded by the barbed wire of fruitless hopes and endless waiting. The sun was there, a minute point at the edge of the continent – where Europe ended and the sea began.

PART FIVE

Chapter Thirty-six

Leaving. Getting out. No matter where he was, in the café, on the pavement, in a queue at the pharmacy, it was the only thing anyone ever talked about. Tickets, captured ships, ships that never arrived, visas, false passports, distant states and countries that welcomed refugees. All of that discussion only served to make the waiting less intolerable – it kept hope alive. In these days the Luftwaffe attacked England, Pétain dissolved the labour unions and prohibited consumption of alcohol in restaurants, windows of Jewish shops were shattered in the name of the national revolution. But the assorted refugees of Marseille never spoke of these things. When Benjamin brought up one of those topics, he'd get a shrug; and whoever he was talking to would resume a story about a friend who'd snuck onto a ship but then got thrown overboard, or about the travel agent at Thomas Cook who for two hundred francs would sell you a fake ticket for the States on a non-existent boat, or of that little office on rue Saint-Ferréol that sold Chinese visas for one hundred francs. After a number of weeks someone finally translated the ideograms on the embossed documents, only to find that it read:

'The bearer of this paper is prohibited under any circumstance to tread on Chinese soil.' And yet, using this visa, someone had managed to procure transit papers for Portugal.

'Obviously if the Portuguese in Marseille don't know a word of Chinese . . .'

Laughter was how you tricked time, how you pretended to the same people that you met over and over again in the bars or in the consulates or in the squares – while hiding from the wind – that desperation hadn't won out.

Benjamin spent his first days in Marseille at Mont Ventoux, a café on the corner of the Canebière and the quai des Belges. He sat there for hours contemplating the white houses around the old port, the sun shining over the forts, the bobbing ships' masts, the fishing nets drying on the docks. While out on the streets, spies patrolled, the police walked the boulevard looking for people with *boche* accents and no papers. If he thought about his discomfort, focused on the anguish of being caught in that trap, Benjamin would have drowned in the acid that gripped his insides, he would have been dragged down to the very bottom. But there were books still to be published, his notes and essays tucked into his black bag. He didn't say it aloud, but he clearly felt that in those pages there was the cry of a prophet condemned to repeat again and again his vision of the future – until it would be eventually fulfilled. This was why he had to go on, why he couldn't abandon it all. So he telegraphed the Institute in Geneva and had them send money for his journey. The next day he went to the American consulate in the place Saint-Ferréol.

There was a table in the lobby, groaning with piles of papers, at the top of the stairs leading to the main offices. A formidable clerk regulated the crowd, pushing the table aside with his hip when it was time to let a lucky person through. Walter timidly approached the clerk.

'Good morning. I am Doctor Benjamin,' he said, holding out the telegram he'd received in Lourdes. 'There should be a visa here for me.'

'Wait over there with the others.'

The few chairs were already occupied. Men, women, children, old people were all gathered there, cleaned up and ready to make a good impression on the consul. They came and went impatiently, they watched the table and examined their papers; they spoke quietly among themselves wondering whether or not to hide an illness or a pregnancy, to conceal or explain that they'd been driven into poverty. The faces were pale, tense, as if everyone had just emerged from hiding – some were familiar, he'd seen them hundreds of times already on the road or in the cafés. Benjamin exchanged ironic smiles with them, knowing, as they all did, that they would be seeing each other again.

'The consul is a good man, you'll find. I know him,' said an elderly man with his hat in hand, who Benjamin recognised from the day before at Mont Ventoux.

Walter smiled faintly, nagged by the guilty knowledge that he was among the elected; that he practically already had a visa in his pocket. Soon he would be walking down those stairs with a document in hand, sealed and tied with a red ribbon, a man who still had a chance for life. It was two hours before the clerk called his name and pushed aside the barrier. He went into a waiting room on the second floor that was already full. He'd have to be patient for another bit. Soon a woman looked out and called him in to meet the consul, a slight, indifferent man in an oversized suit, who seemed lost behind a desk that was too big for him. Walter stood before him, gasping for breath, what felt like ice in his stomach, the anxiety scratching at him like a fingernail, while trying futilely to remember that everything would work out and that there was no way the hunchbacked dwarf had followed him all the way here.

'So,' began the consul, as he shifted through a folder, 'I see that you have very good sponsors. Why don't you hurry up and get through the paperwork with the young lady and then we'll talk again.'

The lady was already waiting in the doorway as the consul spoke. She was very young, with a head of brown curls like lettuce. She politely led Benjamin into the next room, where, without ever lifting her eyes from the typewriter, she began soberly grilling Benjamin on every last detail of his life. The questions were so comprehensive, so inescapable, almost a web, that Benjamin was on the verge of telling her to forget it and just leaving. But instead she stood and sat him in front of a little table for fingerprinting. She showed him how to press his finger to the paper, just hard enough but not too hard, and then each of his fingers and his palm. He began to feel more relaxed, less like he was facing Saint Peter and waiting to learn whether he'd be admitted to heaven.

'Will I receive a red ribbon now?' asked Benjamin.

She laughed and brought him back to the office where the consul was standing as solemn as a priest. There was some more tapping on the typewriter, and then the pens came out, a flourish of signatures and seals. And there he was at the top of the stairs, looking out over the heads of the jealous crowd. Benjamin looked at his festooned visa and then stuffed it quickly into his bag. Eyes lowered, full of humility, he cut through the swarm and burst out the front door. The square was deserted. There was no one standing under the trees in the middle of the garden, there was no one by the news-stand. Everyone was in the café and they stared at him silently when he entered, sought out a table in the back of the dining room, placed his bag on the floor and sat. Among all those stares, he felt forced into that terrible kind of empty time when everything that was happening seemed unreal, and he would have to start waiting again.

A week passed before the money arrived from Geneva, seven endless days spent in the café, the backdrop of his destiny, surrounded by smoke and the conversation of other refugees, or, if his lungs felt strong, strolling among the tangled streets of the old port, from cours Belsunce to boulevard d'Athènes and along the quai de la Joliette. He would scrutinise the empty docks, allowing himself to sink unarmed into anguish and the urge to end it all, to be done with it. He gritted his teeth and resisted the urge. He thought about all the books he would be able to publish in the States, the articles he'd write for money, of his name being bandied about with admiration in the important circles. This was the only way he was able to summon the strength to spend his days checking to see if the money had arrived. Until that Tuesday morning in September when his money arrived and he raced to the travel agency. It was too late; the queue was already out the door and the Corsican clerk had just posted a CLOSED sign in the window. He would have to return at dawn, join the queue in the cold morning, stand with shivering people who were complaining that the port of Lisbon had been blocked and that the *Alexandra* would be the last ship out – and wait until nine when the yawning clerk opened for business. The office was minuscule, divided down the middle by a worn wooden partition. For hours on end, Benjamin listened to prayers, threats, bribes, begging – people jammed up against that partition who had visas but no money, who had a ticket but whose pass had expired but they still wanted a pass for the steamer. When it was his turn the clerk, his hair stiff with pomade, yawned.

'Do you have money?' he asked rudely from behind the window.

Then he became polite when he saw Benjamin's money. He stopped yawning and explained that he would of course go ahead and book his passage, but he wouldn't issue the ticket until he had seen all of the papers necessary. Benjamin could have a receipt in the meantime.

Out on the street the air was still, the shutters on the houses were all closed, a gloomy silence hung heavy over the afternoon. Benjamin sighed and pulled the damp shirt away from his sweaty back. It was done. He could put down another marker in this chapter of his existence. What a strange chapter too, full of paradoxes and trap doors though which his life might disappear. A dark desire inside of him urged him to bring an end to it all, to let him have the last word. And something else drove him to keep writing, to keep fighting. Following the second way, he may never reach the end of this chapter. It could all still be irretrievably lost in this maze of visas, files, ships, tickets and consulates.

He sat at the Café Cuba near the Rotonde reflecting and lingering over an olive and anchovy pizza that he had bought with recently acquired coupons, when he thought he saw her – just beyond the window. Her face was tense and worn; she almost walked with a hunch. The late afternoon light fell on her black hair, catching on the bronze reflections with every step of her quick gait. Benjamin quickly paid, grabbed his bag and raced out onto the cours Belsunce. He was panting as he overtook a group of four or five legionnaires out walking. He called out,

'Hannah,' he shouted, and bit his lip. He knew it was dangerous to have done that.

She turned but didn't see him at first. When she recognised him, she smiled and spoiled him with hugs and kisses that she never would have dared before.

'You're here, too?' asked old Benjamin emotionally.

'That's a stupid question,' she answered seriously. 'Not at all your style, but I'll forgive you.'

Later, in a little café on place Jaurès, Hannah told him about how she had escaped from Gurs along with a hundred other prisoners the night before the Gestapo got there. She had walked across the south of France, from Pau to Tarbes to Montauban, sleeping out in the open or in barns, begging bread and eggs from farmers. She'd travelled alone because she thought it was safer that way. In Montauban she met up with her mother and her husband, Heinrich. She'd been in Marseille for a couple of weeks already and had managed to procure everything – tickets, visas, passage on a ship that eventually would go on to Lisbon. All she needed now was a visa for her mother.

'What about you?' she finally asked.

Walter shook his head. What could he say? He still didn't know the answer himself. The truth? Maybe. The sun outside was setting over Fort St-Nicolas and it had already grown dark over their corner table. Benjamin held his chin in his hand, rested his elbow on the table, and draped his other arm over his black bag. He wanted a cigarette, or some tobacco for his pipe.

'Me? I can't go on,' he said. 'I wasn't born for situations like these. The misfortune just clings to me. Enough already.'

'Oh Walter, you can't still be going on about the hunch-backed dwarf. Look around. Don't you see all these people? No one is taking care of them anymore. They have to extricate themselves all by themselves. At least you have friends in the States. You have a visa and money. You'll see. Soon you'll be able to leave.'

The evening cast a grid of shadows and fog over the streets and the little gardens off the square, extending out to the sea beyond the lighthouse. Walter scraped the sugar at the bottom of his coffee cup and sighed.

'It's easy for you,' he said in a low voice. 'But not for me. You know that you were right last year when you said that I wasn't cut out for these dark times. Modernity, the epoch of hell. It makes me think certain things sometimes. I just want it all to be over with.'

Hannah shivered. She knew that Benjamin had been harbouring the idea of killing himself for years now. Scholem had told her that Walter had got very close back in 1932 in Nice, and that he'd even written up a will. On opposite side of the square from them a queue of about twenty people had gathered by a dock. Hannah stared at them for a while, and then looked out at the pale light coming from the street lights that had just gone on, at the last dusting of blue at the edge of the horizon. Then she spoke.

'Look over there,' she said. 'You know what they're doing? They'll be standing there all night long hoping to buy some bread or a handful of sardines. Just think that you will be free from this torture before long.'

Walter didn't answer. He just opened his bag and started ruffling through it.

'Can you do me a favour?' he finally asked.

She nodded and twisted a lock of her hair around her finger. Her hair was dirty. She could have used two hours of shampooing.

'When you get to New York, will you deliver these papers to Adorno? There are two articles and my *Theses* – some ideas about history. Promise me you'll do it. These are the most important things in the world to me.'

'Yes, Walter. Don't worry.'

Hannah folded the papers in quarters and tucked them into her pocket. She noticed the old man wince at how she treated the papers but didn't comment. She just glanced nervously at her watch and slid forward on her seat.

'You must leave, right?' he asked.

'Yes. I do have to go. But don't worry, we'll see each other again on Fifth Avenue,' she said with a smile. 'Good luck,' she said and planted a kiss on his cheek. He noticed how run down she was, unkempt, worn thin by life's beating. Walter didn't follow her. He sat at the table watching her walk out and head down toward the Canebière and the quai des Belges. A thicket of flossy clouds blew southward over her head.

Chapter Thirty-seven

'Come back next week, okay.'

An entire week spent huddled in a queue on the pavement. Two shirts on his back and a bundle of newspapers blocking out the cold. His jacket filthy and tattered like a flag on a battlefield. All of this just to hear some coarse Portuguese man with a piercing voice tell him to come back in a week.

Once outside the consulate, Benjamin pushed his way back through the crowd of waiting people and headed grimly to cours Belsunce, where he felt a sudden gripping on his heart and his legs folded under him. Someone revived him and settled him at a table in the Café de la Rotonde, ordered him a glass of water and helped him swallow a pill.

'Feel better?'

'Yes. Thank you. Much better.'

The moment had passed. Now all he had to do was sit quietly, breathing slowly, and watching the crowd swarm over the Canebière through half-shut eyes. The shadows gathered in doorways. The light was polished by the wind. A man and a woman walked by hand in hand. A legionnaire passed, he looked – too much – like Arthur Koestler. Walter stayed calm. He was used to such sightings by now and had cultivated a thicker skin. Three days earlier on the rue de Rome, Hilde Berthon appeared suddenly in front of him. And later that same day he spent the evening chatting with Kracauer in a pizza parlour. More or less everyone was, like him, the luckiest of the scum of the earth, and sooner or later they all ended up in Marseille – the gigantic funnel. All you had to do was sit on the Canebière and you'd meet someone.

'Arthur!' he called. The man didn't answer, but walked right by absorbed in his newspaper. Maybe Benjamin had been mistaken. Maybe he had heatstroke, or his heart hadn't settled yet. A few minutes later the man was sitting next to him at his table.

'Seeing you here,' he said. 'It's like you're from another life. But don't call me Arthur. I'm now Legionnaire Albert Dubert.'

He was wearing a handlebar moustache just like Vercingetorix, but the perennial cigarette was still hanging from his lips. So now he was a soldier? And the legionnaires – Koestler or Dubert – had a ration for a pack of cigarettes a day. Benjamin couldn't resist.

'Would you mind terribly offering me a cigarette?'

He inhaled slowly, savouring the smoke as it circled his mouth. He took three, four, five, six puffs before thinking to ask what day it was.

'It's Tuesday, why?'

'Today they can sell alcohol and we should celebrate. Shall we have a pastis?'

To hell with his heart. They toasted to their meeting, to their salvation, and then Koestler told him about having escaped a couple of times from jail and how he'd come to enlist. He said he'd gotten the idea from a Jean Gabin film. He told about how he got to Marseille, and about Daphne who he'd lost track of near Biarritz over two months earlier. Now he wanted to get to England so that he could join the Allied forces.

'It's all set. I sail at midnight,' he whispered into Benjamin's ear.

Yes, thought old Benjamin distractedly. Koestler had ants in his pants. He had the whole world in his head and had his head stuck out into the world. He'd never managed to separate thought from action. Now Benjamin would be alone. The others would all sneak away and he'd be left to disentangle himself between visas and consulates. But how long would those ships still be leaving? How long would he have to wait?

Evening had fallen almost without him noticing; it was a brown-blue evening, warm and quiet. A dense black sky stippled with bright high stars extended over the street.

'Where are you staying?' asked Koestler.

'In a welcome centre, a school. It's an awful place, but all the hotels are full.'

'Maybe you can take over my room. It's just around the corner from here. Could you come now, or do you have to go fetch your bags at the school?'

'All that I own,' answered Benjamin wryly, 'is here with me now.'

They slowly made their way down cours Belsunce, Koestler leading and Walter walking behind. They passed two empty fishmonger stalls, circling the stones that pinned the nets flat while they dried. The wind caught and grew fierce in the dark alleys so narrow that the walls of facing buildings almost touched. They rounded three, four corners and then climbed a steep staircase and went through an open door into a poorly lit entryway. There was a fat old lady with curlers in her hair sitting behind a counter and leafing through a newspaper with long fingers. Koestler exchanged a few words with her, and then looking up at last she pushed the register across the counter to Benjamin. Her nose wrinkled when she saw him copying out his information from his refugee pass.

'You have to pay a week's advance,' she said squalidly.

He paid. What choice did he have? Koestler took the key with a number written on the side and headed into the corridor which was filled with luggage and screaming children, jumping over the bags and chasing each other.

'They're Spaniards,' he explained. 'A whole group of them are leaving on the same ship I'm on.'

The room was tiny. There was just enough space for the bed and a dresser. A rod with hooks hung in a little niche. Veins of cracked paint ran along the light green wall. And a low-set window with greenish panes looked out over an interior courtyard.

'It's not very much, of course,' apologised Koestler.

'You're joking. It's much much better than sleeping on the ground along with a hundred other people.'

'Good. That makes me happy. Now I must go. The boat leaves at midnight . . . You'll see, the war will be over in several weeks' time and we'll meet again soon.'

Benjamin nodded and fell back onto the rickety bed. On the other side of the door he could hear luggage being dragged and children's voices and the landlady screaming to watch out for her vases.

'If it were to go badly, somehow,' he began without lifting himself from the pillow. 'Do you have something to take?'

Koestler shook his head and stared while Benjamin started rummaging through his bag with a conspiratorial air. He pulled out the bottle of Morphium and counted out seventy-two pills in silence. He took half of the lot and held them out.

'Naturally,' he said, 'I hope I won't have to use them, but just in case I hope these are enough. What do you think? Will thirty-six do?'

'Of course, that's plenty,' his friend assured him as if he were an expert. Even under the circumstances the conversation seemed surreal to Koestler – but only to a certain extent. Walter wasn't the first and wouldn't be the last to prefer suicide to the Gestapo. 'But you won't need to find out. I'll leave you some cigarettes too. And promise that you'll write when you get to New York.'

After he left, Benjamin stretched out on the bed and closed his eyes. He searched in the dull darkness of his eyelids for some kind of sign or clue – something that would make him feel less alone. He tried to recapture the horrible feeling of not knowing how he ended up there – on a bed in a squalid pension in Marseille, not a book to read, with thirty-six sleeping pills in his hand, feeling lost like a kite blown out of a child's hands. He would occasionally open his eyes a slit, trying to catch one of the few objects around him by surprise, trying to locate in the sinister twilight coming in through the window the mystery that connected to his destiny.

He must have fallen asleep because he started when there was a sudden outburst on the other side of the wall – screaming children, a bustle of footsteps and luggage, the muted curses of women's voices. Benjamin put on his glasses and peered out the door. He was in a bewildered state; his hair rumpled, his cheeks red, socks dangling off his feet.

'Sorry to bother you,' he said to an elderly lady in a creased flowered dress standing next to him, 'but what happened?'

What had happened was that the whole group had gone to the port, to the docked ship, with their luggage and all, and suddenly the police arrived and without any kind of warning arrested all their men. The woman fretted as she spoke; she bit her lip, clenched her hands into fists, and shook.

'Hijos de la gran puta,' she spat out. 'They said that there's been an agreement between Pétain and Franco. All Spanish men have to be delivered to arms. Bastards. And what do we do now?'

She'd stopped addressing old Benjamin at this point. She realised that this stiff, funny man with his puffy eyes and the air of a poet would be of little help.

'I'm sorry. Good night,' muttered Benjamin as he disappeared quickly back into his room.

He took off his jacket and shirt, hung his trousers on a hook and climbed back under the covers. But could he sleep? He tossed from side to side as the noise outside faded, and he started ruminating on thought after thought, trying uselessly to navigate his past. Shortly before dawn he fell asleep again and was haunted in his dreams by Dora, Jula, Asja, and himself, then his sister, his brother George when they were all children and posing for a portrait. He woke with a start to a clamour in the street below. The hydrants had been opened to clean and the water was streaming over the pavements, down the kerb, and roaring in the gutters. He was better off awake; because even in his dream he'd come to the conclusion that everything was messed up and that he'd only ever been a visitor in his own life.

Chapter Thirty-eight

Done. The cow with the piercing voice told him where to sign his receipt and then as stiff as could be she handed over a Portuguese visa. So this was taken care of. Now it would be an easy matter to get his ticket. At least that's what Benjamin thought. But when he got back to the travel agency (after another two hours in a queue) the fantastically bored clerk told him that he would still need a French exit visa and that beyond that, it would still be another month's wait.

'Don't blame me. There's no point in getting angry,' he said through his window. His brows drew together and the lines around his eyes grew suddenly deeper. 'Have you been down to the port? Have you seen the empty docks? It's been a week since we've even had the promise of a liner coming through. Why don't you come back with the exit visa and we'll see what we can do.'

Outside on the street, Marseille tumbled toward the sea as if reeling from the pounding sun. The rays were too bright. The sky was a ferocious electric blue. But Benjamin couldn't have cared less about the lovely September morning, about that wicked light that cut through things, revealing them and un-covering their every secret. He was dressed in a complete suit of sadness, pain, anguish, rage. Now what? He might have to make that decision. The moment very well may have come to bid farewell to what he'd turned into — a defeated man, bereft of a future. With that thought spinning in his head Walter walked down the quai des Belges like a sleepwalker. He looked at but didn't see the grey chimneys of a gunboat moored near Fort St-Jean. He climbed the stairs at quai de Rive Neuve and crossed the deserted streets leading to St-Victor, stopping periodically to catch his breath. Now what? he repeated to himself as he sat down on the stairs near the church portico, just a few feet away from a little girl selling matches.

Fittko recognised him first. He saw Benjamin sitting in the shadow of a column, his head in his hands and his gaze glued to the ground, and went over to speak to him — not even bother-ing to check that there were no Gestapo spies around.

'Benjamin? Doctor Benjamin — don't you feel well?'

Hans Fittko and Walter hadn't seen each other since they were together in Nevers. There was about ten years age differ-ence between them, but now, just a few months away from the prison camp, Benjamin seemed like a desperate old rag man, and Hans a dapper son with a beret crowning his pomaded hair, a necktie neatly around his neck, and the stubborn convic-tion of someone who clings to his ideals even in the midst of a storm.

'In times like these I'm not sure anyone can be truly well,' replied Benjamin chasing the exhaustion from his lips with a smile. 'But I'm very happy to see you Fittko.'

'Me too, but we're too out in the open here. Let's walk.'

Walter stood and followed him as if in a dream down to the old port, which was glistening in the sun. He couldn't manage to walk and talk so he asked Fittko if they could sit in a café. At the Brûleurs des Loups sat the same people who were always around, the people who had transformed the city into a grim seaside prison. There were heroes and thieves, poor people, doctors and writers, Germans and Italian spies. There was the stink of smoke and sweat. They chose a hidden table some distance from the bar. As they sat Hans tossed a pack of Gauloises on the table and old Benjamin's eyes glittered. He hadn't had a cigarette in four days – they weren't to be found anywhere. The ones that Koestler had left were long gone, and it was usually futile to ask for them. Whoever had cigarettes kept them for themselves. It would be criminal to give them away.

'May I?' he spluttered quietly.

Hans indicated the pack with an open hand and watched Walter light it and hungrily inhale.

'So how's it going?' he asked.

'Badly,' answered Benjamin disconsolately, but then he shook himself and sat up. 'I would be perfectly fine but I don't have an exit visa and without that they won't issue the ship ticket. Now I have to go to the prefect tomorrow.'

'Are you out of your mind?' interrupted Hans.

'Possibly. Why?'

Fittko sighed. He always had to explain everything to Benjamin. It was incredible that as bumbling as he was the old man had managed to survive this mess this long.

'Where are you staying? You'll never get that visa. They process them at Vichy. You might as well wrap yourself up and hand yourself over to the Gestapo. Not to mention the fact that the ship will never leave and in two or three days' time they say this port will be shut down.'

Walter was frozen with his cup of coffee mid-air. He looked at Hans, stunned, as if Hans was revealing a secret.

'What can I do?' he whispered.

'The only way is to cross the border illegally. You have to go over the Pyrenees. The border guards in Spain aren't too bad. Sure they might invent some kind of way to give you a hard time – this document isn't the right kind . . . we can't read that stamp – but they always let you through in the end. Do you have a Spanish visa?'

'No, I don't.'

'Well, get one then.'

Walter was so taken aback that he let the Gauloise extinguish between his fingers. He brushed ash from the table and then inhaled, blowing out the smoke with a long sigh. He thought as he watched Hans scribble on the corner of a newspaper and when he looked up, Benjamin ventured a smile.

'Have you taken a good look at me?' he asked. 'Can you really see me crossing the Pyrenees like some kind of bandit or spy? That's not for me; it's useless.'

Fittko didn't answer. He just tore off the piece of newspaper and slid it across the table.

'What is this?' asked Walter pushing his glasses up onto his forehead. Fittko noticed the red marks they made on the side of Walter's nose.

'It's Lisa's address at Port-Vendres near the border. You remember my wife Lisa, don't you? She's been there for a few days and she can help you. But you must get moving. Marseille isn't safe anymore. The Kundt Commission's put up at the Hôtel Splendide on the boulevard d'Athènes.'

Even Benjamin had heard this news. Under the pretext of liberating Nazis in prison camps, the commission drafted lists of people that would be delivered, wrapped up in a bow, to the Gestapo.

'But the Pyrenees,' he protested without a hint of irony as he looked out the windows of the café over the port. A man was arguing with two dark men and wagging his finger, 'no,' then he brought both hands to his chest and stretched them skyward again.

'I won't claim it's easy,' admitted Hans after a moment. 'There are already German patrols on the border and the Vichy troops are giving backup. But for now it's still the safest route. I'll be going over too in another few weeks.'

The arguing man outside was now being led away by the other two, his head bowed low.

'Did you see that?' asked Benjamin with concern.

'Pretend you didn't see it,' Hans whispered. 'Bastards, damn bastard sons of whores. Finish your coffee and we'll leave. Stay calm. I'll take you back to your pension.'

Fittko stood, and Walter put Lisa's address in his bag and followed. The sun was already low, the sky was heavy, just a few immobile clouds gathered on the horizon. Two lone fishing boats were out on the water pitching in the northwesterly. As Hans walked he kept looking around him, checking around the corner of every alley all the way down the cours Belsunce. Benjamin hobbled behind him, his heart in his throat. It was dark when they parted. There was a little sun still peeking through the roofs but the fronts of the houses were stagnant with ancient heavy shadows.

'I'm counting on you. Say hello to Lisa for me.'

Walter clambered up the stairs and arrived gasping in the foyer. The landlady and her lavish bosom were resting on the counter. Her wide mouth was stretched into a smile and she pegged him in a second.

'Ah ha, monsieur, you owe me another week's rent in advance, remember?'

He remembered. And how. Just the evening before he'd looked over his situation, counting for the ship's passage, it wouldn't be long before he had nothing at all. And yet he had no choice. He drew a couple of bills from his wallet and spread them out in front of that bosom and turned to go to his room.

'The key!' she yelled after him when he was already halfway down the corridor to his room.

Walter opened the door and threw himself onto the bed. He crossed his hands under his head and rested his gaze on the ceiling. He was crying. In his own way, making no sound and shedding no tears, as if he were walking on tiptoe so that no one would hear him. Chalk it up to the anguish of finding himself for the first time in his life unable to melt away the strange pain with words, this futureless cry *right now, right away*. It was because of the pity he felt for what had become of his thoughts, as they were made ever less of projects, and fell in ruins around him. Pity for that damned decision he would have to make and that voice inside that told him that there was no room left for error.

He rose when he thought that it was light out, but when he came out onto the street he saw that there was still a faint line of violet dawn over the cathedral hill. He walked for a long time, not knowing where he was going, as the sky turned red, then magenta, while the women lined cours Belsunce to mend the nets stretched out on the pavement. The brightness seemed to come from everywhere and the sky flickered from the hills to the sea. He finally reached a decision, out of a calm that seemed to come from far away and soothed his inquietude. He was serene again, imperturbable, as if he'd just passed through the kingdom of darkness and emerged safe and sound, as if he'd stared death in the eyes, and had nothing more to fear. For now, he'd listen to Fittko. To hell with Marseille and its ships! To hell with Vichy and French visas! One way or another he'd cross the Pyrenees. And that's how he ended up at seven that same morning in a queue outside the Spanish consulate, his face flushed, his hands in his pockets, and his bag tucked between his feet, teeth chattering in the north wind that chilled to the bone, surrounded by the familiar conversations of queues and cafés.

'The visa came,' a boy behind him was saying, 'at the very last minute, an hour before the boat was to leave. He ran and ran but didn't make it in time. In the end he couldn't join his wife — who was already on board. And do you know what she did? She just waved at him, and left. If you could see him now.'

The main doors opened and a thin functionary was letting people through in drips and drabs. Every ten minutes the throng outside took a little step forward.

'Would you like some?' asked the lady in front of him, holding out a package of dried bananas. 'It's not much, but since there's no bread to be found.'

'Thank you. I'd love some. I am Walter Benjamin,' he said, introducing himself with his usual bow.

She was an attractive lady of about forty, blond, but a little hardened. Her face was traced with lines and bitterness. A sullen child stood next to her. His blue eyes shone against his dark skin and unformed adolescent features.

'This is my son, José, and I'm Henny Gurland,' said the woman, brushing her hair out of her eyes. Her pupils glimmered with anger and pain. 'Are you alone?'

Those dry, bittersweet bananas were truly disgusting, off-putting even, but hunger was hunger. Benjamin choked them down, while trying to quell the embarrassment her question provoked in him, like a punch in the heart. He searched her face trying to see if he could trust her or not. He must have liked what he saw there, because he relaxed, smiled, and tears filled his eyes.

'My son and ex-wife are safe in London. Hopefully I'll join them after the war.'

So that was it. That was why he'd gone soft for a moment, a moment long enough to be painful – he'd seen himself reunited with Dora and Stefan. There are some things that a man can neither invent nor forget, the curve of a woman's back, the body of a newborn child sleeping on his shoulder, certain words, simple words that for some reason stick like nails in the memory. Walter just barely noticed that Gurland was talking to him.

'My husband Arkadij was killed in June,' she said looking down, her voice breaking. 'He was in prison in Tours, waiting to be sent back to Germany. They shot him while he was trying to climb over the wall.'

She told the whole story like that in a single breath. José stood next to her staring at Benjamin, his blue eyes betraying him; he tried to keep himself from crying. A man never cries.

'Will you help us, sir?'

It was the first time in his entire life that someone asked him for help. Old Benjamin. But he wasn't even capable of helping himself.

'Yes,' answered Benjamin. 'Don't worry. We'll work it out.'

Three days later, when he went back to collect his visa, Gurland and her son were there again. José waved and called him over, making a space for him in the queue.

'Nice business,' protested an old man from the back of the queue. 'If I'd known how clever everyone was going to be, I wouldn't have got up so early.'

'It's my father,' answered José shaking a fist, and Walter blushed, his cheeks like two tomatoes.

'If they give me a visa today,' he said, trying to mask his embarrassment, 'I'm going to set off for the Pyrenees tomorrow.'

The woman seemed on the verge of tears, but then she smiled, her face smoothing over, like a blast of wind on the sea.

'Will you take us with you?' she asked.

He coughed and stiffened like a pine tree. Her face was like the bright hopeful smile of a small animal basking in a sunbeam.

'Yes, yes. Okay,' he finally said.

José grinned. Perhaps for this short moment, he felt happy.

Chapter Thirty-nine

The first thing that I saw when I opened my eyes was Mercedes' body, dappled in the light coming through the blinds. The sheet was pulled up just to the top of her bottom. Within a minute the troops were deployed. I was twenty-four, what can I say? I rubbed her shoulders then ran my tongue down the perfect curve of her back. I moved down farther, farther, pushing aside the covers. I kept going down. Two hours later, Mercedes was a bundle of cuddles, caresses and kisses. You know women. Even if they deny it, there isn't a one who doesn't like a rumble early in the morning, still wrapped up in sleepy smell, drowsy. I need two cups of coffee and a cigarette before I can shake that thick feeling.

Alfonso had been pacing the kitchen for three hours while doña Pepa, her upper arms undulating like laundry in the breeze, had swept and was cutting zucchini into a pot on the fire.

'Sleep well?' she asked.

Alfonso growled a response then sat across from me and scraped at the sugar on the bottom of his cup with a spoon.

'I'm leaving tonight,' he said. 'I'm going to find Ana María.'

I tried to discourage him, and then Mercedes tried, and then her mother. But it was useless. He was stubborn as a mule. And nothing we could say was going to stop him. He was obsessed.

'I know,' he said, 'what I have to do.'

'But the state you're in now, you can't tell shit from jam,' I argued.

He looked at me angrily, and maybe with envy. 'You're a fine one to talk. You've got your Mercedes.'

Nothing doing. He had to go. And we kept trying to convince him otherwise, until we were interrupted by a little voice coming from the other room – *Mamma. Mamma.*

There she was. María. About six or seven years old. Her pyjamas hung off her skinny body. She was darker than Mercedes and her features were coarser, but her eyes were exactly like her mother's.

'Hello,' I said.

'Who are you?' she spat.

'I'm Laureano and this is Alfonso.'

'When are you leaving?'

'Soon,' I answered with a lump in my throat. 'Don't worry. Soon.'

Alfonso was true to his word. He left that same evening promising he'd be back sooner or later. But where was I going to go? The war had been my life. I didn't have anything else. The only thing I had in the world, Mercedes, was near me now. Everything else was a flurry of heavy, fat clouds, racing through my head and gnawing at my thoughts. I spent the days absorbed in nostalgia, and lived there like a prisoner. I helped doña Pepa in the kitchen, and only left the house at night when I went out into the courtyard to get some air before I dived back under the covers with Mercedes. Little by little I was trying to win over María. Easier said than done. She played pranks, she made horrifying faces whenever she saw me, when she fell and hurt herself she'd tell doña Pepa that I'd got angry and hit her. Not a day went by that she didn't ask me when I was leaving, when I'd stop bothering her, and when I'd leave her mother alone. I wanted to tell her to go to hell, but then I'd think about her misfortunes and I'd smile idiotically instead. I was worse than Judas.

'I'm leaving soon,' I'd say. 'I told you I was leaving. Don't you believe me?'

Meanwhile I was doing everything I could to find out what her story was. You know? I couldn't just keep doubting Mercedes, letting my imagination eat me up. Then I'd go into a panic thinking about what Mercedes might tell me. I tried to find out from doña Pepa, but she just turned her eyes to the ceiling and shook her head. 'My son,' she'd say. And that was it. End of discussion. Until one night I finally gathered my courage and asked outright. We were in bed, just like the old times – maybe with an extra hint of melancholy – but good too. Every time we did it, every time I'd take her from behind on all fours, her face smashed into the pillow, we both went crazy. She seemed even more satisfied than usual one night, and told me for the first time that she loved me and so I took advantage of the occasion. The moon was high and the room shone with a pale milky light.

'If you don't want to answer, you don't have to,' I started, struggling to find the right words. 'But I'd like to know about María, and well . . . who her father is?'

Mercedes sat right up and grabbed for the cigarettes on the

nightstand. She sat at the edge of the bed and lit one. The room was silent and I could only see her back, the cigarette smoke drawing curlicues in the dark. A cloud must have passed in front of the moon just then, because it suddenly got darker and the shadows loomed heavily.

'I'll tell you,' she said. 'But then I never ever want to talk about it again. Understood?'

I nodded yes, my head still sunk into the pillow. What an ass. As if she could see me nod in the darkness. She wasn't even looking at me. But she must have understood my silence, because she went on in a low voice.

'She's my husband Francisco's daughter. The fascist.'

Mercedes was near tears as she told me what had happened. It was a night like this one, August, four years before, soon after the war started. From the beginning he treated her badly. Beat her every night on earth. Yelled at her, called her a whore and a dirty communist, hurled the worst kinds of insults and humiliated her. Mercedes had come to loathe him and was already thinking about how she could get out of the marriage. But these were things that you thought about, or said just to say them. But that one evening she came home early and saw enough. Enough so that she grabbed María and took her to the kitchen and then came back with a gun.

'The baby,' she said. 'The baby was undressed and he was jerking off in front of her. That's it. Do you hear what I'm saying? Later, after María was in bed, I brought his body down to the courtyard. I told everyone that the comrades had ambushed him. Everything was so confused in that period, and they believed me. That's it. That's everything. Hug me now. I want to sleep.'

A great silence fell over the room. Some time passed and then a breeze started making the shutters knock against the wall, and then a storm blew up and made the windows rattle. It was a while before I could take her gently in my arms, hug her, run my fingers through her hair. It was a while before sleep came.

Chapter Forty

If Benjamin had more time, that sunset would have been an enduring memory. Looking out the train window, he had the mysterious impression that he was already looking at a memory. He felt strangely nostalgic for the red, mauve, violet sky stretching out over the Camargue, for the black-rimmed clouds streaking with jagged colour, for the rose puffs, leaden in the bloody light over the plain and the marshes, the horizon and the sea. The country was drenched in an encroaching shadow, and then there was nothing but darkness and the city lights flashing out at him as the train bounced wearily south. Benjamin, Henny Gurland and her son didn't talk. It was easier like that and they all needed to rest. Walter curled up on the hard wood bench and fell asleep late in the night, his emotions twisting and turning in him. He thought they might break him – the missed opportunities, all that he'd lost in this world, and in other potential worlds, everything that teamed at the margins of his life. He slept soundly without dreaming, like a drunk, until he felt José's hand softly touching his shoulder.

'Wake up, Doctor Benjamin. We should be coming into Port-Vendres now.'

It wasn't even light out when they got off the train, wrapped up in their coats, their breath visible. To the south, where the Pyrenees blocked the horizon, there was a faint luminous line, as if some god had been entertaining himself by doodling the silhouette of the mountain range with neat, pen strokes.

'Now you wait for me here. I'll be back in a couple of hours.'

Looking back into the lobby as he left, he could see Henny Gurland slowly pacing the floor, hugging her black bag to her chest, her shoulders sloping. A shadow in the pale light. Day rose gradually as Benjamin walked. Pink, white, blue houses emerged from the shadows, teetering on the cobblestones leading out to the sea, which was still, purplish and smooth as velvet. Benjamin had forgotten how peaceful the world could be. Then two solders patrolling the main road passed, reminding him that he was in France, he was Jewish, and they had to escape.

It was still early when he knocked at the door of the garret room where Lisa Fittko was sleeping. She batted her eyes in the grey half-light that filtered in through the window. That soft knock again. She thought it must be the neighbours' daughter. She rose groggily and went to the door.

'Who is it?' she struggled to say.

'*Gnädige Frau.*'

It wasn't the girl. The Gestapo? Or the border guards? Lisa rubbed her eyes when instead she found standing in her doorway an elderly man, his necktie tight around the collar of a dirty shirt, a grimy threadbare jacket and filthy trousers. It took her a minute to realise that Walter Benjamin was standing before her.

'*Gnädige Frau*,' he said, swallowing his words and rocking back and forth on his heels. 'Forgive the intrusion. I hope that this isn't a bad time.'

Old Benjamin. The world was falling apart and yet he still clung to his courtly ways.

'*Ihr Herr Gemahl*,' he said. 'Your husband told me where to find you. He also told me that you'd help me cross the border.'

There was no doubt that Benjamin wasn't lying. Only Hans would have stuck her in that kind of situation. He was the only one who could be so sure that she'd find a way to sort it all out. Walter stood in her doorway, his head lowered and his glasses sliding down his nose.

'Okay,' said Lisa. 'Let me get ready. Wait for me down at the bistro in the market square.'

Her nervous hands, the hard lines in her face, her sharp curiosity – Benjamin realised quickly that Lisa was a decisive and resolute woman. After she had dressed, walked to the square and had a coffee, the two walked leisurely arm in arm down the street, trying to avoid looking suspicious. Although, by then, Port-Vendres had seen hundreds of fugitives pass through and the people of the town harboured no hostility toward them. A clingy slow wind was blowing but the scattered clouds in the sky didn't stir. They hovered over the mountain peaks, stuck in an almost pristine blue.

'My husband,' said Lisa with a smile, 'certainly does get me into sticky situations. But he's always right in the end. Though there was no way he could have known that I had already found a route into Spain.'

Benjamin didn't answer. He walked next to her, staring at his shoes, or lifting his head now and again to take in the warm air. Meanwhile, she explained that two days earlier she'd heard about the Lister Trail from Monsieur Azéma, the mayor of Banyuls-sur-mer, a nearby town.

'He's quite a man, an old socialist who spent hours with me going over everything to the last detail. He said that the old road that runs near the Cerbère cemetery has become dangerous. Over the past few months many people have used it, but now there are agents of the Kundt Commission patrolling that route.'

'And so?'

They reached the beach, where the sea was beating slowly against the shore. There was no one there. Just the sour smell of seaweed washed in by the tide to die. Benjamin sat on an overturned boat, stuck his hands in his pockets and crossed his legs.

'And so?' he repeated.

'So,' said Lisa, sitting next to him. 'So there is the Lister trail.'

'Pardon my ignorance, but what is that?'

Lisa fluttered her lips and smiled. 'Don't worry. I'd never heard of it either. The mayor explained to me that Lister is a general in the Spanish Republic, and that many of his troops used this smugglers' route to escape. It's just a little bit to the west and there's some climbing involved. It's not easy.'

'Well, as long as it's safe, the rest doesn't matter. But I should warn you that my heart is unwell and I can't walk fast. Also, I came here with two people, Henny Gurland and her son. He's about fifteen. Will you bring them too?'

The waves swelled a few metres in front of them, and two seagulls drowsily sunned on a buoy. It seemed so calm and peaceful.

'Of course,' answered Lisa. 'We'll go together. But do you trust me? I'm not a guide and I've never been on this trail. All I have is the map Azéma drew for me, and his directions – take a right, watch for the shed on your left, you get to a clearing with seven pine trees, skirt the vineyard until you get to just the right point on the ridge . . . It's risky. Are you sure you're up for it?'

'Yes,' said Benjamin without hesitation. 'It would be more of a risk not to go.'

It was useless to discuss it further. Old Benjamin was pig-headed like very few others that Lisa knew. She still remembered certain scenes he'd made in Paris the few times they'd met, how nasty he could be in his convictions and how easily offended he was. Intolerable. So she let go of her doubts about him surviving the crossing, whether his heart would hold out through the hours of hiking. It was better not to think about it too much.

'You know what we should do?' she proposed.

A quarter of an hour later they had decided to go back to Azéma together and have him explain the whole thing again. There were too many signposts, too many details to keep in mind in order to stay on the path. It would be better if there were two of them trying to remember the instructions. They would just have to tell Eva, Lisa's sister-in-law, who was back at the house with her daughter Titi waiting for them.

'I'll come back to get you once the road is safe and then we'll go.'

They departed in the late morning, Lisa walking ahead, followed by Henny and then Walter along with José – who wouldn't leave his side – bringing up the rear. The sea shone in the distance, while the hills above it dripped with green vines already stripped of the ripe grapes, dotted with shapes of the women dressed in black who were working the vineyards.

It was a few kilometres to Banyuls over flat ground, but Benjamin was winded halfway there. His skin had grown pale and his lips were purplish.

'Do you feel all right?' asked Lisa.

'Perfect,' he answered seriously.

When they got to Banyuls they found three rooms in an inn that looked out over the sea – green, intense blue, under the beating sun. Benjamin could have stayed there watching the water until his eyes ached from the reflections, until the worries boiling in his head had quieted down and dissolved into that innocent blue like the sea itself, newborn. But they had to keep moving. They met again back down on the street just past noon.

'Doctor Benjamin and I,' began Lisa, 'are going to go speak with someone who will help us. Wait for us here. Don't go anywhere.'

'I want to come too,' said José. But his mother shot him a withering look. That was that. They set off. Mayor Azéma was in his office on the main road through Banyuls. A very thin man with strong hands and the face of a clever peasant, features carved deep by the sun and age. He held half an unlit cigar in his mouth. It wasn't the moment for smoking. He shut the door, locked it, and then called the two over to the window.

'There it is. You see? That's the Pic Joan, and just a little beyond that is the clearing with the seven pines. Keep the clearing on your right and go straight on to the ridge.'

'It seems so easy from here,' observed Lisa. 'But then we have to climb that peak.' Azéma laughed and stretched out his arms. 'I can't do anything about that. Spain is over there, on the other side of the Pyrenees.'

He returned to his desk and sat down under the flag and a very old photo of Pétain that hung on the wall. He glanced up and Benjamin thought he saw a crooked smile play over his lips. He wasn't wrong. The mayor was still smiling as he perched on the edge of his chair and said in a low voice, 'It might be a good idea to go now and check it out while there's still light. Go up to that point,' he said, underlining the place on the map he'd drawn. 'That way you can see if you're up to the walk or not. When you come back we'll talk again. I would just add that it would be better to leave very early tomorrow when it's still dark, that way you'll blend into the workers walking up toward the vines. Just bring a backpack and lunchbox. Don't talk – not a word. This is the only way to slip through the border patrols.'

And yes, he was now satisfied. He'd said what he needed to say and he sank back into his chair, struck a match against the wall behind him and took a couple of drags on his cigar. He must have realised that Benjamin was drooling, but would never dare ask for a cigar.

'Would you care for one?' he asked. 'It's good stuff. Contraband on the black market from Spain.'

Walter stood and leaned across the desk toward Azéma's lit match. Finally. But he couldn't taste anything and then he couldn't breathe. Had the smoke gone down the wrong pipe or had his heart suddenly been gripped with fear that he couldn't make it.

'How long,' he choked. 'How far is it up to that clearing?'

'An hour or two at the most. You'll see. It's quite a stroll.'

And it was over. They all shook hands.

'*Je vous remercie infiniment, monsieur la maire,*' he heard Lisa saying.

Chapter Forty-one

'Are you sure you don't want to stay behind?'

'Yes,' said Benjamin decisively.

'You know that we have to get up very early tomorrow morning and we'll have a long walk ahead of us. Wouldn't it be better if you conserved your energy?'

'No. I want to come. I want to see it personally so that I don't have to worry about what's in store for me. And I feel fine now, really fine.'

Lisa looked at him, from head to toe. He did seem genuinely rested. His face was relaxed and he'd regained his natural colour. Apart from that – what would be the point of arguing with someone like him? They left early in the afternoon, walking slowly up the softly sloping path like tourists taking in the landscape, the wind lifting dust clouds over the hill, the gaudy September colours, the olive grove, the fig trees, the carob bushes along the road. José ran back and forth, suddenly overcome by nervous happiness – an uneasiness that he seemed only able to express by careering about, running ahead and then running back along the languid curves. His mother called out to him asking him to stop and stick with them, but it was useless. Lisa thought it would be better to keep quiet. Fortunately the wind blowing around them diffused their voices and masked the sounds of their bedevilled language: four German Jews in flight.

'Around here,' she said, in order to distract herself, 'they believe that the north wind drives people crazy – it carries madness.'

'Where we're from,' responded Benjamin with a smile, 'you don't need the north wind . . .'

Lisa turned to look at him. An ass brayed in the distance – down by the village they'd left behind.

Old Benjamin seemed so out of place there, walking a trail, his tie tight around his neck, his jacket unbuttoned, his walking shoes worn through, carrying the bag that seemed chained to him. It was obviously heavy because he was listing to one side, grimacing, and panting with the effort of carrying it.

'Can I help? I'll carry the bag for a while.'

Benjamin stopped and breathed deeply. 'No thank you,' he said. 'My manuscript is in here. The last one.'

'Well then,' asked Lisa, 'why are you lugging it? It's useless. And we're going back to the hotel tonight anyway.'

Walter looked around as if he didn't know there was no one else there – just a wayward swallow and a tuft of hay lying in the field.

'I wouldn't trust leaving it behind,' he answered with a sparkle of mystery in his eyes. 'It's precious to me. I can't possibly lose it. The manuscript must be saved. It's more important than I am. Do you understand?'

No, Lisa didn't. That man and his damn obsessions. Things looked bad for their journey. But it was better not to think about it. What was important now was to lock every tree into her memory, every rock that might help them find the trail the next day. They walked, each of them closed in a bubble of silence, along that precarious path, cutting their way among the weeds, pines and locust trees. Even José grew quieter as if the mountain looming over them had suddenly frightened him. Benjamin got more and more winded, as he remembered his hikes through the mountains of Giura with Gerhard Scholem, and his outings in Ibiza with Paul Gauguin – the great painter's nephew. But he had been younger then and wasn't being dogged by the Nazis. What could he do? He'd been cursed with a miserable life, getting down and being put back up on one cross after the other.

They had been climbing for almost three hours when a flash of light from a cluster of trees on the hill startled them.

'The clearing!' cried José running out in front of them.

'Shut up,' said his mother.

But José was right. A hundred metres in front of them lay a circle of grass, delicate green and shining like a coin in the light of the advancing afternoon.

'Hurry, let's move,' said Benjamin suddenly. He seemed as if he'd been reborn. His gait became elastic; his heart for a moment beat regularly. He was almost running. Then, without warning, in the middle of the clearing, he fell face down into the grass. Exhausted.

'Are you sick?' asked José. 'Don't you feel well, Mr Benjamin?'

Walter stayed where he was, legs splayed and his torso heaving. Nothing else on his body moved, but one finger extended and wagged back and forth. No no, he was trying to say. I'm fine. Henny stole a glance at Lisa.

'Let's rest for a bit,' she winked. 'I can't go on, I'm so tired.'

So they sat for half an hour in the grass watching the fluffy clouds unfurl in the south wind as if a giant comb were passing over the sky. The strong scent of myrtle and mint rose from the earth, wafting peacefully in the luminescent air.

'Do you want some water?'

'Yes, thank you,' he answered.

Benjamin turned over onto his back and they could all see his skin had puckered and his cheeks were red as peppers, but he was breathing well and was smiling stubbornly again. Lisa perked up. And it was starting to get late, they had to make sure they got as much sleep as possible before leaving the next day.

'Let's go,' she said, standing. But Walter didn't move. 'Are you still tired?'

'No. No. I'm fine. You three go on back.'

'What about you?'

'I'll stay here. I'll spend the night and we can meet back up tomorrow.'

Stubborn, stupid old mule. There was something in his voice, a totally unnatural serenity, and a magic intransigence. What was Lisa to do now? He would be impossible to dissuade.

'We are high in the mountains, Doctor Benjamin,' she said, carefully choosing her words. 'It's risky, there are wild animals, stray bulls, smugglers who might attack you. And it's cold, you have nothing to cover yourself with, and there's nothing to eat. It would really be quite absurd to stay here.'

Walter didn't budge. He just stared back at her, the barest hint of a smile softening his gaze.

'My decision,' he explained, 'is irrevocable. And it's logical. Listen: What is my goal here? To get over the border so that my manuscript and I will not fall into the hands of the Gestapo. I have now covered a third of the trail. If I leave now, I may not be able to make it this far tomorrow. Thus I will spend the night here and then start in the morning from here. Does that make sense?'

Lisa sat back down and crossed her arms. 'Well, then I'm staying too,' she burst out. But only got an amused, indulgent smile in response.

'A *gnädige Frau*,' Benjamin finally said. 'You will stay in order to protect me from the bulls and smugglers?'

How much had he already analysed this decision, examined every pro and con, every alternative? He had it figured to the smallest detail. He must have, because now he was calm and not to be budged. He went on telling her the way things had to go, 'It would be irrational for you to stay with me. First of all, you have to see Azéma again to review the map. And you must get a good night's sleep in order to lead us safe and sound over the border. So you see there's no question that you must leave.'

He was right and Lisa knew it. She had to go down to Banyuls to get some bread, tomatoes and jam on the black market to bring along the next day. She'd tried her best, but there were no alternatives. She resigned herself to heading back down with Henny before it got too dark.

Benjamin waved broadly as the group slid down the pebble path and disappeared into the forest. He was alone now. Alone like a spy. Alone with the big black stain slowly enveloping the mountain from the other side of the valley, the cluster of peaks around him growing grey and soft in the reddening light, striking the tree trunks at a rakish angle and hovering on the horizon, brandishing a sumptuous peacock tail of light. Setting to the husky murmur of the wind, the sun was sad and dreadfully solemn. A faint cowbell echoed in the valley, his thoughts were thick and padded, the crickets pierced the silence like sharp needles.

Chapter Forty-two

Mercedes had said *never*. And we never did speak of her husband again, or of that night four years before. I was understanding. I had probably killed a lot of good people during the war – who was I to judge her now for getting rid of that son of a bitch? No. And this wasn't what was wrong between us anyway, not what was making me feel out of place in that house. It was that after ten days I couldn't take it anymore. Couldn't take eating off charity. Couldn't take this being practically buried alive. I had to be careful where I walked and be careful where I sat. I washed up in the kitchen because the courtyard wasn't safe. I'd go into a room and Mercedes or her mother would rush to close up all the blinds.

'We have to watch out for Enrique,' they told me twenty times a day – a drone.

Enrique was Enrique Viadiu, a short man with a long moustache that hung down the sides of his mouth. He was the town policeman and he lived right across the street from us next to a thin building from which hung the sign HOTEL FRANCIA. Some mornings I'd peek through the blinds and watch him putting on his cap, kissing his wife, happy and pleased with himself as he set out on the two-hundred-metre walk to head-quarters. He'd always stop by to say hello to Juan Suñer, the owner of the hotel – a Falangist of the first order, the local contact for the Nazis. What a bunch. Viadiu was a pig in his own right, but he held a grudge as far as 'reds' like us were concerned – two of his brothers had died in the war. If he found me, chances were it wouldn't go well. So there was nothing else I could do but creep around in the dark behind closed blinds, shut up for days at a time, twiddling my thumbs and trying to survive my pitched battles with María. What else could I do? I wasn't used to being shut up like this. The longer I stayed the more nervous and worked up I got.

In the meantime, I had a horsefly of an entirely different stripe buzzing around in my head. My imagination was running wild. I couldn't figure what we were living on. Where did the meat, wine and cheese come from? The delicious mountain *jambon* that doña Pepa put out on the table every lunch and dinner? It was obvious that Mercedes had left her job at the hospital when she'd dumped me in Barcelona. So what was she doing now? She went out, stayed for a few hours, and when she came back her eyes were guilty and she was practically breathless. I didn't want to ask. There are only so many questions a man can ask a woman. So I started spying on her, going through her things, watching her from behind the blinds when she left. And I found her out. I'd been posted at the window for an hour, looking out over the yard, when I saw her sneak back in, quiet as a mouse, packages tucked under her arm that she hid in the hen house. It was late; there was no one out. I had seconds to weigh my options and I decided to go out to her. There wasn't anything she *didn't* have in that chicken coop: cold cuts, cigarettes, medicine, sausages, meat and vegetables – a cornucopia. Now I got it.

'What is this stuff?' I asked stupidly. 'Are you in the black market?'

She jumped when she heard my voice. But she turned back and stared at me calmly in the half-shadows. Her lips curled, she was almost snarling.

'Well, what did you think, your Excellency? That our food came directly from heaven? That the Holy Ghost was watching over us?'

'No, not that,' I stuttered.

'So what, then?' she answered. 'What doesn't make sense to you. Come to think of it – you're about due to start pulling your weight around here.'

Me? How? I don't know if it was fear that was suddenly choking me, or what. I might have been seeing myself in one of Franco's jails. Maybe I was thinking about Enrique Viadiu and his moustache, about the French army, the Gestapo. Maybe I had changed and after six years of recklessly tempting death I couldn't do it anymore. I felt like I'd been reduced to a shadow of myself.

'Me? How?' I asked in a tiny voice.

'You could make a run, for example, that way I wouldn't have to split the profit.'

'A run? Me?'

And that's how I came to find myself in the course of one day in the smuggling business. Twice a week, I'd leave in the middle of the night, a knapsack on my shoulders, going out the back door. Three or four bored stray dogs would keep me company to the outskirts of town. By morning I was in France. I was all set up. Mercedes had contacts. I brought cigars, eggs, salami, meat and sugar to Port-Vendres and came back to Spain with a sack full of perfume, buttons, tobacco and medicine. I'd travel at night and come home in the dark. For the last stretch on the way back into town, those same dogs would meet me by the train tracks and walk with me. I'd deposit the take in the hen house and crawl exhausted into Mercedes' bed. Fifteen days and I knew the route by heart. Except the more time that passed the more I had to keep my wits about me to avoid getting caught. The border had by then become the last chance of escape for hundreds of Jews, Belgians, Poles running from the Nazis and the Vichy army. And the patrols over the area had got heavy. It was the perfect moment for me to embark on this new career! And there was Enrique. That bastard must have known something was going on. I could tell from the sideways looks he'd cast at our windows when I came home and from the tight-lipped exchanges he had with his wife before setting out for the stationhouse. Lucky for us that in town Mercedes was above all else the widow of a martyr, a hero, and so Enrique Viadiu wouldn't dare come searching the house at gunpoint. But for how long?

The one thing that started improving was my relationship with María. Beats me why she changed her mind about me. Maybe it was just getting to sleep with Mercedes on the nights I was out. Or I'd finally worn her down by smiling over and over again. Or maybe she'd just got used to my face and now that I was part of the family business it didn't seem appropriate to torture me. I don't know. Fact is that she stopped making faces at me and stopped asking me when I was going to leave. One evening, in fact, when I was about to set out for France, Mercedes came over to me all sweet and flirty, kissing my cheek and smiling.

'Why don't you go say goodbye to María,' she whispered in my ear.

I went. María was already asleep, her mouth open, her head rolling back, her arms stretched out over the pillow. Mercedes leaned against the open door, watching me. What was I supposed to do? I knew what she had in mind. So I fussed with the blankets and kissed María softly on the forehead. I've got to admit, it didn't feel right at all. It felt a little obscene, as if I were usurping something, acting out these motions that a father should do. But María responded.

'Papà,' she mumbled in her sleep. And I blushed.

'Sleep, my treasure,' I managed to say. But then, just to be clear, I let her know it was me. 'Sleep, my treasure. It's Laureano.'

For better or worse, I passed that exam. And as soon as I left the room Mercedes hugged and kissed me. I wasn't comfortable. Actually I was seething mad. My stomach was in knots and you couldn't have blown the sadness and disgust off my face with cannon fire.

I headed out a little earlier that night. My dogs followed me. The sky was icy and lit by just a sliver of moon. I climbed quickly, trying not to think of anything – to concentrate on where to put my feet, on my breath, and the darkness around me, the sounds of the night and the twists of the trail, up to the ridge. The breeze cleaned the air and shook the leaves in the trees. I was shivering as I started the descent, and I had to proceed by sheer memory, putting one foot in front of the other on the loose stones, I hugged the escarpment all the way to the clearing. It wasn't far after that. Then I saw him. I found myself standing in front of your philosopher.

Chapter Forty-three

Darkness. Weariness. The heart. Jula Cohn's shadow. Asja, who'd unearthed him in that far corner of the universe where it seems he's ended up. In the Pyrenees, under a pine, watching the sunset. What was he doing there? Shivering in a threadbare, insubstantial suit, tie strung tightly around his neck as if he were going to the theatre or the movies. He'd been out of place like this his whole life. Now the cold, the grim exhaustion, the stars in the sky, pale next to the comma of a moon. The image that smiled upon him now was Dora, the first of many failures with women. And Stefan – how was he? Poor boy. What a wretched father he'd been. It seemed only yesterday when he held Stefan in his arms, watched him take his first steps. Then his heart. The asthma. The darkness. A shiver went down his spine, a wave of discomfort, irresistible – like so long ago in Nice when he'd gone to say farewell – that's enough – the end. There was no way he'd ever get to America. Hunger. The cold closing in on the clearing. This countryside lost in silence. But this wasn't that easy calm he'd always futilely sought out in real life. It was a taut, threatening silence. Heavy and as piercing as a word. The dampness of sunset dug into his bones. He couldn't think about anything but the cold. His teeth chattered and he flapped his arms until finally defeated he curled up in the grass, motionless and panting. He knew he couldn't give in – that he had to walk, to move about. But he – *he* – was too tired even to think! As if he knew how to do anything but think, as if he hadn't spent his life consuming thoughts as voraciously as he could – as if life itself were on loan, borrowed. Now, that life, that body, its heart, muscles, lungs were demanding payback. He tried to stand and fell heavily back to the ground, his head rolling on the black bag. Oh God. Would the manuscript ever make it? He might die there and wouldn't be able to carry it safely to the States. But what did that matter? And thus he arrived at the absence of all desire – he no longer even felt the desire to die. A sudden wave of heat, oh, the treacherous beatitude of those final moments.

Laureano practically stepped on him. Absent-mindedly he'd cut through the clearing, hugging the tree line, in order to cut a little distance off the trail. When he suddenly found this man between his feet, his first reaction was to cuss through clenched teeth. Then he got scared – but recovered instantly because his eyes were used to the dark and he could make out the stranger's face, frozen into a grimace that could have been a smile, spectacles askew on his nose, soiled clothes, mud covered, dust shoes. He was too old to be a threat, and he was clearly unwell. Laureano reached down to touch the man's hands; they were icy. He felt for his pulse; it was faint like sparrows passing in the distance. He had to hurry. Setting his backpack on the ground, he took off his coat and spread it over the man, then started rubbing him from his chest down to his feet. When he thought he saw the man's eyes flicker, he grabbed him under his arms and pulled him upright, then forced him to start walking.

'Are you better?' Laureano whispered. 'You should sit now and drink some wine.'

Trembling, the old man looked up as if he were surprised to still be there. In the white light of the moon, his face was a maze of wrinkles and exhaustion out of which shone terrified eyes. Could he trust this stranger? He had to.

'I would like to extend my thanks,' Benjamin said, mustering the little bit of Spanish that he'd learned back in Ibiza. 'My name is Benjamin, Doctor Walter Benjamin,' he added with a slight nod.

Laureano stifled a laugh. Where had this little man come from – with his funny accent, his courtly manners, as if they were in an eighteenth-century salon instead of in the middle of the Pyrenees in the middle of a fucking war.

'The pleasure is mine, Doctor,' he said at once, a little playfully. 'Laureano Mahojo. I'm a smuggler. And you?'

He couldn't keep himself from laughing with his eyes – silently so that the patrol wouldn't hear. Benjamin thought that this frank, light-hearted laughter must be a sign, the last sign perhaps that life was still calling him and that he wasn't ready to abandon it. His heart beat too quickly. His arms were tingling but he felt better. He could finally drink in the silence, the candid light over the top of the trees, the lush grass covering the clearing, the voice of the young man offering him a piece of bread.

'I am a Jew,' he said between bites, 'escaping . . . If only I could tell you,' he sighed.

But even as he spoke these words he realised that he didn't want to. That his nervousness had hardened him and he was already thinking of everything that lay ahead.

'But I won't make it,' he added, lowering his head. 'I can't.'

'Why do you say that?'

'Because my heart isn't strong, I have asthma. For four months now — really for years now — I've been running and running and now I'm tired, too tired. That's why I say it.'

'But there isn't much farther to go now at all,' said Laureano, trying to comfort him. 'More importantly, are you all alone?'

Old Benjamin waggled his finger, because his mouth was still full, to indicate that he wasn't alone. 'They'll join me tomorrow,' he added after swallowing. 'I'm with a lady and her son and another lady who is our guide. Might I have some more wine?'

'Good,' said Laureano. 'But you shouldn't worry, the trail isn't hard from here. Another two or three hours and you'll be at Port Bou. Just walk slowly and stick to one pace — don't vary. Walk for maybe, I don't know, ten minutes, then rest for a minute and then start again. Understand?'

Benjamin pursed his lips and stared back wide-eyed. Could he trust this man or not?

'You think so?' he finally asked.

'There's no reason why you shouldn't. The important thing is your state of mind — whether or not you really want to make it or not.'

Benjamin sat back silently for a moment, sweating cold in the darkness, trying to find a comfortable position against the tree trunk. Then, with a start, he found himself fending off a sudden, stubborn thought, wedged hard into some crevice of his brain — he had to make amends with the hunchbacked dwarf from the nursery rhymes, the one tugging at the worn threads of his existence, his destiny. What was he getting worked up over? Maybe his life was even being controlled by the hunchback – like in that story he'd written about the automaton playing checkers. Something shook him and he emerged from that fleeting battle as if from a bad dream, a nightmare.

'Yes, yes,' he said almost to himself. Then, lowering his voice and drawing near to Laureano, added, 'You see, if it were all about me then there'd be no problem. I wouldn't be worth doing this for. It's not me, it's this manuscript.'

'Manuscript?'

'Yes, my book. It's in this bag, you see. I left a copy in Paris with a friend, but who knows what the Nazis will do with it. But I have this one – with me or without me it has to get to New York. My book must escape the Gestapo. You see why it's so important?'

No, Laureano didn't entirely understand, but he also didn't have time to decide how to answer—

'Get down to ground and keep quiet!' he whispered gruffly, shoving the old man into the brush behind the pine tree.

The voices were coming from below, on the path, not even fifty metres away. There were two of them, they were laughing. Benjamin's heart pounded in his chest and he buried his face into the grass – but he couldn't stay like that long and soon lifted his head and managed to catch a glance of the moon flashing on the bayonets. Then the voices started to fade and disappear entirely around the bend in the path.

'French,' said Laureano, 'the *Garde mobile*.'

They sat motionless, flat to the ground, without talking for almost half an hour. As Laureano listened to the little man's rattling breath, he thought he could almost touch his sadness. When he thought Benjamin had fallen asleep, he stood and gathered his things quietly. But Walter was still awake even though he was keeping his eyes shut against the darkness. It was frightening now, the way the darkness wrapped around them like a blanket. The daylight always made everything seem more familial, comforting – but not this.

'Don't leave,' he implored. 'Wait until it gets light.'

Laureano nodded and sat back down, legs splayed, his back against the pine. He stayed until the sky swallowed the stars and turned chalky grey and the first, wet glimmers of light fought their way into existence, articulating the dark mass of trees around the clearing.

'I have to go now,' he said. 'You will make it; you'll see. But you must promise me that you'll take your life a little more seriously.'

Benjamin looked at him, or perhaps he looked into the emptiness behind him, his absent eyes seemed to be harbouring other thoughts.

'I lived,' he said at last as if reciting a poem, 'but never saw life. I was swept away, like dust.'

Laureano smiled. That was just what they needed – a poem.

'Lovely words. Did you write them?' he joked.

'No, Dostoyevsky did,' answered Walter soberly.

'You read too much, Doctor Benjamin,' he said with a smile. 'Farewell and good luck.'

'Yes,' he mumbled.

And he watched him disappear into the forest, walking with the elastic gait of someone who could walk half of Europe, someone with a lot of time left before him and more than that the will to enjoy it. Lucky him, he thought. And then realised he was alone again. Fortunately there was a streak of pink and violet already coming in from behind the mountains, illuminating just the peaks that Walter had yet to climb. He breathed deeply and stood to piss against a tree. When he looked up again the sky was almost blue, the wind almost warm and from the valley came the faint sound of a rooster crowing. He felt better now. Alive. He fell asleep with his spirit strong, clinging to his bones.

PART SIX

Chapter Forty-four

He was already awake when he heard José's voice calling him. Just a few minutes earlier he'd opened his eyes when he felt the sun on his nose; pulling his watch from his pocket he saw that it was ten to seven. The air was cool, the sky clear, not a cloud, not a remnant.

'Hallo, Doctor Benjamin,' cried José.

'Will you please keep quiet,' hushed his mother, who was walking behind with Lisa.

With considerable effort, Walter made his way to his feet and headed to meet his companions with a smile. He could feel his bones creaking.

'It is quite a pleasure to see you again,' he said to José, tousling his mop of hair.

A few yards away still, Lisa started waving but as she drew near she cast her eyes to the ground and grew silent. He tried to guess why she was looking at him with such a terrified expression.

'Ah ha!' he said, taking off his glasses and wiping his face with a handkerchief. 'It's the dew. The colour on these frames runs when it gets wet.'

Thank goodness. The two dark rings around his eye sockets against that yellow complexion reminded Lisa for a moment of her uncle's colouring right before he died. But they were already gone.

'So, will you be joining us?' she asked with a smile.

'I believe so,' answered Benjamin gaily. 'I think a lovely stroll to Spain would do me some good.'

Not exactly a *stroll*. The path became much more difficult after the clearing and the trail itself got lost among the rocks and the escarpment. At a certain point they realised they were heading downward to the right of the very crest they had to climb. They were walking away from the trail and had made a mistake.

'May I have a look at Azéma's map?' asked old Benjamin. 'Here, you see? We have to go back.'

It was a good twenty minutes back to the fork in the road where they had taken the wrong turn. To call it a trail at this point would have been an exaggeration. Sometimes it was steps barely etched into the rock, at other times it was a thin crack between two boulders through which you could only pass one at a time. But the mayor had been right that this was every-thing else notwithstanding the safest route – it crossed below the most highly trafficked roads and was hidden from the police and border patrol behind the perilously jutting cliffs. Occasionally the two paths would run close and the group would have to keep very quiet.

Benjamin walked slowly and kept a steady pace. He stopped periodically to rest and then would take up again at the very same calm pace.

'Are you tired?' asked José.

'No. I figured out last night how to get through this. I have to stop and rest at regular intervals before I actually get tired. This is my system for getting to Spain. Do you know what I wrote many years ago? – *Nothing can conquer my patience*. I wrote that.'

Benjamin could feel Frau Fittko's sharp eyes on him, and he could guess what she was thinking: what a shame that a man with so much strength of will couldn't be slightly less inept. This is what Lisa was thinking – but old Benjamin was used to it. And he didn't have the time to dwell on it because José kept talking to him.

'You're a writer?' he asked.

'Let's say I'm a critic; I write essays.'

'José, stop bothering Doctor Benjamin,' his mother reprimanded him.

'Don't worry about it,' said Walter.

The little triumph lit up the boy's cheeks and he perked up. 'Do they pay you to write?'

Benjamin could barely keep himself from laughing. 'Sometimes,' he muttered, and he began to reflect sadly on the fruitless results that all of his ideas and effort had produced. What use had thoughts and ideas been? It all came to nothing. Not even survival. Not really, no. He just hadn't been born into the right time-period.

'Can I help carry your bag?' he heard the boy ask.

This time he consented because the sun was beating maliciously on his neck and there was the steep vineyard Azéma had marked on the map in front of them. This would be, he'd warned, the hardest part of the journey. There was no path, just the slippery ground under their feet. They climbed among the vines dripping with almost ripe Banyuls grapes, black and sugary, hanging at an angle that seemed almost horizontal to Benjamin. He gasped for air, a grim sound that came straight up from his lungs. He stopped, moved forward but his legs stayed behind and buckled. He stopped again to let his heart slow down, moved forward on hands and knees and then stopped again wheezing for air.

'This is it. I can't go on,' he calmly announced between breaths. 'This climb is beyond me. A person knows when it's time to stop, when he's reached his limit.'

'Don't talk nonsense,' Lisa called to him as she came down again with José to assist him. They each took a side, draping his arms over their shoulders and they dragged him, tripping and puffing, to the top. Benjamin opened his mouth, but no words came out. He didn't even complain. Though he wouldn't take his eyes off the black bag, which Lisa was now carrying.

They stopped to rest on a narrow overhang above the vineyard. It was hot and the sun was high. They had been walking for more than four hours. According to the mayor they should have already reached Spain, but they knew they were still quite a distance from Port Bou.

'Mountaineers,' grumbled Benjamin when he recovered his breath and could feel his heart slowing down, 'they make it look easy.'

'Yes,' agreed Lisa. 'But we still have time. We could eat now if you want.'

No one was very hungry. After all these months, the camps, the flights, the bombs and rations, their stomachs had shrunk and yet they had to eat something.

'May I serve myself *gnädige Frau*?' asked Benjamin.

There was old Benjamin as ever standing on ceremony. Absurd. Lisa pushed the tomatoes toward him, and something caught her eye just over his shoulder. What was it? The bleached skeleton of a goat? Two vultures swept across the blue sky overhead.

'We'd better get moving,' she said.

The path had grown less steep, but Benjamin was worn from the accumulated effort of the morning and was having more and more difficulty. His pace grew slower and his rests lasted longer. It seemed that he only cared about keeping his rhythm regular. Lisa was walking out in front of the group when they hit the crest between the Coll de Rumpisa and Pla del Ras. She stopped short and caught her breath, thinking she might be looking at a mirage.

'Come!' she allowed herself to shout. 'Come up and see.'

Behind them in the distance lay the brilliant blue sea of France, the green, yellow and ochre of the vineyards they'd passed through. Below her, as far as the eye could see, there was the Spanish coast, rows of jagged cliffs standing over a turquoise sea, calm and transparent. Beyond that a delicate veil seemed to have burst from the horizon, shooting a milky blue between the water and the sky.

'It's marvellous,' said Lisa.

They were almost there. Port Bou lay below them, hidden behind a knoll. They just had to walk straight from there and they would arrive in no time. It was done. They passed their umpteenth frontier. They were almost saved. Lisa would have to turn back now. Their visas and papers were all in order. But hers weren't. She couldn't possibly run the risk at that point. Imagine being caught in Spain. But they all agreed that she would walk with them another bit.

Twenty minutes later, they passed a greenish, stinky puddle, thick with mud and fungus. Right there Walter kneeled and, waving the insects away from his face, prepared to drink.

'What are you doing? Can't you see that the water's filthy? It's polluted.'

Lisa's canteen was empty now, but Benjamin hadn't even asked her for a sip. Now it suddenly seemed that drinking had become a matter of life or death.

'I'm sorry,' he said calmly, leaning over the puddle. 'But I don't have a choice. If I don't drink, I'm not sure I'll make it.'

'Listen to me,' begged Lisa. 'Please just stop a minute and listen. We're almost there, just one last stretch and then you can have all the water you want. Think about it. Do you really want to expose yourself to typhoid now?'

For a moment, Walter lifted his head to look at her. His icy blue eyes were rimmed with red, inflamed with conjunctivitis. Black dust had settled into his wrinkles.

'Of course, I might get sick,' he patiently explained. 'But you must try to understand. The worst case is that I'll die of typhoid once I cross the border. But at least my book will be safe. Forgive me, *gnädige Frau*, but I must drink now.'

They didn't speak after that as they descended the easy slope. Only after they'd hit the edge of the ridge, Lisa turned to speak. It was two thirty. They could see the white shape of the Port Bou train station below them, gleaming in the sun, the web of tracks, a church spire, the low houses coasting the sea and the bay.

'I must leave now,' said Lisa. 'There should be a real road after this. It's an hour's walk at the most and you'll be there. Go straight to the police to present your papers and get an entry visa stamp on your passports. After that, get on the first train to Lisbon. But you already know all of this. Good luck.'

'Good luck to you,' they all answered simultaneously.

Lisa watched them for a while before turning back. Her three companions climbed down to the road over the rocks and around the ditches. There was a gentle breeze, heavy with brine, the perfume of capers and mint, the dried summer weeds growing along the path. They were too tired to talk or even to enjoy the view. But they could sense eyes on them. Benjamin turned around, his heart in his throat, and was relieved to see four women a hundred metres behind them. They were Jews, like them. Jews in flight. But . . . yes! He knew at least three of them from Paris, quite possibly from longer ago, from Berlin. There stood Grete Freund of *Tagebuch*, and Birmann and her sister, Frau Lippmann. They all seemed exhausted too. Grimy with dust and leaning on sticks they'd picked up along the trail. He stopped, breathlessly, to wait for them, motionless under the sun and rubbing his eyes with his hand.

'Most happy to see you here,' he said with a bow. 'If one can be happy at all under these circumstances.'

'When did you leave? Are you alone? Do you think we're almost there?' asked Grete in a rush. 'We've been walking since early this morning. We're so tired. No one told us which way to go.'

The metres closed between them before either Benjamin or José could answer, meanwhile Henny Gurland was calling to them.

'Let's go. It's getting late. We'll catch up later.'

They walked together for a short distance but Walter was moving too slowly. He'd take ten steps and then stop to rest.

'Please don't worry about me,' he said. 'You all go on ahead and I'll join you in town.'

An hour later, with Gurland leading the way, and José practically glued to Benjamin's side, they reached the first houses of the town. There were the train tracks and then, far off, the tops of two palm trees on the beach. They could hear the sound of dishes being washed, the strong scent of garlic and fried fish wafting from the windows. They passed a gallery and then followed the tracks that led into the station. There was a great silence under that vaulted ceiling, their dragging footsteps, a few people scattered on the benches and one train parked at the last platform. A yellow light fell lazily in through the windows.

'Thank you, José. I'll take my bag now. Thank you very much.'

The room where the police were stationed was long and narrow with two benches, three desks and two bored-looking soldiers in conversation. A poster hanging on the wall read, 'Primera Cruzada,' and 'España espiritual del mundo.' The sergeant's office was at the far end behind a partition. The three ladies and a fourth friend of theirs were already sitting on the benches, and the expressions on their faces said everything. There was trouble.

'What's happening?' asked Benjamin, still standing in the doorway.

'They say,' sobbed Frau Lippmann, 'that they won't let us in. There were new orders.'

In the meantime, one of the policemen had come over to Benjamin and the Gurlands and asked for their papers. He stood slowly flipping through them and shaking his head with an expression somewhere between sympathy and scorn.

'Sergeant, can you come out a minute?' he finally said.

And the scene repeated itself. A tall man, his officer stripes on his shoulder, irritably examined the blue and pink documents. He shook his head and let out a long sigh.

'There's nothing we can do,' he said without looking up. 'A new order came in yesterday,' he explained quietly. 'It says that *sans nationalité*, everyone without a French exit visa should be handed over to the French police to be sent back.'

It was as if another piece of the world crumbled with every word and now as he finished an avalanche of ruins fell around them. Benjamin had done everything in his power to climb down off this one last cross and now he would have to climb up on another – this one perhaps the last for real. He felt like he'd reached a dead end and this was perhaps what gave him sudden strength, enabled him to gather up what little adrenaline was left him as the women wept and begged.

'You know very well,' he cried in a broken voice, 'that for a triviality, for a silly stamp on our papers you are condemning us to death! By sending us back you are delivering us hog-tied over to the Gestapo. You are a murderer!'

Then shocked, even a little scared of what he'd said, Walter lowered his eyes and fell back onto the bench, gasping loudly. The women were silent now, and José's eyes were wide with fear. And the sergeant stood there, pretended to review their documents again and then sighed.

'There's nothing I can do,' he finally said. 'Really, I'm sorry, but I have orders to follow.'

Silence. A heavy, desolate silence, like that of a cemetery or a desert inhabited only by thoughts that whirled but never settled – unable to find their form, to become an idea, a word . . . Until someone dared speak.

'But how can we leave now?' stuttered Frau Freund. 'You can see that we're tired and there's a child with us.'

'And they're women,' Benjamin interrupted.

The sergeant seemed to consider it and then said, 'One moment.' He disappeared behind the partition into his office and emerged again five minutes later.

'Okay,' he said. 'You can stay here tonight and rest. Obviously, we'll be guarding you. Núñez and Alcina will bring you to the Hotel Francia. Then tomorrow we'll take you back to the border.'

It was just a few hours, but it was another reprieve from their meeting with death.

'Please follow me,' said one of the policemen, taking his hat from the hook on the wall.

Before leaving, Benjamin turned to the sergeant who was standing still in the middle of the room. 'I should apologise for before,' he said, 'I seldom lose control.'

The man nodded and smiled perhaps. Then he looked up at the old man with the long beard and dishevelled hair and crossed eyes, his suit in tatters and a tie dangling over a filthy shirt. He stank. The sergeant looked at him with dismay and whispered, 'See you around,' and bowed ceremoniously.

Chapter Forty-five

Outside in the dark hall, stopping on the stairs leading from the station to the street, Walter batted his eyes against the light flooding the entry and shining in the square beyond. Then he grew pale. He had a gripping pain, a wicked spurt in his stomach that stole his breath. The women and José watched him with concern while the two policemen snorted nervously.

'Are you sick?' asked Henny Gurland.

Benjamin leaned on the rail and wheezed. 'Not really,' he murmured. 'I just need a moment to collect myself.'

'José, go and help him. Carry the bag.'

But Walter motioned that the moment had passed. He started timidly down the steps, pausing on each one, then slowly following the group down a street lined with burnt plane trees, across the square and past the market stalls. A few passers-by turned to look at the dejected procession of foreigners being escorted by two policemen – an elderly man in a beret, hands clasped behind his back, a child playing with a dog, and a man who seemed to be rushing toward the board-walk. A train whistle blew behind them. Benjamin lifted his gaze and looked ahead. Grete Freund was pointing to her left: the Hotel Francia, a narrow two-storey building, a crumbling edifice crying out for a new coat of paint. When they reached the door, the two policemen had already disappeared inside making the beaded curtain rattle. One of the two men, Núñez or Alcina, poked his head back out the door and called to them.

'Are you coming?' he said.

Walter entered last, leaning on José's shoulder. They found themselves in the main room of a tiny restaurant with red-checkered tablecloths, the still blades of a fan in the middle of the ceiling, walls painted halfway up with a steely matt grey. Two old men were sitting by a turned-off radio. In the back of the room, by the counter where the women were already gathered, a man with heavy eyebrows and the grin of a rabbit stood recording their names in his register. Benjamin sat with his bag on his knee, eyes shut, to wait for his turn. He was thinking that he should call the American consulate in Barcelona when Núñez, or Alcina, called him over.

'Señor,' he said as Walter dragged himself to the counter and presented his documents to the owner.

'Benjamin, Walter?' asked the man with a smooth smile, bending the name to accommodate the Spanish vowels. But Walter didn't care about that anymore.

'Yes,' he answered, attempting a bow. 'Mucho gusto.'

The man looked at him without lifting his head from the register. What ceremony? Didn't the old man in the glasses realise his predicament? Was he joking? No. He wasn't joking.

'Juan Suñer at your service,' he forced himself to say. 'Room number four, first floor.'

He pulled away from the counter and opened a door off to the right.

'Through here,' he said.

'We'll be staying here. No one leaves the hotel. Is that clear?' directed one of the two policemen – the one with the moustache who looked like a mouse. Was that Alcina or Núñez? It didn't matter. Now he needed to concentrate on climbing the steep narrow stairs in almost complete darkness, waiting and gasping for breath while the owner got the women settled. Finally Juan Suñer opened the door to number four.

'It's the smallest. I apologise, but it's all I have.'

'It will be fine,' answered Benjamin breathlessly.

Once he was alone, Walter looked around. They certainly were spare accommodations: a narrow, almost rectangular closet over by the window, a little bed, a nightstand and a rickety wardrobe, a table pushed against the wall. Benjamin put his bag down on the table. Outside church bells struck five.

He practically collapsed on the bed with a sigh of relief. But as soon as he was horizontal that gripping in his stomach came back, and then he felt a pushing as if something inside him was writhing to get out. He tapped his stomach and it seemed a little swollen. Maybe Lisa had been right that he shouldn't have drunk from that puddle. But now he had to go back downstairs and get some kind of help. He had to call the consulate, write to Juliane Favez in Geneva. He had just stood up when he heard a knock on the door.

'Come in,' he said.

The door slowly opened and Henny and José peered in from the dark corridor.

'Forgive the disruption. How are you doing? Do you need anything?'

'No thank you. I'm on my way downstairs too.'

It was all torture: the stairs, asking Señor Suñer for a telephone line, then listening to the phone ringing in the empty American consulate, trying to explain the situation in a few lines on a postcard to Favez in Geneva, and then going back up to his room and feeling that pain in his stomach come back like a knife digging out his intestines. He removed his jacket and shoes, and loosened his tie, scanned the room to make sure his bag was still on the table and lay down on the bed. The pain just got more intense. The hunchbacked dwarf inside him was elbowing. He turned on his side and brought his knees up to his chest waiting for the pain to subside. It was like an echo, a distant beating drum that he could only feel. Benjamin exhaled. This was just colic, ridiculous colic. But he couldn't worry about his stomach now. As soon as he regained some strength he put his shoes back on and looked desperately out the window. The low light of first sunset brought out the shadows and corners of the alley below and laid bare the stairs leading up to the church in the high part of town, lit the wall of a courtyard across the way where he observed a dark-haired woman going into a hen house and emerging with a pack under her arm. The woman turned for a moment and Walter could see her green eyes and high cheekbones. Then she disappeared into the house. It seemed strange that people were living out there, and that the wind carried the perfume of the sea and that his world was slowly drumming to a close. It was all slowly coming to an end.

There was the sound of footsteps out in the hall and then two soft knocks at the door, barely audible. It was Frau

Lippmann, small and pale. She wanted to know if he would be joining them for dinner. There was something about her eyes, he wasn't sure what, that reminded him of his mother. So he agreed. He'd come down so that he wouldn't have to be alone, though he wasn't hungry and another pain, somewhat diminished now, made him fold over.

'Are you sick?' she asked.

'No. Thank you. It's nothing. I'm coming now.'

Walter looked around before sitting in the dining room. They were the only ones there at dinner. Núñez and Alcina were at a table in the corner playing cards with a blond man and a *guardia civil* whose moustache hung down the corners of his mouth.

'Buon appetito,' said the waiter as he almost furtively deposited a tray in the middle of their table.

For a while, the only sound was that of cutlery against the plates, and the clicking of the bead curtain in the doorway. Sooner or later the questions would begin. A minute passed, then two. The women all kept their eyes down, and José stuffed food into his mouth. Walter scraped his plate with a spoon. He was alone again, suspended in a time that didn't belong to them. His future raced through his head – there wasn't the slightest opening to let in the messiah who was supposed to save him. He was overcome again with an asthmatic wheeze, it crept up from deep in his lungs, and that mute pain in his stomach wouldn't go away.

'Have you come up with anything?' Grete asked finally in a whisper. 'Do you have any idea about what to do?'

Their voices seemed to arrive in Benjamin's ears as if muffled, like the wake of a ship silently leaving port. Was it Henny who was speaking now?

'Maybe if we leave when it's still dark tomorrow morning we might be able to make a break for the six o'clock train to Barcelona.'

'Sure. Even if we somehow manage to get out without those two seeing us, don't you think they'll just stop us at the station?'

Now Benjamin thought that Frau Lippmann was speaking and he lowered his eyes when he realised that she was looking right at him, expectantly, waiting for his answer. He tried to shrug her off, to deny everything. He looked at his plate but all he saw were those eggs and peas floating in a watery sauce, and the fear of death.

'I'm not leaving,' he said angrily with trembling lips. 'I'm not going anywhere. Whatever happens happens. I'd rather have it over and done with here.'

No, no. This was not what he was supposed to say at all. He wasn't asking for pity. But what . . .

'Doctor,' protested Frau Lippmann, 'you'll see that when we call the American consulate tomorrow . . . And don't you have a letter for the Dominican prior? We can call them too. Don't worry. We won't be sent back.'

This was not how it was meant to go. He was almost relieved when he felt another pain shooting through his stomach, constricting his throat. This pit was his last refuge.

'Will you all excuse me?' he murmured. 'I don't feel well, and I'd like to retire, with your permission.'

He stood and gestured reassuringly to the women. Then he headed back toward the stairs, struggling to hold himself upright. Later, in bed, when the pain finally let up a little he realised that he could barely remember dragging himself up to his room, or flinging open the window or gasping for air before falling onto the bed and drifting off into a restless half-sleep. The shadows of night were now creeping over the walls and darkness was consuming the ceiling like a terrifying invading army. The church bells rang nine o'clock. How slowly time moved. Then it started racing. Walter suddenly felt like he was being strangled. There was a hoarse whistle coming from his throat, an almost animal sound. In the dark, with these stomach pains and short breath, his body became a silent battleground. He sat at the edge of the bed, gasping through an open mouth, stretching his jaw and holding his neck in his hands. Enough! What had he done to deserve this kind of suffering? He sat there, frozen and frightened, waiting for the grip of pain to ease enough so that he could lie back on the pillow. He was a wreck – sweaty and weak. The sounds of people eating dinner floated up from the restaurant. Then he heard the shuffle of footsteps on the stairs, coming to a stop in front of his door, which he'd left open. Frau Lippmann pushed it open very slowly, and peered into the dark room.

'Excuse me. Did I wake you?'

A bald, lanky elderly man, dressed all in black, stood behind her.

'We thought,' she said, tripping on her words, 'that you might need a doctor. We took the liberty of . . . Well, this is Doctor Vila Moreno.'

'No,' spat Benjamin. But he looked at the woman and was again reminded of his mother. 'I am grateful to you, madam,' he added a little more calmly. 'But I don't have any need of a doctor.'

'It may be necessary,' insisted the woman, 'in this case. Perhaps the doctor could give you a certificate so that you could stay on in the hotel a few more days.'

He understood. So he let the doctor take his pulse and tap his stomach and abdomen, listen to his chest with an icy stethoscope and then measure his blood pressure.

'Breathe deeply,' he heard him ask.

'Easy for you to say,' he answered with a forced smile. 'I have a bad heart and asthma. There should be an X-ray in my bag.'

But the old doctor ignored him, going on with the examination, communicating in monosyllables and gestures. He finally looked up and removed the stethoscope with a deep sigh.

'I'm going to give you a shot,' he explained. 'And tomorrow we'll take some blood. Your blood pressure is extremely high, you know.'

When Frau Lippmann returned with a syringe and kettle, Vila Moreno had already turned Benjamin on his side.

'Do you have something to take,' he asked as he prepared the needle, 'in case of another asthma attack?'

'Morphium,' answered Benjamin between clenched teeth.

'That will do.'

Vila Moreno replaced his instruments in his bag and snapped it shut. As he headed toward the door, he said, 'I'll be back tomorrow morning. Try to get some sleep.'

Frau Lippmann walked the doctor out, leaving Walter alone. He looked about for the watch he'd put on the nightstand. It was ten thirty. The dull light from the straw lampshade on the nightstand fell on his head and cast broad circles on the ceiling. Then he felt another twinge come on and then a doubt which he tried to beat away the minute he saw Frau Lippmann reappear in the doorway.

'Did I pay the doctor?'

'No,' she answered. 'But he explained to me in horrible French that he'll charge it to the hotel bill.'

'Ah ha,' mumbled Benjamin as if that were reassuring. 'You must be exhausted.'

'A little,' she admitted. 'But I wouldn't dream of leaving you alone.'

'Don't worry about me. I feel better now. Go on. I'm fine.'

They went back and forth like this until they finally agreed that she would go to sleep under the condition that Walter would bang on the wall if he needed anything. Her room was right on the other side and she would come at the slightest tap.

'Okay,' said Benjamin as a new shooting in his intestines made him wince. He tightened his lips to keep the shivers away, while Frau Lippmann brought him water, pulled the covers over his legs, put her hand on his forehead and shyly rubbed his temples.

'Has it passed?' she asked. 'Promise that you'll try to get some sleep now.'

Back into darkness, left alone again to wrestle with the hunch-backed dwarf and the thoughts racing crazily through his head. He counted the bells: eleven o'clock. He tried to face his destiny. There was a bustling of footsteps down in the alley, and the howl of a dog in the night. Walter didn't move. He stared at the dense shadows with bulging eyes. He strained his ears as if he were worried about being surprised in his sleep by some sound. He knew that the creaking and whining wasn't the bed. It was death, he thought, with a shiver. It was the slow, steady gait of death growing inside him.

Chapter Forty-six

'You're back early. It's only midnight. Is everything okay?'

Mercedes was sitting in the shadows on the edge of her chair, one elbow resting on the table. She was smoking. Doña Pepa, plump in her apron, was over by the fire peeling potatoes and tossing them one by one into the pot.

'Everything's fine,' answered Laureano as he took off his coat. Quickly he put his backpack down on a chair and sighed. He was beyond tired — and irritated. 'Is there anything new here?' he asked, just to make conversation.

Mercedes shrugged and pursed her lips. 'Nothing much,' she said, shaking her head.

'What do you mean, nothing?' said doña Pepa turning around, knife in mid-air, and looking severely at her daughter. It wasn't right not to mention what had been going on in town.

'What do you mean, *nothing*?' she said. 'What about the refugees?'

'What refugees?' Laureano asked, releasing a puff of his cigarette. His eyes were suddenly flashing in the firelight.

'Oh, yes,' remembered Mercedes. 'But refugees, all these people in flight — it isn't news anymore.'

'Except that,' said doña Pepa sharply, 'this time they want to send them back to France. Fine men they are, doing that to women and a child. The blacksmith Miguel saw the lot of them. He says there's even an old man. A very sick old man. Doctor Vila Moreno was just there.'

'An old man,' said Laureano.

'He must be the one I could see from our courtyard. With glasses, all rumpled. He's staying in the room across the way.'

Mercedes had barely finished speaking, but Laureano was already at the door, wrestling with the doorknob that seemed suddenly stuck.

'I'll be right back,' he said as he left.

'But where are you going? Are you crazy? There are policemen and guards over there. You have to watch out for Enrique.'

But he was gone. If it weren't for the lamp swinging in the wind and the laughter of the last diners in the restaurant, he would have been alone in the silence, in the dirty darkness of night-time before the rain comes. He crossed the street, hiding in the shadows of the alley. Hugging the wall he edged around the hotel. There had to be a back door. In fact there was, and it was open, propped open. Someone, a cleaner, was going in and out, carrying out the rubbish. The first moment he could, Laureano lurched out of his shelter and burst inside. A corridor, a door in the back on the left, a stairway. One, two, three, go. He pretended he was still on the battlefield, a rifle between his hands. The dark over the stairs hid him. From below he could hear the door scraping and the sound of a man dragging something.

'There's another bag here, Luis, are you going to get this one?'

He reached the top of the stairs. He could just make out a long shadowy hall. It wasn't hard to find his friend's room — the sound of his heavy tortured breath could be heard through the door, which was ajar.

'Doctor? Doctor Benjamin,' he whispered, sticking his nose in.

'Who is it?'

The voice was feeble and pasty, barely audible.

'It's me, Laureano.'

'Well then, come on in.'

'Would it bother you if I turned on the light?'

And he saw him: pale, hair falling in clumps over his forehead, a grey beard carving hollows into his cheeks. His nose seemed to have grown sharper and his lips were wrinkled, his eyes red and tired. Laureano knew what he was looking at. He'd seen so many of them during the war, the wounded, two steps from death, their faces already marked by death — hanging on, like a fly to a mule.

'How are you?' he asked.

'Honestly, I don't feel well.'

Walter tried to find a more comfortable position on the bed, and to distract himself from the sharp pain that wouldn't leave him be. He looked around the room, nodding at the crumbling walls, the rickety wardrobe, the flies buzzing around the light. Okay. He'd ended up here, but when precisely along the way did he get so lost. How did he get to this room in this sad hotel — he asked himself that as he watched the shadow dance over the wall. The watch on the nightstand read one thirty.

'Where did I go wrong?' He seemed to be asking himself. There was a tense smile on his face.

'We all make mistakes,' said Laureano under his breath. 'I've made mistakes in my life. If I ever stop to think about them I get a stomach-ache. But at a certain point it's no use to rehash the past. It's better to look ahead. Believe me.'

'Ahead? There's nothing in my future.'

Benjamin shook his head and cast a sideways glance at Laureano who was leaning against the table. Very far away there came the sound of thunder rolling off the mountains.

'Don't talk nonsense. You didn't think you were going to make it last night and yet here you are.'

'I'm at the end of the line. I've finally hit the end of the line.'

His mind was a-flutter like a wasp locked in a jar, his arms were tingling and there was a heaviness in his chest. Walter exhaled a deep, sad sigh. He'd already decided. He'd weighed all the possibilities and at last his thoughts had fallen into place in his mind. At least that's the way it seemed to him.

'It just doesn't make sense anymore,' he added slowly. 'Do you know what Kafka said? *I never redeemed myself through writing. I've spent my life dying and now I die for real.*'

Laureano blanched and then recovered himself. He tried to smile.

'And do you know what my uncle Adolfo said? A live dog is better than a dead lion. That's what he said.'

'Apologies to your uncle, but that line comes from Ecclesiastes.'

'From what?'

'Ecclesiastes.'

Okay so that hadn't worked. He still couldn't give up. Laureano stared at the damp forehead and expression of ultimate disorder that the old man wore on his face.

'So,' he said. 'We should stop joking about these things.'

Walter coughed, gasped, then closed his eyes for a moment – just enough time to see Dora, Stefan, Asja, Jula, Lisa Fittko, the sergeant, Scholem, Koestler, Henny Gurland – a silent crowd waving to him.

'I'm not joking,' he muttered when he caught his breath. 'I've lost and I must surrender.'

'Losing,' said Laureano with a sigh. 'What does that mean. I've grown a thick skin over it. I make a habit of losing and yet I'm still here.'

They sat in silence for a while thinking of the way time moved so slowly in that room, as the church bells rang two, and the wind scratched the glass. Then, there was the sudden sound of footsteps on the stairs and Laureano flattened himself against the wall by the closed door until they faded and he returned to the bedside.

'I can't stay long,' he whispered.

Walter lowered his eyes and nodded. It was true; there wasn't much time.

'Listen,' he started talking again in a rough voice. 'Even if I were able to make it through until tomorrow morning. Do you realise what's waiting for me? Spanish customs want to send me back to the Vichy police who will make a fine present of me to the Gestapo. And then, after days and days without food or drink, crammed into freight cars, we'll get to Germany, to one of those camps where my cousin has probably already died. I'd rather not even think about it. Do you really think that in my condition I could make it? And to what end? So that I have to work even harder to die?'

Benjamin paused to catch his breath. Grinding his teeth, he

leaned to one side, trying to bear the torment of his stomach. Who knew if the dumbfounded boy standing by him now had understood any of what he said. But his eyes seemed honest. He had more life accumulated in his pupils than his years. If he could only try to explain.

'Does it seem so wrong to you,' he whispered, 'to want to die with a little bit of dignity?'

What could Laureano say? Was there any use insisting? There wasn't a crack in his logic. Doctor Benjamin wasn't one who shirked from looking at things straight on and calling them by their first and last names. A pity that there was no point to living. Laureano sighed deeply and stayed quiet. Then he cast his eyes down and Walter saw in that blink of an eye the beating wings of his angel – the angel watching over his last journey, the angel of the prophet, the messenger. Yes, the boy had understood everything.

'My bag,' he said. 'Will you hand me my bag from the table?'

He got up and sat panting in the middle of the bed with the bag on his lap and started opening the buckles as if he were handling a sacred relic. Then he pulled out a blue folder stuffed with papers and tied shut.

'This is my manuscript.' Benjamin's voice was a wisp. The words like stones unmoving in his mouth. 'It is the most important thing in the world to me. You must promise that you will get it to Teddy Adorno in the United States. I've written the address on that piece of paper.'

'Of course,' stuttered Laureano, embarrassed. 'But wouldn't it be better to give it to one of your friends? One of the women you came with?'

Benjamin shook his head slowly. He'd thought of this too.

'If they—' he began with difficulty. 'If it doesn't go well, they could end up like me. But I must be sure that this book gets to the States. Understand?'

No, he didn't know how those pages full of tiny writing could be more important than life. But if he were to say that . . . How could he possibly leave the man on that bed, pretending he didn't know what he was thinking?

'Perhaps it would be better,' he murmured.

But old Benjamin wasn't listening anymore. He lowered his head softly onto the pillow, closed his eyes, and started breathing slowly. He began to die right in front of him.

Chapter Forty-seven

Laureano didn't speak. He laid a hand on Benjamin's shoulder, turned out the light and left. When he was alone, Walter let the dark back through his eyelids. There, in that obscurity, he looked for the only thing that could emerge – he looked at his future, now as irrevocable as his past. The church bells rang three, then four, as he lingered feebly in a kind of lucid doze, balancing between threads of pain and the fear of not being able to breathe until he heard more thunder from even farther away shaking the glass. He opened his eyes and turned on the light. His pipe, passport, papers, identification, two books, the X-ray – it was all there. The pills, even though the phial had got bent in the bag. He sat on the edge of the bed and dumped two pills into his hand, and then he put them in his mouth. He picked up the glass of water and swallowed, closing his eyes and breathing deeply. He stopped a moment to watch the night shadows flying slowly about the room, then swallowed another two pills and took another sip of water. Then he paused again – like a cere-mony, a ritual, still more pills, water, and more. The thought occurred to him that perhaps for the first time in his life he was making a decision that wouldn't end in catastrophe. But then again, he had done nothing more than manage to follow in the footsteps of the hunchbacked dwarf. To trace what was already written in his book of destiny. But what big words were these. The important thing now was to stay calm, prepared. Many years before he'd experimented with drugs with his friend Fränkel, so he knew very well what was waiting for him. There would be lucidity initially, euphoria, and then a pounding heart and little by little, thirst, a headache, the sensation that both his legs and arms were being broken, and then something like paralysis followed by sleep, slowed breathing, asphyxia. There wasn't much time. He had to hurry.

There was a moment when, breathless and sitting up in bed, he spied death and wasn't afraid. He clenched his teeth to bear the new rush of twinges then took a white sheet of paper and his pen from the bag. 'In a predicament without recourse,' he slowly wrote, 'I have no choice but to end it.' He inhaled deeply before continuing. 'I beg you to convey my thoughts to my friend Adorno and to explain the situation I find myself in to him. There is no more time left for me to write all the letter that I wanted to write.'

There it was done. He carefully folded up the paper and wrote on the outside 'For Henny Gurland', and then set it on the nightstand with a glance at his watch. It was almost seven. A beam of pale light floated hesitantly in the room, like in an aquarium. As he looked for a position to relieve some of the pain, Walter removed his glasses, cleaning them meticulously with a handkerchief. He was surprised by the enormous weight of his arm when he tried to pull it back. There was very little time. The sound of his fist against the wall echoed loudly and sombrely in his head until he heard the footsteps of Frau Lippmann in the hall and her knock at the door.

'Can I come in?'

'Come,' he stuttered from the bed.

'My god,' said the woman. 'What have you done?'

In the shadow she saw instantly his swollen face, the phial abandoned on the covers by the wall. She went silent and dropped her face in her hands, not daring to ask more.

'Good morning,' spluttered old Benjamin. 'Would you be so good as to call Frau Gurland for me?'

Eyes shut from the effort, and his throat parched, Walter thought about what he might tell her. Not much. Just to keep going. To make it through. And then there she was next to him, her pale hair hanging down over one shoulder. Frau Lippmann stood in the doorway behind her chewing her fingers. She was crying while Benjamin explained about the pains and the pills – and his decision.

'Frau Gurland, you must forgive me,' he whispered. 'I would have only been a burden. Without me you might make it.'

'You're going to make it too. You'll see,' she replied in a husky voice. 'I'm going to call the doctor.'

Benjamin didn't have the strength to shake his head. He said no with his eyes.

'It's useless,' he added as soon as he found some strength. 'Will you instead promise me that you'll keep the pills a secret? It could be a problem. Say that I was sick. Okay?'

Henny nodded, frightened, then reached out for the phial and hid it in her pocket. The bells outside struck seven. The day was struggling to emerge from behind the gathering storm clouds – the sun never came through that wan grey.

'Something else,' resumed old Benjamin. 'I wrote you a letter, it's on the nightstand. You should let Teddy Adorno and my son Stefan know what happened.'

That was it. He couldn't manage any more. His sickness moved into his eyes. Henny picked up her letter and bit her lips so she wouldn't cry. She didn't know what to do. With a nervous gesture she rearranged her hair, then looked at him, shaking her head with disbelief. This was the last image of the world that Walter saw before his eyes closed and he plunged into stillness, broken up by voices, footsteps on the stairs, all of it distant like his life – a sudden shock of pain, like a punch. And he knew that there was no coming back; he'd taken himself beyond the limits of repairable. Kafka, he thought without irony, and then he let himself be consumed by sleep, by the storm of images that he would never be able to recount.

'Everyone,' wrote Eduardo Galeano, 'goes into the death as they lived. Some go in silence on tiptoe, others go fighting, others ask permission and forgiveness. Some go in arguing and making excuses, and there are some who raise their fists and cuss. Some embrace death. Some close their eyes and others cry.' Benjamin faced death with dignity, with courtly manners – he walked her streets as if he'd been walking them his whole life, following his destiny, limping and trying to hide his in-eptitude at dying. For years he'd imagined that moment as a kind of seismic explosion, a moment of light that would have clarified his existence. But instead it was a slow-moving canal, a loop in a long river, where you can barely perceive the memories that bob together to the surface, the heart that slows its beat, the stretch at the end that grabs you by the throat and drags you out of time.

Chapter Forty-eight

So that's how it was with your philosopher. Unlucky. If he had crossed the border a day earlier, he would have been able to get on a train to Lisbon without a hitch. If he'd stayed one more day in France, he would have heard about the Spanish police's new orders, and then he and the Gurlands would have waited before climbing over the Pyrenees. You see? It was a matter of one day, just one damn day that brought your philosopher to disaster. And in fact his friends — the ones he'd met up with along the way — were brought to the border in a flood of a rainstorm — and then, it's not clear what happened. Maybe it was the storm or maybe the guards wanted to make a little money. Maybe the orders changed again. They were released and went on to Lisbon, safe and sound. What luck. Destiny dealt Benjamin a bad hand; the deck was stacked against him. Fuck it. He did the right thing. I agreed with him. It was better to have it over and done with in that hotel than to be killed by the Germans. But his bad luck followed him, even after death.

When the doctor got there, soaked from the rain, thunder and lightning close on his heels, Benjamin was already in a coma.

A strange light like steel pushed weakly in through the window, stippled by fat raindrops on the glass and dissipating as soon as it hit the opaque silence of the room. The only thing that Vila Moreno could do for him was call the priest to give last rites. They assumed he was a Catholic! They'd found that famous letter for the Dominicans in his bag. Frau Gurland ended up on her knees praying next to don Andrés and the altar boys trying to hide the fact that she didn't know a word of the liturgy. She watched the priest with the holy oil and tried to follow his gestures mumbling confusedly in Latin.

Your philosopher died in the afternoon. The rain had already become a steady downpour – a monotonous, dense litany gathering in the sky like time. I don't even know if Vila Moreno understood or not – maybe he was pretending – but he certified the death as being caused by a cerebral haemorrhage. Committing suicide back then was a crime, you know? Think about the trouble Frau Gurland would have got in if the real story ever came out. But thanks to Vila Moreno they let her and her son leave for Lisbon the next day.

Benjamin was left alone in that damn hotel. The judge came in that night just before eleven and the corpse was already dressed and laid out on the bed. He set the funeral for the next day and rented a plot in the cemetery with money they'd found in the black bag. Instead of a ticket for the States, Benjamin bought himself a grave in Spain. He had francs and dollars on him. Not much, but it was enough back then in Port Bou. The priest, the doctor and the carpenter who built the casket made out fine. Juan Suñer, the hotel owner, actually presented the judge with a bill for five days in the hotel and the expenses for disinfecting the room. What a son of a bitch. Mercedes and I got these details from doña Pepa. She went out and asked around. People in town knew things and she didn't mind sharing.

'*Ay pobre*,' she said, making the fat under her chin wobble. 'They steal from him and then they bury him like a dog.'

'When?' I asked.

'Today at three,' she answered.

That was the first time I went out in the light of day. I took advantage of the lunch hour when everyone was inside eating to creep out of town and climb the hill opposite the cemetery. I had my binoculars, the only relic of war that I hung on to. The rain the day before had cleaned the air. The sky and sea that I saw from up there was dizzying. And those white tombs sticking out of the hillside, motionless in the wind, teetering over the transparent water – it made you want to die. There was a lone woman among the graves, changing the water in the flower vases, weeding, and polishing her loved ones' headstones. Eventually don Andrés appeared on the road leading up to the hill, followed by two altar boys with their incense and six men carrying the casket on their shoulders.

Machado. Don Antonio's poem came to mind. He was dead now too, betrayed by his heart and lungs, by the terrible sadness of exile. Died not a month after I'd seen him, just a few kilometres from there at the end of the war. Damn border. Now I watched don Andrés offer benedictions, and the gravediggers lower the casket, the altar boys bow their heads, and Machado's verse came to mind: 'It struck the bottom with a sharp sound, solemnly, in the silence. The sound of a coffin striking the earth is something unutterably solemn.'

And do you know the final mockery, the last low blow destiny dealt your philosopher? The priest, judge and doctor all believed

that his name was Benjamín and that Walter was his surname.
In the town hall and even on the death certificate, there's no
trace of Doctor Benjamin. Even the corner where he's buried
is marked Mr Walter. And so no one will ever find the grave.
When they shut him in there, they sealed away his name, his
legacy, the only thing we leave behind. Luckily I still had his
manuscript and I thought that it was up to me to restore to him
a little of the legacy he deserved.

They quickly recited the requiescat. A quarter of an hour
later the only person left in the cemetery was the woman
dusting her relatives' headstones, a black shape moving slowly
under the blazing sun. I stayed until nightfall. It would have
been too risky to go back into town during the day. What else
was there to do in the bright light, surrounded by those odours,
under the clouds spinning in the sky so fabulous you couldn't
even follow them? I thought. That's what I did – about Mercedes
and me and about Benjamin and how I didn't want to ever end
up in his shoes. I never wanted to have to make that kind of
decision. I realised that I didn't have much time. I couldn't
really stay there in Port Bou, buried alive in Mercedes' house.
I only had one life and I shouldn't waste a moment of it. I
know. Those are the kinds of things you say, but it's true that
life is like a freight train: it passes so slowly, you watch it, and
it seems like it's endless, and then all of a sudden you're staring
at the red brake light of the last car as it's disappearing. Then
for the first time with dismay I recognised that I would have
to go into exile. I might have to go to Mexico, Cuba or
Argentina. If I wanted to live, I would have to resign myself
to the fact that I couldn't go back to Spain for a long time. I
went home late that night with a long face. I couldn't even

smile or talk to María who was dancing around me, wanting to play.

'What's the matter?' asked Mercedes.

So I told her: I said that I had to leave and that I would go to Mexico and I wanted her and María to join me once I got settled. Mercedes agreed. She didn't argue, she didn't ask for explanations, she didn't cry. Nothing. It was as if my declaration was made of soap bubbles. She even smiled. And she was good – because it had taken me two months to come to that decision. It's as if women don't have to learn how some things have to go. They just know things and that's that – they just hang on, like fish on a hook. So I prepared my backpack with my few things and put it by the bed. One day passed and then the next and there was always a reason to put off leaving, even if it was heavy to have to stay in the house all the time and even though with every trip I made over the border I could feel the cops' breath on my neck closer and closer. Until it happened one December morning so quickly that I didn't have time to think about it. I'd come back from a trip in the middle of the night. I was freezing and dog-tired and I lay down on the bed without bothering to undress. But I stayed awake, as if I knew. I tossed under the covers and cursed at the fact that I couldn't fall asleep. But that's how I heard them at dawn. I heard their footsteps under the window, their breath condensing in the cold dry air, the whispered orders. Shit, it was Enrique. I jumped up and Mercedes complained in her sleep, 'What's wrong? What happened?'

The time it took to put on my coat, grab my backpack and fetch the manuscript from its hiding place under the mattress and I was out the door in the courtyard. Mercedes put a hand on my shoulder and held out something to me in the darkness.

'Here. This might help,' she said.

It was only after I was already running frantically up into the mountains and I had the chance to shoot a glance backward and see how much of a lead I had on the cops that I stuck my hand in my pocket and saw that she had given me a picture of herself. Mercedes, I thought, shaking my head. But I couldn't stop longer, it was more important to keep moving, watch my back, keep out of the open and cover my trail. At noon, I stopped on a ledge, sheltered by a clump of locust trees and took out my binoculars. Very far down, where the path coasted a little stream, I saw three policemen in a row. Enrique Viadiu and his moustache was in the lead. He must have realised that I was more than just a regular smuggler, that I was a Red son of a bitch because he'd set after me as if I were worse than Jack the Ripper. The chase lasted two days. I headed west to avoid passing through France and they stuck behind me the whole time as if catching me were the most important thing in the world. The farther I got from the sea, the colder it got; the higher I climbed, the fiercer the wind, getting under my clothes and whipping at my face. By nightfall I was walking between ice puddles embedded into the north-facing ground. I was hungry, cold, sleepy, thirsty and the bag was heavy on my back. The worst of it was the second night. By then I was walking through snow almost a metre deep. Before, when there was still some light, I'd seen the shadow of the cops on the other side of the valley behind me. I had a couple of hours' advantage but no more, so I stopped to rest against a pine tree. Just ten minutes I promised myself. Just enough time to catch my breath.

I didn't pay much attention to the first gust of wind whistling through the gorge, but then the wind started building. The branches were bending over my head and a fog like cotton rolled up from the bottom of the valley covering the moon. Then came the whirls of heavy snow, coating my face with icy dust. It must have been ten or twenty degrees below zero. I had to get moving or I would freeze, but that was easier said than done. The gusts threw me back to the ground. I was exhausted and gave up. I found shelter under an overhang. It's not worth it, I said. Why should I go on? I can't make it. There. I'd become just like Benjamin. There was no room for flattery in a situation without remedy. I really thought my time had come up on that mountain. I'm going to die, I said to myself, but I also remember being calm, as if I was ready. I only had one regret. I put my hand in my pocket and pulled out Mercedes' picture. I lit a match in the crook of my hand to look at it; it was one of my last matches. I stared at her high cheekbones and her eyes when it suddenly occurred to me in a flash that I could light a fire. I was sheltered and with that fog the cops would never see me. I just had to gather a little wood – nothing easier you say. I crawled out into the dark and started looking desperately in the snow around my shelter, digging with bare hands through the snow until I'd gathered a handful of branches but when I tried to light them I realised I would die first – they were too wet and useless. The effort of gathering them had taken my last strength. I was finished. I felt my eyes closing, treacherous sleep wrapping slowly around me with its false peace. With a last burst of awareness I reached out for the backpack and pulled out the manuscript. I only hesitated a moment before spreading the blue cover out under the circle of branches. The cover will work, I thought. Instead it curled in the faltering flame and faded into the snow. There was nothing else to do, I thought, it was Benjamin or me. My future against his memory. I began with the first three pages, then another five, six, a stack of pages, and more until finally one of the thinner twigs sparked to life. By the light of the fire I could see well enough to collect more wood, which at first just smoked and finally started burning. My hands were slowly warming; the ice melted, the water dripped over my eyebrows. I was saved. It was all thanks to your philosopher. What greater gift could he have given me?

When the sun rose, the blizzard had passed. No one was chasing me any more. All I could see around me in the clear, brisk air was the brilliant whiteness of the landscape. The trees listing under the weight of the snow, the drop into the valley where four little houses perched on a crag overlooking a plain. The backpack was light on my shoulders now, and I walked more quickly. But it became evident that my lot in life was to travel Europe by foot, all the way to Lisbon. I never did manage to get on a train or bus, or get a lift with anyone – nothing to save me even a hundred feet of heel-toe. There was always some danger lurking, a *guardia civil*, policing the trains, the blue shirt of a Falangist behind the wheel of a truck. I cut across fields, followed streams, secondary roads, trails cut into the side of the mountain range. It was just like when I was in France a few months before except that there was no Mercedes waiting for me at the other end. Now I was leaving my home for ever.

I got to the sea in the middle of March by following the Tagus River down to Lisbon. But it was another month before I could get on a boat. It wasn't until I saw the Torre di Belém disappearing in the distance, and the river and white houses cluster on the hills – only then I started breathing easily. Although there was only so easily I could breathe when thoughts of Mercedes clogged my throat. It was a crystal clear evening in April. The water was murky and still, the stars were thick in the sky. I was out on the bow, the wind whipping my clothes and blowing the hair of a woman leaning on the parapet. Her hair was black as pitch. She leaned over, twisted, folded in two – struggling to light a cigarette.

'May I?' I offered, a match already lit in the crook of my hand.

The woman inhaled and stood back to look at me.

'Thank you,' she said in French. 'My name is Hannah, Hannah Arendt. You are Spanish.'

I nodded yes while I lit a cigarette of my own.

'Where are you from?'

'Port Bou, near the border.'

I don't know why I answered that way but it was the first thing that came to mind. Deep down I really didn't know where I was from anymore. I vaguely, but vaguely had a sense of where I was going.

'Port Bou . . . I've been there,' she slowly said. 'A friend of mine died there. I even went to the cemetery. It's lovely, but I couldn't find his grave.'

I went white like a coward – as if the evil beast itself had appeared before me. What luck. But of course I would meet her, this friend of his. She might well have thought that manuscript was worth more than my life.

'Maybe, if you looked harder,' I stuttered.

But she had already turned away. A man was coming toward her, smiling.

'So long,' I said and breathed again.

For the rest of the trip I did nothing but try to avoid her and I managed to do that. But once the ship docked and I set foot in Veracruz, I realised that I had stopped running, that I would be here my whole life. I would stop now, and wait. But for what? Have you ever felt that sensation that you are waiting for something but you don't know what? I do. I've felt that way for more than fifty years. At first I thought I was waiting for Mercedes, but when she and María joined me two years later, I discovered that I was happy and at the same time that feeling I was waiting for something never left me. I thought of Franco. I thought maybe I wanted to go back to Spain as soon as he fell. But no. When that old son of a bitch died I realised that I was happy here and too old to go back – exile had become a part of me. Over all these years I've thought often of your philosopher. We couldn't be more different but there was something that linked us. I guess that we were each in our own way two hairs off the same dog, two faces of the same Europe. Then everything fell apart. They say that the world won't end for a long time yet. But ours already collapsed in a heap. Since then there's been no place for people like us. Time killed him; his moment in time killed him. Who knows why I got lucky. I got lucky but I've been condemned to survival and little by little I have had to absorb all of the defeat and wait, and wait some more. But I've seen things that maybe I'm the only person who's seen them left to talk about them. And fuck if I won't talk about it. At least as long as I am here, I'll keep at it, keep going, even if it's not always easy. Memory isn't like a dog; it doesn't come whenever you want it to. It hardly ever comes when you call. I know this is probably useless, all this storytelling and taking up so much time, boring nice people like you. But you can forgive an old man for that, right? Later, you'll make your own peace with the memories, decide what you want to do with them. That's your business. When it's all done, I've won one against time. And this, my son, doesn't seem like a small thing.

Acknowledgements

Like all of its counterparts, this book is also a son and brother to other books. I am naturally indebted to Walter Benjamin, the critical work on his thinking (especially Agamben, Tiedemann, Solmi, Arendt and Adorno), his biographers (notably Scholem, Brodersen and Witte, as well as the worthy research provided by Scheurman), and to numerous historical works about Spain and France in the 1930s. I'd also like to make mention of several novels and accounts that have proven invaluable to my work. I drew extensively on Arthur Koestler's *Scum of the Earth*, Anna Seghers's *Transit*, Lisa Fittko's memoir *Escape Through the Pyrenees*, and the work of Max Aub. But I also 'stole' a great deal from Mariano Constante's *Los años rojos*, Franciso Pérez López's *Españoles en los campos Nazis* and *El Mexicano*, Jay Parini's *Benjamin's Crossing*, from *Exil im Exil* by Hans Sahl and *El Pasajero Benjamin* by Ricardo Cano Gaviria as well as from the testimonials collected by Eduardo Pons Prades in *Republicanos españoles en la segunda Guerra mundial*. Pillaging these texts made it possible to bring times I didn't live through and places that I've never visited to readers. Is this not also the purpose of literature?

I owe Paco Ignacio Taibo II for introducing me to a great deal of this writing of Spain, as well as for additional information, and much much more. I'd like to thank Giuseppe Russo for several tremendously useful photocopies, Gabriella Catalano for her patience helping me translate from German, Cristina Guarinelli for her technical generosity and Manuel Cussò-Ferrer for having agreed to meet up with me in Barcelona and providing me with invaluable suggestions for my scouting in Port Bou.

It's almost necessary to emphasize the fact that this is fiction, albeit based on actual events. Thus I have taken many liberties with history, convinced that, as Manzoni once said, 'the writer must benefit from history, not be in competition with it.' Which is why some of the characters who appear in the book are entirely made up and others bear the name of historic figures – even those, however, are ultimately products of my imagination.

I'd also like to thank, my little 'circle of readers' (Antonio C. and Antonio F., Giovanni, Laura, Mariano, Paolo, Pietro, Silvio and, of course, Marco Tropea), that private institution, formed out of respect and affection, without which no book and no writer would be what they are. Finally, the greatest thanks are due to Iaia: only she and I know deep down why.